NECROMUNDA

CARDINAL CRIMSON

WILL McDERMOTT

For Don and Jan, my most loyal fans, who have read nearly every word I've ever written. It's safe to say that without their contribution many years ago, my life and career would not be what it is today.

A BLACK LIBRARY PUBLICATION

First published in Great Britain in 2006 by
BL Publishing,
Games Workshop Ltd.,
Willow Road, Nottingham,
NG7 2WS, UK.

10 9 8 7 6 5 4 3 2 1

Cover illustration by Clint Langley.

A CIP record for this book is available from the British Library.

ISBN 13: 978 1 84416 372 4
ISBN 10: 1 84416 372 5

Distributed in the US by Simon & Schuster
1230 Avenue of the Americas, New York, NY 10020, US.

Printed and bound in Great Britain by
Bookmarque, Surrey, UK.

See the Black Library on the Internet at
www.blacklibrary.com

Find out more about Games Workshop
www.games-workshop.com

In order to even begin to understand the blasted world of Necromunda you must first understand the hive cities. These man-made mountains of plasteel, ceramite and rockrete have accreted over centuries to protect their inhabitants from a hostile environment, so very much like the termite mounds they resemble. The Necromundan hive cities have populations in the billions and are intensely industrialised, each one commanding the manufacturing potential of an entire planet or colony system compacted into a few hundred square kilometres.

The internal stratification of the hive cities is also illuminating to observe. The entire hive structure replicates the social status of its inhabitants in a vertical plane. At the top are the nobility, below them are the workers, and below the workers are the dregs of society, the outcasts. Hive Primus, seat of the planetary governor Lord Helmawr of Necromunda, illustrates this in the starkest terms. The nobles — Houses Helmawr, Cattalus, Ty, Ulanti, Greim, Ran Lo and Ko'Iron — live in the 'Spire', and seldom set foot below the 'Wall' that exists between themselves and the great forges and hab zones of the hive city proper.

Below the hive city is the 'Underhive', foundation layers of habitation domes, industrial zones and tunnels which have been abandoned in prior generations, only to be re-occupied by those with nowhere else to go.

But... humans are not insects. They do not hive together well. Necessity may force it, but the hive cities of Necromunda remain internally divided to the point of brutalisation and outright violence being an everyday fact of life. The Underhive, meanwhile, is a thoroughly lawless place, beset by gangs and renegades, where only the strongest or the most cunning survive. The Goliaths, who believe firmly that might is right; the matriarchal, man–hating Escher; the industrial Orlocks; the technologically–minded Van Saar; the Delaque whose very existence depends on their espionage network; the fiery zealots of the Cawdor. All striving for the advantage that will elevate them, no matter how briefly, above the other houses and gangs of the Underhive.

Most fascinating of all is when individuals attempt to cross the monumental physical and social divides of the hive to start new lives. Given social conditions, ascension through the hive is nigh on impossible, but descent is an altogether easier, albeit altogether less appealing, possibility.

excerpted from Xonariarius the Younger's
Nobilite Pax Imperator – the Triumph
of Aristocracy over Democracy.

PROLOGUE:
END OF THE WAR

JOBE FRANCKS PLACED his two metre, ninety kilogram body square in the doorframe, blocking the only exit. It was a shabby, rundown building. More crumbling stone and dusty mortar than anything else. But it did have one luxury – a single access point.

In the Underhive, finding a building that hadn't had a hole blown through the side, back, or roof was definitely a luxury. He and Syris had stumbled into this luxurious abode three years earlier while running from members of the New Saviours gang. As they hid in a dark corner, listening to the heavy footsteps of their Cawdor rivals pounding the streets outside, they both knew they had found a new home, a hideout for their own gang, the Saviours of Humanity.

'You're not going anywhere until we talk this out,' said Francks. 'What you're considering is insanity. It's got to be a trap, and you know it.'

'If you know it's a trap, then it's not really a trap… at least not a very good one.' Syris smiled his normal, lopsided grin as he threw an arm around Francks's shoulder. 'Lieutenant,' he said. 'Everything will be fine. You stay here and guard the hideout.' He swept his other arm out in a grand arc, gesturing at the crumbling, five-room structure as if it were a palace.

Several juves sat at a table, trying desperately to concentrate on the weapons Francks had them cleaning, rather than the confrontation between their leaders across the room. The rest of the gang members were either sleeping in the crowded siderooms or on patrol in the streets around the hideout.

'You're in charge until I return. Don't give them an inch, you hear me? Stay here, keep your head and everything will be fine.'

Francks stared deep into the cloudy, grey eyes of his friend and leader. A frown curled his lips as he narrowed his eyes from stare to glare. 'Are you just trying to reassure me or have you "seen" something?' he asked.

Syris winked at him, which probably did not have the effect that was intended. It was a slow wink, the eyelid fluttering on the way down as if it was reluctant to close over that eerie, almost milk-white eye. It didn't help that Syris's scraggly, sand-coloured hair practically floated in a tangle around his head, or that his complexion had turned almost blue in the last few weeks. He looked, for all the world, the epitome of the crazed wyrd that the New Saviours continually railed against. The entire effect was somewhat unsettling, even to Francks, who knew that much of it was an act.

'There is a plan for the Universe, my friend,' Syris said, his eyes now definitely focusing on something or someplace far beyond Francks. 'I have barely glimpsed the edges, but there is a plan. And our part in it is far from over. Stay here. Keep the gang safe. We will be together again.'

FRANCKS CROUCHED BEHIND a chimney on a roof near the meeting place and stewed. He realised he was doing something he had never done before – disobeying a direct order. But there was no way he could let Syris attend this meeting alone. The danger was real. How could someone with the 'sight' not see that?

It had sounded too good to be true, which meant it definitely was. Jules Ignus, leader of the New Saviours, wanted to meet with Syris Bowdie, leader of the Saviours of Humanity (or as Ignus had called them 'The Old Saviours') to discuss peace terms. He had said he wanted to meet one-on-one – no lieutenants, no gangs – just the two of them on neutral territory so there would be no chance of the meeting erupting into another gang war, which neither of them could afford.

Francks wished he could get closer, but past this building there was nothing but the acid pools that gave this settlement its name. Nobody knew where the acid had come from originally. It might have been a reservoir hidden beneath the dome that finally ate its way through the dome floor or it might have leeched out of a toxic waste pipe running down from the factories in Hive City.

It didn't matter. Wherever the acid came from, it had been pooling up in Acid Hole for generations, simultaneously dissolving away the settlement and providing its residents with their only livelihood. Acid mining was dangerous work that killed more people than it made rich, but when you're poor and desperate, a chance at a better life is worth any risk, even your life, and that pretty much summed up the situation for nearly every soul in the Underhive.

The pools had claimed almost half the settlement in the last hundred years. Even now, acid licked at the foundations of the building where Francks hid. Soon, it too would crumble. Then the rubble would be used to extend the stone pier that ran into the middle of the pools, allowing the miners to reach their claims.

At least Francks knew that Ignus would have to keep his end of the bargain. There was nowhere his gang could hide out in the pools. As far as the eye could see, there was nothing but acid criss-crossed by stone paths. But that also meant he couldn't get any closer. So, Syris stood in the middle of the acid, alone, waiting for his rival to arrive for the peace talks.

It was getting late, which made Francks worry even more. This had been Ignus's meeting. Where the hell was he? Probably trying to addle Syris by making him wait. If that was the case, then Ignus knew nothing about the leader of the 'true' Saviours. It would take more than an hour at the edge of the acid pools to make Syris Bowdie panic.

The sound of a stone skittering off the edge of the roof made Francks whirl around, laspistol in hand.

Jerod Bitten, Ignus's own lieutenant raised his hands over his head, palms forward to show he had no weapon. 'You're not supposed to be here,' said Bitten.

'That makes two of us,' sneered Francks. 'No lieutenants, remember? Only I don't trust your boss to keep his end of any bargain. And it looks like I was right.'

'You don't understand,' said Bitten. He moved forward, but then stopped as Francks re-aimed his weapon at Bitten's head. 'You're not supposed to be here. You're supposed to be protecting the gang. Now, it's all going to hell.'

'What are you talking about?' asked Francks. The pit of worry that had been festering in his stomach all day cracked open and bloomed into full-scale paranoia. He knew exactly what Bitten meant. 'Syris wasn't the target at all was he? Dammit. I should have seen this coming... Syris should have seen this coming. Only he did; that's why he wanted me to stay away from the meeting.'

Bitten stood beside him now. Francks was so caught up in his own guilt he hadn't even seen the rival lieutenant cross the roof. 'We can still stop the rest of it,' he said. 'But you have to trust me.' Bitten was talking fast now, either because he was telling the truth and they didn't have much time, or just to get his story out before Francks melted his brain with the laspistol. 'You have to warn Bowdie. Get him away from the acid pools now! Before it's too late!'

Francks stared at Bitten, still processing the ramifications of everything that had been said in the last few moments. 'Rest of it? Warn Bowdie?'

Bitten grabbed Francks by the shoulders and shook him. 'Your gang is already dead. Ignus is on his way here now to kill your leader. I can't stop him. I just... I can't. But you can. If you act now.'

Francks shook his head to stave off the impinging darkness and then rolled his shoulders to wrench himself away from his enemy. 'This is preposterous. Ignus wouldn't dare murder another gang leader. Nobody is that insane. He'd be dead in an hour. If that's your story, I'm not buying it. If not, tell me why I should trust you.'

Bitten shook his head. 'Because you have no choice. Because Jules Ignus is that insane. I came here to try to stop a murder, but I can't. I... I'm terrified of him. You can stop him, but only if you trust me. Now go!'

Francks stared at Bitten for another heartbeat and then turned toward the pools. Syris was too far away to hear him call. He had no way to get his attention. He looked down at the weapon in his hand. Maybe he did have a way. Francks aimed for the middle of the pool next to Syris. If he didn't hear the blast, he would at least notice an eruption of acid ten metres away. At least then he'd be on guard for whatever Ignus had planned.

As he steadied his grip with both hands to be sure of the shot, Francks thought he saw something move in the distance. No time to lose. He squeezed the trigger. Nothing happened. He squeezed again. Nothing. 'Scav!' Francks flipped open the bottom of the grip to check the power cell. It was empty. He'd checked it before he left. What was wrong? 'Those damn juves screwed up the recharge.' He snapped his head toward Bitten. 'Hand me your weapon.'

'But...'

'Quickly!' He snapped his fingers. 'You have to trust me, right?'

Bitten pulled out his own weapon and handed it, grip first, to Francks. His trust obviously only went so far, though, because as soon as Francks had the weapon, Bitten backed out of sight around the chimney.

Francks turned back toward the pools again, ready to fire a warning shot, but it was too late. Jules Ignus had appeared out of the acidic haze, perhaps another hundred metres past Syris. He must have been waiting out there near the edge of the dome the whole time. He had something in his hands, something metallic that glinted in the dim light. He raised the item up to his shoulder. It was a rifle!

Francks aimed, but had little chance of hitting Ignus from such a distance with a pistol. The two shots rang out almost simultaneously. Francks's bolt slammed into the pool next to Ignus, sending a spray of acid into the air. The blast from Ignus's rifle hit Syris in the back. Bits and pieces of armour flew off as the shot bored through to flesh. Syris's head snapped back and his mouth opened. Francks knew his friend was screaming, but all he could hear was the pounding of his own heart.

He shot again and again, hitting the stone walkway in front of Ignus and then the rival leader's arm. That shot finally stopped him. But the damage had been done. Syris crumpled to the ground.

Francks screamed and continued firing, but in his rage, he never even got close again. He saw Ignus look up at him and raise his rifle again, pointing it at the roof. Still he fired, standing beside the chimney in plain sight, no longer caring for his own safety.

The bolt erupted from the end of the rifle, and Francks could smell the air sizzling beside him as it passed him by. He laughed and took aim again. This time he wouldn't miss. This time he'd hit more than just the devil's arm. This time...

Something hard and sharp smacked Francks in the back of the head. He felt himself falling, felt his eyes closing and the darkness seeping in around the edges of his consciousness. For a brief moment, he felt the rough pebbles of the rooftop on his neck and arms. Above him he saw Bitten, a large chunk of stone held in both hands. He was saying something; something important.

'I'm sorry. It's all I could think of...'

FRANCKS ROLLED OVER and groaned. It had happened again. The dream. No, it was a nightmare. Or was it a vision? It was so hard to tell anymore. But this one he remembered from the previous ocassion. At least he thought it was a memory. So much cluttered his brain that it was nearly impossible to sort out fact from fiction, memory from vision, present from past... from future.

The Universe had a plan for him alright. And that plan seemed to be to roam the ash wastes as a madman. At least that had been the plan for as long as he could remember. Beyond that there were only vague shapes and fleeting images.

But today, something was different. He felt different. The images from his dream didn't flee at the first signs of consciousness this morning. That dream *had* been a memory from before. He had been someone – someone important – before becoming a wandering madman.

He had worked beside a great man. He had led men into battle in a righteous struggle. He had even begun to believe in this plan that the Universe had supposedly laid out before him. The reason behind that belief escaped him at the moment, but he knew with a clarity he hadn't had for years that once he had believed.

And now it was time. Time to be someone again. Time to do something important with what was left of his life. Jobe Francks stood up and opened his eyes – his cloudy, grey eyes – and gazed at the endless stretches of white stones and boulders surrounding him. He picked a direction and began walking. It was time to return to the hive.

1: BIG TROUBLE

It felt to Jobe Francks like he'd been walking through the ash wastes for days. In truth it had probably been a lot longer. The ten mile high cone of Hive Primus had loomed ahead of him all that time, seemingly just at the edge of the horizon, never appearing to get any closer. Like a magnet that had changed its poles, it drew him in just as it had pushed him away so many years ago. Now, the home of his youth towered above him.

The tattered remains of his leather trousers and jacket barely covered the old man's stooped body. Scabs from decades-old blisters dotted his ruddy feet, chest and arms. But his face, perhaps protected from the harsh environment of the wastes by the massed tangle of white hair that enveloped his head, was both clear of blemishes and milky-white in complexion.

Francks looked up at the imposing structure of Hive Primus, now mostly shrouded by the layer of poisonous clouds that surrounded it some five miles up. These clouds were testament to the hardworking men and women of Hive City, who toiled in factories so that the nobles could live luxurious lives high up in the spire, well above the poison and filth beneath them. These foul gases also made the ash wastes what it was – an inhospitable hell where even the dregs of society dare not live.

The magnetic attraction drew Francks on toward the Hive. But he knew, deep inside, that it wasn't the Hive that drew him back now. No, it was the body.

'It is time, old friend. It is time.'

He mumbled the phrase over and over as he trudged across the final stretch of wastes. He slipped through the same crack he'd used all those years earlier and trudged on. Now shrouded in darkness as he unconsciously followed the circuitous route from the ersatz entrance toward more habitable areas, he continued mumbling. 'It is happening again. Just as you said it would. It is time. Time for the Universe to pay its debt. It is time, old friend. I am coming.'

'Are you talking to me, old man?' asked a guard.

Francks looked up at the question. Somehow he had found his way to the Hive City docks. A ship flew past him, headed for the mooring berths where its cargo would be unloaded, inspected, catalogued and then stored in one of the many warehouses lining the wall of the dome.

A distant memory pulled at his mind. Smugglers. Sometimes cargo needed to bypass inspection. Ships landed in the Wastes and the special cargo got smuggled into the Hive through tunnels beneath one of the warehouses. The Saviours had done some work for the smugglers back in the day. Francks had used that connection to escape the Hive. Now he was back.

Why was he back? The Body. The Bowdie. He shuffled on again, mumbling. 'It is time, old friend. It is time.'

The clanking of boots running across metal was followed quickly by a hand on his chest. Francks looked up, trying to focus his cloudy eyes on the shape in front of him.

'Okay, gramps,' said the guard, his other hand on the butt of a gun still in his holster. 'I think it's time you stopped walking and tell me what in the Spire you're doing here.'

'I have returned from the wastes to reclaim that which was lost,' said Francks. 'The body of Bowdie will return. You will see.'

'Um, yeah,' said the guard. 'Well, I think you'll have to wait for your buddy in a cell until someone who makes more creds than me figures out what to do with you.' The guard grabbed Franks by the arm and twisted it, trying to turn him around.

Francks whirled around, easily slipping his thin arm out of the guard's grasp. From the look of surprise on the man's face, Francks moved much faster than the guard thought was possible. He pulled the guard forward and gently kissed his forehead.

When Francks released his hold, the guard slumped to the floor at his feet. 'Be at peace,' he said as he stepped over the unconscious guard. 'The Universe has a plan and the time draws near.'

KAL JERICO LONGED for the day in the not so distant past when he had been hanging from a catwalk with his faithful, yet disgusting sidekick Scabbs holding on for dear life to Kal's trousers, which had slipped down to his ankles after they both tumbled over the edge. Ah yes, that day was infinitely better than this one. Or the time that Scabbs had almost blown them all up when he kicked a grenade off the street. That was a fun time… compared to today.

'Have we lost them yet?' asked Kal, not wanting to look back and confirm his worst fears.

He heard a slosh, which might have been Yolanda turning in the waist-high muck to get a look at their pursuers, or his cyber-mastiff Wotan breaking the surface to make sure everyone was still with him. Or it might have just been Scabbs going face first into the dross. Again.

No report was forthcoming from either of his bounty hunter companions, so Kal cocked his head and took a look back. One of the blond braids that framed his wide face fell across his eyes, but he could still see clearly enough.

Yolanda, his brash, amazon-like, sometime partner jogged through the muck beside him. Impossibly long legs kept her loincloth-covered waist just above the brackish, oozing liquid. The scowl on her face and the creases running through the tribal tattoos above her eyes told Kal that she was no happier about this situation than he.

A wake in the muck to the other side showed Wotan's progress. Just then, Wotan's metal nose broke the surface and the mastiff let out a sharp, tinny bark. He was none too happy either, it seemed.

'Good thing Wotan doesn't need to breathe,' said Kal. Scabbs, on the other hand, did need to breathe, but was probably so used to his own stench that he wasn't bothered by the smell of this place. In fact, his constant dips into this muck could only improve the little half-ratskin's odour.

Scabbs was just pushing himself up out of what Kal now suspected was raw sewage, gauging from the brown clumps sticking to his scabby, pudgy face. If it weren't for the ashen colour of his skin, it would be hard to tell where Scabbs left off and the sewage began. Unfortunately, he had fallen behind the other two and was now dangerously close to their pursuers.

Which brought Kal to the crux of the problem. The Goliaths – six angry members of the Grak gang to be exact – were not slowed down by the muck as much as

Kal had hoped. These huge, barrel-chested behemoths with their hulking frames strode through the deep muck as if it were no more than a puddle. The sewage barely reached the Goliaths' knees. Luckily, they only had frag grenades and shotguns, and were still out of useful range for both. But that wouldn't last for long.

'Great plan, Jerico!' yelled Yolanda beside him. She grabbed the edges of her tight-fitting vest and puffed her already well-endowed chest out a little further in what Kal soon realised was an attempt at imitating him. 'Let's cut through these pools. The Goliaths will never follow us through this muck.'

Kal glanced down at his leather coat, the bottom half of which he realised with a groan was beneath the sewage. He was certain he had never stood clutching his lapels like some soft, Spire-raised politician puffing up before a speech. His poses were much more awe-inspiring.

He grabbed the pommel of his sabre, nearly dipping his hands in the muck, and cocked his head just so before replying. 'They wouldn't have chased us in the first place if you hadn't shot half of them in the chest,' he said. 'You know that just makes Goliaths mad.'

Yolanda whipped around toward Kal, sending her cascade of dreadlocks flying in a vicious circle around her head. 'And I wouldn't have had to shoot any of them if you hadn't spent so much time cutting the head off Grak.'

'Do you know how thick their hides are?' asked Kal. 'Not to mention their steel-like bones. And that head is worth thousands of creds–'

Scabbs cut in. 'Uh, Kal?'

Yolanda and Kal turned on the little man, who had caught up with them as they argued. 'What?' they yelled together.

'Grenade!' cried Scabbs, pointing to a round object dropping toward the muck behind them. He dived forward into the ooze.

Kal and Yolanda looked at each other for a split second before following Scabbs under the dross. A muted explosion made Kal's ears pop and the resulting wave forced his body down to the slimy ground beneath the sewage.

He broke the surface of the muck a moment later, sputtering and fuming. Chunks of what Kal desperately hoped was mud clung to his coat and stringy bits of something greenish-yellow dripped off his braids, nose and beard.

'Alright, now I'm mad,' he said. 'Time to finish this. Come on.' He ran on ahead, trying to get back out of grenade range.

Scabbs swiped a scabby hand over his slimy face as he ran, which did little more than smear the brown chunks, like a paste, across his flaky skin. 'So, you have a plan, Kal?' he said more as a statement than a question.

'Yeah,' replied Kal. 'I'm going to kill them and then go get drunk and forget about this day.'

'Another great Kal Jerico plan,' retorted Yolanda, easily keeping pace. 'We needed a grenade launcher to take down Grak, and that got scavved. How exactly will you kill six Goliaths before they rip your arms out and beat you to death with them?'

Kal glared at Yolanda, but somehow the slime and organic matter had completely slipped off her body when she came out of the muck, leaving just a liquid sheen covering her bare arms, midriff and heaving cleavage. He quickly lowered his eyes toward her weapon belt, which held about a half-dozen grenades. He then smiled as a plan formed in his head.

'With that,' he said, pointing at her waist.

'No way, Jerico,' said Yolanda. 'I'd rather die standing, if you don't mind.'

'Not that,' said Kal. 'Get your mind out of the sewage.' He smiled at his joke, but neither of his companions were laughing. 'Hand me your grenade belt,' he continued. 'You, too, Scabbs.'

His companions looked like they wanted to protest, but both knew better than to fly in the face of a Kal Jerico, live-by-the-seat-of-your-pants plan. Kal took the two bandoliers and reached under the muck for his mastiff. Finding Wotan, he knocked on his steel head. The cyber-mastiff surfaced and looked up at Kal, metal jaw open showing a row of sharp, spike-like teeth. Kal was certain that if Wotan had a tongue, it would be lolling off to the side right about now.

Kal draped the bandoliers over Wotan's head, pointed at the oncoming Goliaths, and commanded, 'Wotan! Deliver!' He then pointed toward the muck. 'Stay down!' he added.

The mastiff's head slipped back under the muck. Kal watched as the wake moved off to the side and began heading back toward their pursuers, who were getting dangerously close to grenade range again. Kal glanced at Yolanda and Scabbs, and smiled as he pulled out his twin laspistols and twirled them both at once. He stood facing the Goliaths. 'This should be fun,' he said.

Yolanda obviously didn't trust in Kal's plan because she kept slogging through the muck. 'Enjoy your death by dismemberment,' she said. 'I'll come back for Grak's head after they're done with you.'

Scabbs, who had stopped when Kal stopped, looked back and forth between his two protectors. He shrugged, which dislodged several large muck-covered flakes of skin from his neck. 'To the end, Kal. To the end,' he said.

'Thanks, Scabbs,' said Kal. 'You don't know how much that means to me.' But Kal could tell by the way Scabbs kept glancing behind them at the retreating Yolanda that his heart wasn't really into it. But he knew the plan would work. It had to.

A moment later, the muck in front of the Goliaths erupted as Wotan soared into the air, spraying the giant gangers with slime and refuse. The mastiff's impressive leap carried it over their heads. The stunned Goliaths could do nothing but watch as the metal beast soared above them. Wotan whipped his head back and forth at the apex of his jump, shedding the bandoliers, which fell on the heads of the two leaders.

As soon as Wotan hit the muck behind the Goliaths, Kal opened fire with both weapons, sending blasts of superheated particles racing toward their pursuers at the speed of light. His shots slammed into the chests of the two leading gangers, which would have had little effect if they hadn't both just acquired new bandoliers full of explosives.

The resulting cascade of explosions ripped through the entire gang as the initial blasts set off the rest of the ordnance carried by the giants. Once the smoke cleared, Kal was quite pleased to see not a single Goliath standing in the muck.

Then he noticed the wave of sewage headed toward him from the blast site.

'Oh crap!' muttered Kal.

'WHY ARE THOSE men standing there?' asked the foreman, a large, beefy man by the name of Grondle. Foreman Grondle had a thick shock of black hair that covered his entire head except for his eyes, nose and bright red cheeks. His stomach extended just slightly out past his huge chest. You might call him rotund, if you were absolutely certain he couldn't hear you.

When the small man beside him didn't answer, Grondle pointed a pudgy finger at a group of workers milling around near a three-storey pile of rocks, concrete blocks and other debris that spilled out of the side of the dome. He'd just recently come on the job and had specific instructions from his boss to get the work back on schedule. This twenty year-old rockslide, most likely caused by a hive quake, was his first priority. 'Those men, there, Dinks.'

'They say the rockslide is unstable,' replied Dinks, the crew leader. He was a short and officious looking fellow, with toothpick arms, no chest to speak of and a ring of short-cropped hair running around his otherwise bald head. 'We're waiting for the engineer to show up and inspect it.'

'We have to get that cleared by week's end,' he grumbled. The masons were scheduled to come in and begin to shore up the dome after that, and if he slipped even a day on the schedule, it would take months to reschedule them – months that he would be out of a job. 'The engineer was here yesterday and declared it safe. Get them back to work.'

'But…'

The foreman glared the crew leader into silence. Staring down at the little man, who seemed better suited for library work up in the Spire than construction, the foreman realised Dinks must have got the job of crew leader because he wasn't physically able to actually do any work. 'No "buts" except yours and theirs up on that pile of rubble, clearing rocks!' demanded the foreman.

Dinks looked like he wanted to argue, but decided it would be easier to clear rocks than to sway Grondle's decision. He turned and skittered away toward the rockslide. A moment later, the crew began climbing up the rubble. They formed a chain with Dinks at the bottom, a decision he probably regretted when the first, huge chunk of masonry was handed to him and he had to lug it over to the bin.

Tavis would just love that. Waiting for an engineer inspection. The nerve of that Dinks. Guilder Tavis was not the easiest man to work for. He knew what he wanted and had enough money and power to make everyone's life miserable until he got it. Right now, he wanted this old dome cleaned up for a huge new manse. As if the palace where he lived now was too small for him. *Hmmph*, thought Grondle. Probably too small for his ego.

A series of low rumbles snapped Grondle out of his reverie, but they ended as abruptly as they had started. Grondle looked around at the various work areas. It hadn't sounded like a hive quake, it had been too regular and too short. Then he heard screams and turned to look at the rockslide. Men, rocks, and chunks of concrete tumbled down the hill toward poor Dinks, who stood rooted to the spot in fear, screaming, his face ash-white.

Grondle ran toward Dinks, screaming, 'Get out of there, you fool! Move!'

But it was too late. The chunks of rubble rolling down the hill from the top unleashed even more rocks and even a few boulders as the avalanche swept over the line of men, building momentum and growing ever larger as it careened down the hill.

Halfway to the foot of the hill, Grondle screeched to a halt and began backing away. Debris piled up where Dinks had once stood as more rubble spilled down the hill. A head-sized chunk of rock bounded past Grondle as he turned and ran from the continuing avalanche.

And then it was over. The ringing in Grondle's ears from the continuous rumble of rocks cracking against one another came to an end. He looked back at where Dinks and his crew had been just moments before, and saw nothing but what seemed to be an even larger pile of debris than before. Grondle pulled a cloth from his back pocket and began to wipe the seat from his forehead. 'I'm going to need more men again,' he grumbled. 'Tavis won't be happy about that.'

'HOLY UNDYING EMPEROR!' said Nickle, 'What in the Spire is that?'

This brought a clap to the ears from Staven. 'Never take the name of the Undying Emperor in vain,' he said, adding a moment later, 'Holy scav! What is that?'

'That's what I asked,' said Nickle. He was the taller of the two by almost a head, but was obviously the subordinate in this relationship. Nickle pulled the hood of his blue cloak down around his neck to get an unobstructed view of the old man wandering through the Hive City docks, and then scratched at the bare skin around his sore ear. 'Ow. That hurt.'

'Maybe you'll remember next time, then,' said the shorter Staven, also pulling his hood down to get a better look.

Both men wore identical blue, hooded cloaks and orange body armour. They also had haircuts that made them look like someone had inverted a bowl full of yellow noodles over their otherwise bare heads. They were Cawdor, part of a local gang called the Soul Savers whose territory included the docks. It was a prestigious area for the Soul Savers. They were entrusted with saving the souls of the dock workers, who were well-known for their sinful ways. They did, however, have to curb their more physically instructive styles as violence was frowned upon even in this rough area of Hive City and the gang was forced to masquerade under the guise of a legitimate security operation.

Nickle and Staven had been standing outside Madam Noritake's House of Fun, verbally instructing its patrons about how much more satisfied they would be in the embrace of the Undying Emperor than in the clutches of the unclean women inside. Most people either ignored the two and hurried inside with their faces averted or just glared at them, perhaps quashing a violent instinct or two of their own.

But this strange man walking toward them with wild hair that seemed to almost float around his head, ripped and ragged clothes that barely covered his thin, blister-covered body and a far-off, almost lost look to his eyes – this was a man that Staven thought could benefit from being saved.

He stepped away from the building as the old man shuffled forward. It looked to Staven like he was headed inside Madam Noritake's, which seemed ludicrous considering his age and condition, but the old guy stopped right in front of Staven. He was mumbling something, but Staven didn't bother to listen. He just started into his speech, modified somewhat on the fly for this special lost soul.

'Have you ever considered that perhaps you are lost and need someone to show you the way to a better place?' Staven was quite pleased with himself on his modified opening, but before he could continue, the man grabbed his face and forced him to look into his eyes – those piercing blue eyes shrouded but not obscured by hypnotic, milky-white swirls.

It felt like he was falling through a blue sky toward white, fluffy clouds. It was at once the most blissful feeling he had ever had, as if he were safe in the embrace of the Undying Emperor, but also the most terrifying experience of his life, like falling through eternity, out of control.

And then it was over. The old man said, 'You are "Saviours". It is true.' He smiled at Staven, who looked over at Nickle. The other Cawdor must have been caught in the same trance because he still had a far-away look in his eyes. 'The Universe has a plan, boys. It has brought me to you. The Bowdie will return. You will see. It is time. The Bowdie will return. Now, take me home.'

Staven turned and began leading the old man through the streets of Hive City, glancing back only once to make sure that Nickle had followed as well. They shouldn't have left their posts, but they did. They were forbidden to bring converts back to the Saviour headquarters without express permission, but that's what they were doing. His life seemed to have turned into a walking dream where the rules of the real world were suspended.

As they walked, the old man continued his mantra and an old memory stirred inside Staven about the return of a mythical body. It wasn't from the scriptures. It was more of a story told to young juves from a time in the past. He remembered an old ganger talking to him and a bunch of other new recruits years ago. What was his name? Burton? Benton? Bitten! That was it. Bitten. Staven wasn't sure if Bitten was still around, but someone must know. He'd send Nickle off to find out when they got the old man back home.

KAL WAS FEELING much better about life in the Underhive. Both he and his clothes had been washed – at the same time but by quite different female hands – and he was now sitting in his favourite watering hole with a drink on the table, a girl on his lap, his cyber-mastiff at his feet and a wad of credits from the bounty on Grak burning a hole in his pocket.

The Sump Hole was the Underhive's premier bar, which was to say it was a rat-infested refuse dump that served what tasted like watered-down lighter fluid in bottles that were only clean by the virtue of holding something so toxic that nothing could live inside. The barmaids were slightly cleaner than the bottles and slightly better looking than the rats, but made up for any shortcomings with short skirts and shorter blouses.

Kal's home away from home was constantly filled past capacity with gangers and bounty hunters, and the next brawl was always just an insult or accidental bump away. There'd been so many knock-down, drag-out fights in the Sump Hole over the years that the tables and chairs were now bolted to the floor, which made it somewhat harder to hit someone over the head with one, but a lot more deadly when you did.

'I love it when a plan comes together,' he said, stroking the bare shoulders of the redhead on his lap.

A voice stung him from across the room. 'A Kal Jerico plan doesn't so much come together as fall into place – from a great height with a loud splat.'

Kal smiled. As long as the redhead stayed right where she was nothing could ruin his mood, not even Yolanda's strained wit. 'Hello, partner,' he said. 'I didn't see you come in.' Wotan's head lifted under the table at Kal's voice, but then dropped back down with a clank when it became obvious his master was talking to someone else.

Yolanda pushed her way through the crowd with ease. Even with dreadlocked hair framing a face dominated by an intricate Escher clan tattoo that ran across her forehead, Yolanda was still far more attractive than any of the barmaids, especially with her tight-fitting vest and tantalising leather loincloth. But the combination of her incredible height, well-toned muscles and array of holstered weapons made even the uninitiated patron wary as she crossed the room.

After staring down one juve who got a little too close or smiled just a little too broadly as she strode across the room, Yolanda kicked one long leg over the back of the empty chair opposite Kal and slid down. This was Kal's table, and no matter how crowded the Sump Hole got, there were always at least three chairs open. Kal's was the one with it's back up against the wall of the bar.

'Where's my cut, Jerico?' she asked.

Kal toyed with the idea of telling her that only those partners who stood by him in his hour of need would get a cut, but the narrowness of her eyes and the creases running through her tattoo told him she wasn't in a joking mood.

'I've got it in my pocket,' said Kal. 'Roberta here is guarding it for me, aren't you darling?' The redhead purred into Kal's ear and shifted quite comfortably on his lap. 'As soon as Scabbs shows up, we'll get down to business. For now, get a drink and enjoy life a little. It doesn't always have to be about business.'

'With you, Jerico, it's never business,' said Yolanda. 'Everything is a big game to you.'

'And what's wrong with that?' asked Kal, refusing to let her bring him down. 'Life *is* a game, and the one who has the most fun wins.'

'And you're bound and determined to win at any cost, aren't you?' she asked, but a slight curling of Yolanda's lips indicated she was enjoying the banter. It was the closest Kal had seen her come to smiling in a long time.

But Yolanda's proto-smile disappeared completely when the juve sat in the last open chair. He didn't look at Yolanda, though. In fact, it seemed to Kal that the young ganger was deliberately avoiding eye contact with her. The kid's blue cloak and too-shiny, orange body armour should have rung warning bells in Kal's head, but he'd been distracted by Roberta's tongue in his ear. He didn't realise the danger until the juve started speaking.

'Hi, my name is Georig,' he said in a rush, continuing without even taking a breath. 'I couldn't help but over-hear your conversation. Did you ever think that you might be on the wrong path? Have you ever considered basking in the glory of the Undying Emperor instead of living a life of drunken debauchery? As the teachings of our spiritual leader, the holy Cardinal Crimson, state…'

The room went suddenly quiet as both Kal and Yolanda drew their weapons in a rush at the mention of the Cardinal's name. Roberta slid to the floor with a thud as Kal stood and glared at the young Cawdor. From beneath the table, Wotan growled between the juve's legs, which sounded like a chainblade screaming to life.

'Because you're so young and so obviously stupid,' started Kal, 'I'm going to give you to the count of three to get out of this bar before I fire. Of course after one, Wotan will make sure you can never debauch again. Ready?'

As Kal breathed in to begin the count, Georig fell off his chair and began scrambling across the floor on all fours, proving he wasn't as dumb as he had first appeared. The crowd kindly stepped aside, probably more to get out of Kal's line of fire than to help the kid escape. Kal holstered his laspistols and sat down with a resigned thump.

'I hate Cawdor,' he said, waving off Roberta as she tried to sit back down on his lap. He was no longer in the mood. 'Useless bunch, the lot of them. Undying Emperor, hah! What a bunch of hokum. And Crimson? Holy? Scabbs is more spiritual than that two-bit hack.'

An odd odour wafted across the bar, one that Kal instantly recognised. 'Although his purity is definitely up for debate,' he added as Scabbs took his seat. 'Helmawr's rump, man. Five hours of bathing and you still reek. Did they find another layer of stench under the first ten?'

Scabbs slid into the chair that Georig has just vacated. Jerico didn't know how he did it, but even with a bath and clean clothes, Scabbs still looked like he had slept in trash for a week. There were obviously some stains in his dingy, grey shirt and trousers that would just never come out. If Kal cared more, he'd buy the little rodent some new clothes out of his share, but that money was earmarked for drunken debauchery.

'Nice to see you, too, Kal,' said Scabbs. He pointed behind him. 'That your handiwork I saw running out the front like a scared scavvy?'

'Damn Cawdor!' spat Kal again. He was about to go into another tirade about their holier-than-thou attitude, but Scabbs cut him off.

'So, where's my cut?' he asked, holding his hand out over the table. A few flakes of skin fell from his arm onto the booze-soaked table and floated there like little boats.

'Right down to business with both of you,' said Kal, shaking his head. 'What? Don't you trust me?'

Two heads began shaking across from him. 'You spent our shares of the last big score before we even saw it,' said Yolanda.

'Those were business expenses,' protested Kal. 'I lost my pistols and had to buy new ones.'

'Pearl handled?' asked Scabbs. His hand was still hovering over the table, releasing more boats into the Wild Snake sea below.

Kal looked back and forth at his two partners and saw that he was not going to get any compassion from either of them. But, as he dug into his pocket to pull out the bounty money, he thought he heard his name from over by the bar. He looked up and saw another new face.

This person definitely had no place in an Underhive bar. For starters, his clothes were clean. And not clean like Kal's scuffed leather coat was clean. Clean, like new. And these clothes were expensive. They looked like cotton or silk instead of denim and leather.

'Oh scav!' mumbled Kal, and then quietly slipped under the table. The only people who could afford clothes like that lived in the Spire or acted as agents for one of the Hive City Houses. Both spelled trouble.

'What in the unholy Spire are you doing down there, Jerico?' cried Yolanda.

'Shhhh!' hissed Kal. 'That guy at the bar is looking for me.'

There was a pause before Scabbs answered. 'So?' he said. 'He's almost as small as me. You can take him.'

'You don't understand,' said Kal. 'I owe money... a lot of money... for my new laspistols. That's got to be the debt collector from the Re-Engineers, the Van Saar gang that sold them to me.'

'You're in debt to a Van Saar gang?' asked Yolanda, her incredulous voice still too loud. 'Are you insane? You're lucky to still have all your limbs.'

But Kal didn't answer. He was too busy crawling to the next table. As the debt collector came over toward his usual table, Kal skirted around toward the bar. As soon as there were enough people between him and the silk-suited businessman, Kal stood and slipped out of the Sump Hole.

SCABBS TRIED TO act nonchalant as the silk-suited man arrived, which meant he spent a lot of effort picking at some loose skin on his elbow and then cleaning his fingernails with his teeth. His only mistake was spitting the wad of crust and dead skin he'd mined from under his fingernails onto the striped, grey trousers of the debt collector, who was by now standing right next to him.

'Sorry,' he said, looking up into the face of the stranger. The man stood probably two heads less than two metres, which put him about a head up on Scabbs. But his features made him look much smaller. Wire-rimmed glasses perched on a narrow slip of a nose, outlining beady eyes that were so small and dark they wouldn't have looked out of place on the head of a rodent. His thin, dark hair looked like it had been greased to his head and his face showed not even a hint of stubble.

He held a small, black satchel and, after wiping the spittle from his trousers with a white handkerchief, he laid the satchel on the table, placing both hands on it as if that would be enough to keep it safe, if Scabbs or Yolanda should want to take it.

'I am looking for a Kal Jerico,' said the stranger. 'I assume you are not he.'

Scabbs and Yolanda looked at each other, quizzically. Scabbs decided the man must be talking to him. 'That's right, I'm not Kal, and neither is she,' he added, pointing at Yolanda.

'A ha ha,' said the stranger, which seemed to shake his entire skinny body. 'A good joke, Mr Scabbs. Do you know where I can find Mr Jerico?'

Being called by name flustered Scabbs. Was he getting famous, finally? 'You just missed him...' he started before a quick kick to the shin from Yolanda brought him to his senses. 'I... uh... I think he went to the little bounty hunter's room,' he said, pointing at the back of the Sump Hole.

The stranger looked back where Scabbs pointed, which when Scabbs looked, he realised, was just a blank wall. Did the Sump Hole even have a bathroom? Scabbs had always done his business in the alley outside. The stranger drummed his fingers on the satchel.

'What do you want with Jerico?' asked Yolanda.

The stranger's eyes scanned the lanky bounty hunter from top to bottom, stopping a couple of times for a longer look along the way. 'We have business that must be attended to in person,' he finally answered.

'Well when you find that son of a scavvy,' continued Yolanda, 'let us know. We've been looking for him all day. We have some unfinished business to attend to as well.'

Scabbs had to admit that Yolanda was a much better liar than he, and the stranger might have just bought it, except at that moment, a whistle echoed through the Sump Hole, and Wotan jumped to his feet beneath the table, nearly knocking the man's satchel to the floor. As the stranger grabbed for the handle, Wotan bolted for the door, knocking gangers and waitresses to the floor in a loud racket as he left.

'That, I believe was Mr Jerico's cyber-mastiff, Wotan, if I am not mistaken,' said the stranger, repositioning his glasses on his sharp nose.

'What's a cyber-mastiff?' said Scabbs, which brought another kick to the shin. He should really just let Yolanda do the talking, he thought. But it was too late.

The stranger had left the Sump Hole, following Wotan into the Underhive night.

JOBE FRANCKS FELT more human than he had in a long while. Of course, for him, a long while was counted in years instead of months or weeks. The Soul Savers had fed him and clothed him, and even given him new boots to wear. It felt odd walking through the world without feeling every stone and sharp piece of glass underfoot. Francks wasn't sure he liked it. It felt a little too detached from the wonder of the Undying Emperor's creation. But he felt like he could get used to it.

He'd refused the body armour, but enjoyed the feel of the new, blue cloak against his neck, which offered a constant reminder of his years of suffering as it rustled against his blistered skin. After supper, Randal, the leader of the Soul Savers, came up to Francks with a proposition. He was a tall, gangly man with wavy, blond hair that grew down to his shoulders instead of being worn short in the normal bowl cut of his men.

'How would you like to preach the return of the body to a large crowd of unbelievers?' Randall had asked. There was a smile on his almost boyish face, but Francks had noticed the slight twitch in the curl of his lips that suggested deceit mixed in with the request. 'The square outside the Fresh Air saloon is the perfect spot to begin spreading the word.'

Francks had let his eyes cloud over slightly as Randal spoke, and peered into the black centre of Randal's eyes. Yes, there was deceit hidden beneath his jovial exterior. Deceit mixed with greed, and just a touch of fear. Randal probably didn't know what to do with him, so was sending him into another gang's territory. It was a brilliant move. Randal had complete deniability if Francks got into trouble, and had much to gain if 'the old man' actually made any inroads into the other gang's home. It was how the game was played. Francks remembered those days well, even through the fog of time.

And so Francks had gone to the square and preached, alone of course. Randal couldn't afford to send any of his men, who would be recognised by members of the rival gang. He'd drawn a small crowd, mostly drunk factory workers who'd stumbled out of the saloon to get a breath of fresh air from the huge fan hanging over the square that pumped recycled air into the area and gave the bar its name.

Francks told of the grand plan of the Universe to save them all and bring them into the glory of the Undying Emperor. He regaled them with tales of the crusades fought through the centuries in His name. He spoke of the messenger – the Bowdie – who would return to reveal the intricacies of the universal plan and light the way home into the bosom of the Undying Emperor.

By the end of the evening, Francks's voice was little more than a whisper and his throat was raw. After two decades of speaking to no one but himself, his vocal cords were too easily strained. He would have to pace himself for a while. Stains dotted his new blue cloak from fruit and vegetables thrown by some of the more passionate members of the crowd. He carried several of the firmer pieces of produce in his cloak to give to the Soul Savers.

As he walked through the dark streets, Francks picked at a line of caked blood on his cheek, remnant of a piece of cobblestone thrown shortly after the produce failed to end his sermon. He had felt the surge of blood, a relic of his youth, course through his veins as the pain from that rock radiated through his face.

He had felt the anger of his old life strain against the self-imposed chains that kept him in check. How easy it would have been to jump into the middle of the crowd and snap the neck of the instigator. But he was here to prepare the world for the return of Bowdie, not to begin a holy war. That was his role in the Universal Plan – at least for now.

Lost in his reverie, Francks didn't notice the dark form detach itself from a shadowy alley and slip in behind him; at least not consciously. But somewhere near the base of his skull, Jobe Francks felt the man's black aura. His mind's eye, which saw more of the world than any sane man should feasibly be able to handle, noticed the intrusion and primed Francks's muscles for action a moment before the assassin's arm shot around his neck.

THE STRANGER IN the silk suit, a man by the name of Sorrento, came rushing out of the Sump Hole just in time to see Wotan lope down the street and turn a corner. Unfortunately for Sorrento, in his headlong rush out of the bar, he failed to notice a large bounty hunter heading into the bar.

'Ooomph,' said Sorrento as his nose and glasses slammed into the bounty hunter's barrel-sized chest. He stepped back and tried to re-seat his glasses around his ears, but the wire frames had twisted in the impact.

As he worked on the bent frame, two immense hands dropped onto his shoulders like the gods descending.

'You smudged my armour,' said a booming voice from above.

Sorrento finally got his glasses back on and looked up at a wide, scraggly-haired face. A scar running from the edge of the man's lip down to the centre of his chin marred the perfect two-day growth of beard. One long eyebrow slanted across his forehead and the tangle of black hair covering his head looked thick enough to stop bullets.

'Um, sorry?' asked Sorrento. The grip on his shoulders tightened, making him cry out in pain. It felt like the fingers had penetrated his skin and were now crushing bone. The street began to spin, or was that his head? It was difficult to tell. He needed to appease this hulking brute before he passed out and ended up dead in a gutter. 'I'm… unngh… terribly sorry, sir,' he tried again. 'Let me… um… buy you a drink to make up for it?'

The pressure eased, but was quickly followed by a new pain as the bounty hunter slapped Sorrento on the back and pulled him into a 'friendly' hug that made him gasp as his chest compressed. They walked back into the bar, where Sorrento proceeded to buy his life back with several rounds of Wild Snake.

KAL'S LUCK HAD definitely changed in the last few hours. After giving the debt collector the slip, he'd wandered the darkened streets looking for a dive where he could drink in peace. By chance, he'd stumbled upon the Lucky Strike Hole. From the front, you wouldn't even know it was there. It was dark, drab and falling apart, making it look like every other semi-inhabited building in the Underhive.

The windows and obligatory blast holes were covered by burlap and tape, which by itself had drawn Kal's attention. Why bother if it was just a flop spot? And a gang would have reinforced those potential incursion points with something more durable than cloth. Intrigued, Kal had gone to the door and knocked. He wasn't too surprised when a small hatch slid open at eye height.

'What's the password?' asked a voice behind the door.

How quaint. A password-protected hole. Luckily, he had the universal password. He pulled out the bounty credits and fanned them in front of the eyes. A moment later, the door opened and Kal walked into the most lavish gambling hole he'd ever seen in the Underhive.

Gambling tables sat on red and yellow carpeting in a huge space that once might have been a factory floor or warehouse. Carpeting! His feet sank into the deep pile, as he stared in awe. Everything looked new. The tables showed no chinks, holes, or scorch marks from previous brawls, and the floor was free of those ugly brown stains that you never asked about and always walked around in other holes.

As Kal revelled in the luxury, a gnawing little voice in the back of his head began to ask some obvious questions. Who would spend this kind of money on an Underhive hole? And if you had that kind of money, why not spend it in the Spire, or at least in Hive City? But at that moment, a waft of lilac followed by a soft touch on his arm pulled Kal from his musings. A beautiful hostess, who made Roberta look like a scavvy, smiled at Kal, took him by the arm and escorted him to a table. She never said a word but it seemed to be understood that as long as Kal was gambling (and winning) she would be his constant companion.

Kal tossed the bounty money on the table and started to play. He was home.

2: OLD FRIENDS

JOBE FRANCKS FELT the sharp pressure of a dagger in his side. The shadowy assailant wrapped an arm around his neck pulled him fast against his body. The point of the dagger dug into Francks's skin through the new blue cloak. Underneath the clean shirt, a trickle of blood dripped down to his waist.

'Don't struggle, old man, and I promise it won't hurt… much.' The arm around Francks's neck tightened as the assailant pulled him back toward an alley. The dagger punctuated the threat, digging further through the blue cloth.

But Francks had no intention of struggling. In fact, his plan called for complete relaxation. He glanced down and back to see where they were headed. When his attacker reached the raised platform at the edge of the street, he paused for a moment and then pulled away slightly as they stepped up. At this point Francks went completely limp in the attacker's grasp and slid toward the ground.

The dagger caught in the folds of his cloak, pulling the attacker's arm down and pitching him forward off the edge of the walkway. Francks groaned as the serrated blade scraped across his ribs, but fought the urge to catch himself. The attacker tightened his grasp around Francks' neck and tried in vain to pull the larger man back to his feet.

Francks gagged and fought off the impending blackness as the arm crushed his larynx, but instead of leaning back to ease the pressure, he bent forward, pulling the already off-balance assailant over on top of him. They both fell to the ground in a heap. Francks rolled away and then kicked out with both feet. His new boots cracked into the assailant's knee.

The man screamed in pain as Francks scrambled to his feet. He stood, facing his attacker, who had also found his footing, but was now favouring one leg. Both men breathed heavily, but the attacker smiled.

'Nice moves, old man, but I still have the dagger...' He brandished the serrated blade. '...and a laspistol.' The assailant raised his other hand, holding a jet black pistol. He held the blade out to the side, poised to strike, and the gun in close to his body, as if protecting it.

Adrenaline coursed through Francks, bringing renewed vitality to his old body and a clarity of mind he hadn't enjoyed in many a year. This was a professional he faced. That much was certain. The angle of the blade, the calm hold on the pistol, the piercing gaze he gave Francks, all said this was a man trained to kill.

Francks knew two things he hoped would help him survive. First, if the attacker was going to use the weapon, Francks would already be dead. For some reason, the pistol was his last resort. Francks didn't know why and didn't care, but he was sure he had nothing to fear from the laspistol. Second, Francks had been trained not to kill, but to survive. The key to winning a gang battle was to not get hit, and in his day Francks had been good at that, one of the best.

The attacker crept toward him, keeping the pistol pointed at his head as he approached. The dagger waved slowly back and forth in front of him in a tight figure of eight as he moved. Francks glanced over his shoulder, as if looking for somewhere to run. He stepped back toward the curb tentatively, trying his best to look scared.

'You can't run, old man,' sneered the attacker. 'I'm younger and faster and I've got the gun.' He tilted the butt of the gun ninety degrees, as if to prove his point.

Francks glanced over his shoulder again as the attacker closed on him. He then pivoted at the waist and took a step as if to run. He heard heavy footfalls behind him. The attacker had taken the bait. Francks twirled around and dropped into a squat, sweeping his leading leg out and slamming it into the attacker's injured knee.

The man dropped to the ground and rolled over in pain. He grabbed at his leg, which pointed in an odd direction below the knee. Francks snatched the laspistol, which lolled in the man's hands, and fell on the attacker. He shoved the gun into the man's stomach between their bodies and fired. The press of the bodies on the gun muted the loud blast. He fired again to make sure, and then rolled off.

A few minutes later, Francks knelt over the body of the attacker in the alley looking at an odd piece of paper. The man had no identification, which was no surprise, but the note he carried gave Francks pause. A simple message scrawled in what looked like blood said: 'This man is a heretic. The heretic must die!'

Francks folded up the note and secreted it, along with the dagger and pistol, in a fold in his cloak. He hurried back to the Soul Savers hideout and dropped the pistol into the gang's armoury cabinet. He kept the dagger, though. It appeared he might need to use the old ways a bit more before this was finished.

JOCK BEAMLER, PIT boss at the Lucky Strike, pulled at the taut collar stretched around his thick neck as he watched the gambling floor. Long ago, when this had been a factory, the rusty walkway he stood upon must have provided access to machinery or the ventilation system. Whatever had been there had already been scavenged, but the catwalk remained – most of it anyway.

It made an excellent vantage point for keeping an eye on the Lucky Strike. He wasn't pleased with what he saw today. Most of Jock's night was spent watching the dealers to make sure they weren't cheating the customers and pocketing their ill-gotten chips. Cheating was encouraged, of course, but a portion – an extensive portion, actually – of any extra credits skinned from a mark belonged to the house.

But this was different. At first, Jock hardly even noticed the bounty hunter sitting with Stella. She was a good girl and always got her marks nice and drunk so they lost all the credits they hadn't already spent on her. He hadn't given that mark a second thought once he saw who was working him.

But now there was a huge stack of chips in front of the man with the long leather coat, and Stella was looking up at Jock and gesturing behind the man's back. From the look on her face, she'd been gesturing for quite some time.

'This is not good. This is not good at all,' said Jock. He swiped a meaty hand across his cheeks and then wiped the slick palm on his neatly-pressed trousers. Jock was a burly fellow, huge upper arms and Goliath-sized chest. In fact, Jock's general size and shape made most people think Goliath – at least until they glanced up at his face. Jock had the smooth skin and rounded features of a child, all set in a head that looked almost ludicrously small sitting atop his massive shoulders and thick neck. Despite his large body and small head, Jock was bright enough to run the Lucky Strike and, more importantly, smart enough to know when he needed help.

He made a quick cutting gesture at his neck, and mouthed the words: 'Cut him off.'

Stella shrugged her bare shoulders and mouthed, 'How?'

Jock shrugged back. 'Think of something.' He turned from the railing and ran toward the ladder. He knew the loud clanking of his hard-soled shoes on the metal would make every eye in the place glance up, but he needed help and he needed it quick.

KAL GLANCED UP at the clanking sound in the rafters, and smiled as he watched the large man run across the walkway and slide down a ladder. He glanced around the room to see what the commotion was about, but all the patrons had the same bewildered look in their eyes. They all watched as the pit boss lumbered across the back of the room. Buttons popped off his coat as he ran, and he tore his cuff as he slammed through a door, leaving a large shred of black fabric hanging from the busted door frame. The coat was very much too small for him, especially with his muscles bulging in the kind of frantic panic that gripped him now.

The hair on the back of Kal's neck bristled. At first he thought it was due to Stella's soft fingers on his nape, but when he looked back at the table, the tingle turned into a full, ringing alarm. His entire stack of chips had been pushed into the middle of the table… and he hadn't made that bet!

He glanced at Stella, who fluttered her eyelashes and smiled at him as she now began stroking his neck. But it was obvious where her hands had been a moment before. Kal had been set up.

Now he understood the reason for the commotion. It was a distraction, and he'd fallen for it. Of course, he knew Stella worked for the house. She'd been pilfering the odd chip here and there all night, but a soft warm body was a soft warm body, and Kal had figured it was worth a few credits to keep her hands on his neck and shoulders, amongst other places. But now she'd pushed him all in and he had no choice but to ride it through.

Kal checked his down tiles one more time to see if Stella had got her pretty little fingers on those as well. All seemed in order. The joke would be on the house this time. He'd carefully built a Full Spire over the last quarter hour, and most of it was hidden from view in his face-down tiles.

All he was showing was a wild scavvy brute, two Orlock gangers, and a single Spire noble – the Catallii princess – whom Kal mused was the spitting image of Yolanda, without all the gang tats of course. So, it looked to the dealer like he had the makings of a fairly strong hand: two pair, nobles and gangers, or three Orlocks, depending on where he put the wild scavvy. He'd been betting strong, but not too strong, to keep the table alive.

But his stack held three more nobles – two House Ty and the Catallii prince. Along with his wild scavvy, this gave him an almost unbeatable full house of Spire nobles. If Stella hadn't pushed him all in on this round, he might have done so himself. The player to his left, who was showing a weak pair of ratskins, blanched at the bet and folded immediately after the commotion died down.

The next two players quickly followed suit, which brought the bet around to the dealer, a short bald-headed man with a thick black beard. He had the strongest hand showing at the table: two Ko-Iron nobles and a Delaque gang leader, along with a Spyre Hunter kicker. But, Catallus beat Ko'Iron, so Kal wasn't worried.

Until the dealer matched the bet, and then reached out and flipped the doubling cube.

'House doubles,' he said. The squat dealer tried to smile, but a nasty scar running from his cheek to his chin made it look more like a sneer.

The rest of the players tossed their tiles into the dis-card pile and sat back to watch the show. The bet came back around to Kal, who pulled at his long sideburn while staring at the dealer. He tried to read the man's face, but the beard left little uncovered. There was a cer-tain gleam in his eye that Kal didn't like, though.

The double cube was a nasty move. It meant that if Kal lost, he would owe the house twice the pot. But if he won, they owed him double. It was used to scare off the weak and those out of money. Well, Kal was only one of those two things.

The real question was had the dealer played him as well? Kal was certain the deal had all been legit. He'd been watching the ugly little dealer like a hawk all evening and hadn't seen a single suspicious move from his hands.

Kal reached out and flipped the double cube again, accepting the bet. His Full Spire was the best hand at the table, he was sure, and the pot would cover the debt for his new pistols and let him pay Yolanda and Scabbs their share. Everybody wins.

Unless…

The tingle returned to Kal's neck, but it came too late.

The dealer smiled again and flipped his hidden tiles. Among them were three House Helmawrs, including old Gerontius himself. He had a higher-ranking Full Spire. Helmawrs beat Catallus every day. Kal had lost. Stella slid off his lap and melted into the murmuring crowd.

It dawned on him too late. He'd been played from the beginning. The dealer must have realised Kal was watching him like a hawk and had to wait for the commotion to make his move. He must have been good to make the switch in those few seconds.

Kal wondered who ran this place. Dirty games didn't last long, but these people were obviously professionals. And now Kal was in debt to them.

But that assumed Kal paid this bogus debt. He'd been swindled, and felt no compunction to play fair at this point. He snapped his fingers under the table, and heard a rasping growl in reply. Kal rose to his feet, pushed open his long leather coat, and rested his hands on top of his twin laspistols. Wotan prowled a circle around him, growling at the crowd of onlookers.

'Clear a path between me and the door,' said Kal, an almost icy calm in his voice, 'and I promise nobody will get hurt.'

But as soon as he finished, Kal knew he wouldn't be able to keep his promise. Somebody was going to get hurt – him. The crowd had thinned as the regular patrons slipped under tables or backed off to the far wall, but he was still outnumbered by the workers. All of them – dealers, hostesses, security guards and even the waitresses and busboys – stood their ground. Almost as one, they drew weapons and pointed them at Kal.

'Let me rephrase that...' said Kal as he raised his hands into the air. 'Don't hurt me and I promise not to do anything stupid. Well, anything else stupid.'

The burly pit boss in his too-small coat pushed his way through the circle with a couple of even taller and thicker guards. He pulled at his cuffs, ripping the torn sleeve even more. 'Come with us, Mr Jerico,' he said. 'The boss would like to see you.'

Wotan growled, and the pit boss flinched, his eyes widening as he stared at the mechanical mastiff. 'Play nice, Wotan,' said Kal. 'We're going to go talk this out.' He made a patting motion with one hand as he spoke and Wotan quieted.

Kal and Wotan followed the pit boss toward the back door, escorted by the two goons. Kal didn't know what to expect past that door, but figured his chances were better once he wasn't surrounded by weapons.

The pit boss opened the door and Kal stepped into a darkened room. 'Now, I'm sure we can all be reasonable about this…' he began.

'I'm nothing but reasonable, my dear Jerico,' said a familiar voice deep in the darkness.

Kal's hopes flew away. He'd been safer out there in the circular firing squad. 'Hello, Nemo,' he said as the door shut behind him.

JOBE DIPPED HIS bloody hands in a bowl of water one of the juves had brought him, rubbing them together beneath the brackish surface to remove as much of the stain as he could. His hands shook, but not from the cold water. With the adrenalin ebbing away after the battle, his old body had begun to tremble. His arms and legs felt like lead slag and the simple act of moving them made his muscles ache and quiver in protest.

Afterward, he sat on the edge of his cot and dried his arms and hands with a dirty towel, contemplating his next move. He needed sleep, that much was obvious. The attack had left him with the strength of a Spire-bred librarian. Even though he had a threadbare blanket to go with his thin towel – which said a lot about the prosperity of the Soul Savers – this was no longer a safe haven.

The Savers were doing well for themselves to afford such luxuries for a total stranger. He had no intention of bringing doom down upon them by overstaying his welcome. Besides, there must be other Cawdor gangs out there.

'The redemption business seems to be going well,' he mused out loud.

'That it is,' said a rasping voice from the darkness by the door. 'But I thought you were out of the business. In fact, I thought you were dead. Half-hoped you were a few times.'

Francks dropped the towel on the bed and stared into the darkness. He could see the man's form well enough with his cloudy eyes, but didn't need the sight to recognise the voice. 'It would have made things easier, wouldn't it?' he said. 'My death.'

'Probably,' replied the figure in the dark. 'But that's not why I sometimes wished it. I just thought you deserved some peace after all these years.' There was a pause, and then, 'How long has it been?'

'Since you tossed me out into the Wastes?' asked Jobe. A smile flickered across his face for a moment. 'I honestly don't know. Twenty years? It's hard to keep track of the days, let alone your sanity, out in the Wastes.'

The silence that followed was broken only by a single 'Hmmph' from the doorway. Then the figure moved into the dim light of the lantern next to Jobe's bed. 'It was the only way to save your life.'

'I know, Jerod,' replied Jobe, his voice barely above a whisper. 'I know. You did what you could to save my life.'

'Such as it was,' said Jerod Bitten, Jobe's old rival.

Jerod's long, black hair had gone completely white and was now cropped short and straight. Blue eyes that had seen too much death in their day looked grey and tired, as did his wrinkled and gaunt face. Bitten's clothes were clean and new, which was quite a change from the torn and dirty body armour he'd been wearing the last time Jobe had seen him.

He sat on the cot next to Francks. 'What kind of life did I condemn you to in the wastes?' he asked. 'I honestly expected you to die out there. I never thought I would see you again.'

'I always knew I would see you again,' replied Francks.

Bitten nodded. 'I know. The plan, the grand scheme of the Universe.'

'You still have one last part to play,' said Francks. 'A vital role.'

'Perhaps,' said Bitten. 'But not now. You shouldn't be here now. It's too dangerous.'

Francks turned to look at his former enemy, staring at a spot just behind the man's temple with his cloudy eye. After a moment, Bitten stood and walked toward the door, back into the darkness, as if that would stop the sight.

Francks wondered how much Bitten knew about the attack. He'd grown to trust this man in the weeks after Bowdie's death, but he had been an enemy; freely admitted that he'd sent Francks out into the Wastes to die. *How much can I trust him now?*

'It's Ignus, isn't it?' asked Francks, deciding to push some buttons to see how Bitten reacted. 'He sent an assassin after me tonight.'

Bitten stopped pacing in the dark. 'You were attacked?' he asked. The surprise seemed genuine. 'So soon after arriving?'

'Do you know anything about it?' asked Francks. The adrenaline began to flow again, calming his nerves and numbing the pain in his arms and legs. 'Was Ignus behind it?'

'No,' replied Bitten after a pause. 'Jules Ignus is gone.' Another long pause followed, but Francks waited. He knew there was more to come. 'I don't know who sent the assassin. Not many people even knew you were back.'

'How did you know?' asked Francks. He leaned back, slipping his hand under the blanket to grab the dagger, just in case.

If Bitten was unnerved by the question, the darkness hid it. 'The Soul Savers sent word. I have a… uh… an arrangement with them. But someone very powerful, and very well-connected must want you dead.'

'Why?' asked Francks. He tightened his grip on the knife. 'What does anyone have to fear from an old man, withered by time and the Wastes?'

Bitten came back into the light, but kept his head bowed, as if he couldn't look Francks in the eye. 'As you said, the redemption business is good. The last thing anyone wants is a prophet coming in from the Wastes with a message of hope. An actual saviour appearing right now would be bad for business. There are many people who wouldn't want that to happen.'

Silence filled the room. Francks stared at Bitten in his new suit, his face clean and freshly shaved. Sure he'd been an enemy, but he'd also been a holy warrior; a leader of the armies of truth. Now who was he? A businessman feeding off the faith of others?

'What happened to you, Jerod?' asked Francks.

Bitten finally looked him in the eye and Francks could see the full weight the years had left on his oldest, and probably only, friend. He released his hold on the dagger. He had nothing to fear from this man.

'I grew up,' he replied. 'I survived the wars and I matured.'

'You mean you lost your faith,' said Francks.

Bitten nodded, slowly. 'And you'll lose more than that if you continue preaching.'

Francks just smiled. 'If that is the will of the Universe, then who am I to argue?'

Bitten shook his head and sighed. 'You won't leave, will you?'

'No.'

'And you're going to continue to preach the return of Bowdie?'

Francks nodded. 'I cannot turn away from the plan.'

'No, I don't suppose you can,' Bitten reached inside his jacket and pulled out a small package wrapped in linen. 'Then take this. It's not much – all the credits I had on hand, plus a list of names and locations. These are gangs who will take you in, no questions asked. Each one knows how to contact me, if needed.'

'More business relationships?'

Bitten nodded. 'That's all I can do, though. If you don't leave, I won't be able to save you this time.'

'It is not I who needs saving.'

GUILDER TAVIS SAT at his desk and tried to concentrate on the paperwork in front of him. His assistant, Meru, had stacked everything into neat piles. There were contracts for him to read, payments on promissory notes he needed to validate, collection requests that had to be signed, and warrants that needed to be approved and stamped.

He pushed his chair back and grumbled. 'How did Meru let this work pile up so much?' He shoved the nearest pile away, scattering the contracts across the desk and ruining the ordered system his assistant had spent so much time upon. He then stood and paced across the room to another table.

Tavis was a heavy-set man with thick black hair that always seemed unkempt even after he combed it. His roundish face slid into a thick neck, with only a thin, greying goatee separating his chin from his jowls. His thick, flowing robes kept him warm in the dank office, but did little to hide the paunch above his belt. He had the look of a former warrior who had gone soft behind a desk.

In fact, Tavis had once been a ganger in the Underhive, and had only disdain for the guilders in his youth. 'They're soft,' he used to say. 'Without their bodyguards, they're not so tough. Just a bunch of money-grabbing, noble wannabes. Bankers? Businessmen? Traders? Hah! They're nothing more than parasites, preying on the poor, I say.'

His tune changed when a lucky strike put a sizeable amount of credits in Tavis's pocket. After removing the competition and his former gangmates from the equation, he'd gone straight to a guilder. They formed a partnership and Tavis prospered, especially since his partner's untimely failing health had removed him from the picture as well.

In the end, Tavis had become the epitome of the soft guilder he had once loathed. He ran the whole operation, with extensive help from Meru who better understood the contractual side of the business. Tavis still had a nose for opportunity, and that nose had brought in a lot of revenue over the years.

'And now it's time to reap the benefits,' he said as he looked at the model spread out on the back table.

A scale model of a dome dominated the work table at the back of his office. The table itself was priceless, made of real wood, but Tavis had no eye for the fineries of his office today. He took for granted the thick pile carpeting beneath his feet and the tapestries that hid the dull-grey metallic walls of his downhive abode. This was his baby on the table.

He slid the top of the dome off the model, exposing the interior. Inside sat a model of his new manse. He'd outgrown this small hab in Hive City and as he was no noble, he'd had to go outside the confines of the City to find enough space for a manse that would satisfy his lavish tastes. The entire dome was to be his playground. Huge pools surrounded by imported sculpture. His own theatre where he would import special plays for his entertainment. An immense new manse that would be the envy of guilders and nobles alike. A shining gold dome topped a glittering three-storey abode with a pillared entrance. The central courtyard, dotted with statues, led to the gardens in the rear, complete with fountains.

Tavis knew that this last was purely extravagance. The cost of procuring and caring for live plants alone was more than a mere guilder could afford, but he loved to dream, and the comfort of a huge manse in his very own dome had long been Tavis's dream.

'Who would have thought that a man of such humble beginnings would own a dome one day?' he said as he gazed at the model.

A cough from the door brought Tavis out of his reverie. He looked up to see Meru, dressed in her customary, sensible, beige trouser suit. As usual, she held a data-slate in one hand and a stylus in the other. Tavis wasn't sure he'd ever seen her without stylus and pad. She was efficient and went to great pains to look the part.

She coughed again. 'Excuse me, sir,' she said. 'A Mr

Grondle to see you.'

'Mr Grondle?' he asked. 'Oh, the foreman. You can just call him Grondle. That's his name.'

'Of course, sir,' she replied. 'Shall I show Mr Grondle into your office?'

'At this hour?' Tavis sighed and trudged back to his desk. 'This can't be good news.' He fell into his chair behind the piles of paperwork. 'Yes, yes. Show him in.'

Meru stepped back and a moment later the large foreman stepped through the door.

Tavis immediately yelled, 'Stop!'

Grondle teetered forward on the balls of his feet and waved his pudgy arms around, but was finally able to stop his momentum without toppling over.

'How dare you step foot into my office looking like that,' continued Tavis. 'You will not soil my carpet with that filth.'

Grondle was indeed a sight to behold. His shirt, which might once have been white was now stained brown and grey with a mixture of sweat, dirt and mortar. His trousers were smeared with more of the same. Grondle's thick beard and hair were matted against his sweaty, red face. Every once in a while a bit of slime dripped off his beard onto his shoulder, while brown streaks ran like muddy rivers down his glistening arms to hands that were practically encased in sludge.

'You will report from there.'

Grondle wrung his hands, which sent a cascade of dirt hurtling toward the rug. Tavis opened his mouth to scream at the man again, but decided it would only prolong the filthy foreman's stay in his formerly clean office. At last, Grondle screwed up enough courage to start his report.

'I'm sorry to tell ye, sir,' he began, 'There's been

another accident at the construction site.'

After all the build-up, this revelation came as no surprise to Tavis. 'How much time will this one set us back?'

'It's worse than time, sir,' replied Grondle. 'We lost a dozen men at least.'

'Lost?'

'Buried, sir. That massive rockslide at the edge of the dome gave way and killed an entire crew.'

'I repeat,' said Tavis, drumming his fingers on his desk. 'How much time will this cost me?'

'I dunno, sir,' said Grondle. 'It all depends… '

'On what?' Tavis stood and came around the desk, staring Grondle down until the large foreman balked and looked away.

'On whether I can get the men I need to do the work.' Tavis opened his mouth to protest, but Grondle pressed on, perhaps trying to get it all out quickly so it would hurt less. 'There's been half-a-dozen accidents in the past six months alone. It's been hard enough to get workers and today I lost twelve men and another twelve walked off the job after we dug out the bodies.'

'Hire more men,' said Tavis. He strode over toward Grondle. You're the foreman. Personnel issues are your problem.'

'That's what I'm telling ye, sir,' said Grondle. He began to wring his hands again and then noticed the pile of ash and dirt on the carpet below him and stopped. 'I can't get anyone else to work for me. The men think this project is cursed. Nobody will work on it anymore… at least not at the wages we're paying.'

Tavis yelled right in Grondle's face. 'We're already paying twice the scale rate!' He stormed back to the model. 'And we're not anywhere closer to this than when we started two years ago.'

'What can I do, sir?' asked Grondle. 'Without men, we can't do the work.'

'Then find men!' screamed Tavis. 'I don't care where. I don't care how. But you get workers into that dome or you'll be scraping waste from the bottom of Dust Falls until your hair falls out and your eyes bulge.'

'How do I…?'

'Whatever it takes, Grondle,' said Tavis. 'You do whatever it takes to get the job done, do you hear me?'

'Yes sir.'

Now get your filthy carcass out of my office. And send Meru in here with a mop and a broom.'

IT TOOK A few minutes for Kal's eyes to adjust to the dim light. The only illumination came from a bank of vid screens arrayed in a semi-circle facing the back wall. Nemo, master spy of the Underhive, collector of confidential information, keeper of arcane secrets, purveyor of archaic tech and personal pain the rump for Kal Jerico, sat in a high-backed chair in the middle of the monitors.

But even though he was bathed in the warm glow of the screens, the spymaster looked like a silhouette. He was dressed from head to toe in a form-fitting, flat black fabric that seemed to drink in the light. He would have been impossible to see against the black chair if not for the reflective helmet that covered his head. Kal could almost make out the images on the screens reflected in Nemo's smoked-glass mask.

The bounty hunter could sense other presences in the room as well. There was the pit boss and his two goons behind him, but a low growl and a snap of Wotan's jaws beside him confirmed there were other guards lurking in the shadows to the side.

'You have me at a distinct disadvantage, Nemo,' said

Kal, adding 'again,' under his breath.

'And you owe me a lot of credits, Jerico,' replied the spymaster. Kal couldn't even tell if Nemo was looking at him or not. Even as Nemo spoke, the chair swivelled back and forth to face one and then another of the vid screens. It was a little disconcerting. 'How would you like to settle up? Cash or an IOU?'

Kal weighed his options for only a second. He had no cash and would never sign a debt note to Nemo; at least not again. He decided to try a third option. 'I don't accept the premise of your statement, Nemo,' he began. 'That game was rigged. I owe you nothing. And if you want to dispute it, I suggest we take the matter up with the local guild magistrate.'

'Oh, there's no dispute,' said Nemo. 'You bet and lost... doubled. I have an entire room full of people who will attest to that.'

Kal barrelled onward. 'But your hostess pushed me all in so your dealer could beat me with his rigged hand. All I need is one person at that table to fold under the scrutiny of the guild magistrate. Do you have that much confidence in your people?'

An odd noise emanated from behind Nemo's mask. It sounded like tar bubbles popping in quick succession or the sound of far-off gunfire. After a moment, Kal realised that the spymaster was laughing. He looked around the dim room, but none of the black shapes had moved or even said anything since Kal had entered. Perhaps there was something on one of Nemo's monitors that had made him laugh.

'What's so funny?' he asked, finally.

'You don't know how right you are, Jerico,' said Nemo.

'So, I'm free to go?'

'No, no. When you called them my people.' The sentence was punctuated with that disconcerting, rapid-fire laugh again. 'There's no one out there who will speak against me. I think you know that. And as for the magistrate, I believe he was the man to your left at the table.'

At that, the entire room erupted in laughter.

'You lost, Jerico,' said Nemo. 'Yes, Stella bet all of your chips. But you went along with the bet, even after the double, and you lost. Now you owe me a great deal of money, and I ask once again, how do you plan to pay?'

'But, but…' sputtered Kal.

'Bring on the magistrate, Jerico,' continued Nemo. 'In fact, Jock, go fetch the magistrate right now. He's probably still trying to win back the money he owes me. We can take care of this tonight, and then tomorrow you, Kal Jerico, will be in the slave pits for failure to pay your debt.'

The pit boss turned to leave. Kal was getting flustered. Why did his meetings with Nemo always end so poorly? 'Wait,' he called out. 'I'll sign the IOU.' At least that would give him some time to find a way out of this mess.

'I have a better idea,' said Nemo. He turned toward the side wall and flipped a few switches on a board. 'I have a bounty that needs hunting. You bring in this man for me and I will wipe your slate clean.'

'One bounty and no more debt?' asked Kal. 'That's a high price for a single head. Sounds too good to be true.'

'Oh, not just this debt, Jerico, but all of your previous debts to me. You still owe me over that little matter with the Underhive vampire last year, not to mention the deaths of several of my best men over the past few years.'

Kal blanched even further. If Nemo was willing to

forgive and forget on all of their past business dealings, then this bounty would be tough to collect. 'What's the catch?' he asked.

'You must bring him in alive,' said Nemo. 'He is of no use to me dead, so keep your buxom partner on a tight leash. There is no half-bounty for a head in a sack.'

'That's it?' asked Kal. 'Doesn't sound too hard. Just give me the particulars and Wotan and I will go take our leave to begin tracking down this dangerous fugitive.'

'Not so fast, Jerico,' said Nemo. He flipped another switch.

The room went white. Kal raised his arm to shield his eyes, but was blinded for a moment by the sudden assault of bright light. Wotan growled and barked, but the rasping sound that Kal had always likened to the revving of a chain blade stopped abruptly. He then heard laughing again, but this time it was almost a childish giggling, and he was almost certain there were two distinct pitches in the laughter.

Kal tried to move toward Wotan, but his eyes were blurry and stars filled his vision. As he wiped the stars from his bleary eyes, hands grabbed him from either side and slammed him into the wall.

When Kal could see again, he found Jock, the pit boss, and his two goons holding him in place against the wall. Nemo was still at his chair, but the other two guards were slapping each other's hands, jumping into the air, and slamming into each other, giggling and laughing like girls.

He recognised the guards, now that he could see them in the light. It was the twins who liked to be called 'Seek' and 'Destroy'. Wotan had sat on one or the other during the whole Underhive Vampire fiasco, giving Kal enough time handle the situation in his own inimitable style.

Wotan now lay at the feet of the cavorting twins, shackles around his legs and a steel muzzle holding his strong, metallic jaws shut tight.

'What is the meaning of this?' asked Kal.

'Collateral.'

'What?'

'It's simple,' said Nemo. 'You bring me Jobe Francks, alive, and you get your cyber-mastiff back, alive. If not…'

3: NEW ENEMIES

CARDINAL CRIMSON BASKED in the adoration of his flock, the warmth of his convictions, and the glow of the molten pits of acid and waste surrounding him.

'We bring not judgement upon the wicked,' he called out to the gathered throng of Redemptionists. 'We bring holy salvation. Let all who have sinned, be they unbelievers or witch-wyrds, blasphemers or debauchers, heretics or mutants, cleanse their souls in the scalding bath of truth.'

He paced back and forth atop a rocky abutment, his dais, and gestured to the hundreds of believers who lined the bubbling, green pools below. As his followers chanted 'Burn their sins, burn their sins, burn their sins away!' Crimson raised his arms above him and looked skyward, as if peering through the miles of rock and metal of the hive to the face of the Undying Emperor himself.

The flowing sleeves of his red robes fell back revealing arms that were little more than patches of blackened skin over exposed muscle and pitted bones. Strips of sinew and tattered shreds of leathery, flaking skin barely held together skeletal hands.

'Let them find salvation everlasting in the flaming fire of our faith,' he continued. 'Let them reflect on their evil ways as we burn their sins away. Let righteous redemption come to them at the end of their wicked days. It is the way. It is the will. It is the commandment of our Lord and Saviour, the Undying Emperor.'

The chanting grew louder and faster at the utterance of His name, becoming a single word over and over: 'Burn. Burn. Burn!'

Crimson tossed back his hood and dropped his robes to the ground, standing half-naked before the fervent mass with his arms raised to the heavens. The burned flesh extended across his entire body. Not a single strand of hair was left on his head or chest. Large chunks of skin seemed to have been eaten away, exposing ribs, muscles, and even organs. What flesh remained was blackened or glowed bright red as if inflamed. His eyes bulged in empty sockets beneath the bare skull of his forehead. His large, hooked nose remained intact, but his lips seemed to have been completely dissolved, leaving the Cardinal with a permanent, grizzly smile.

'I, who have walked through the fire of faith and bathed in the burning acid of truth will reveal the path to the wicked,' chanted Crimson. 'It is the will. It is the way.'

The chanting paused as the crowd intoned the words back. 'It is the will. It is the way.'

Crimson lowered his bony hands and pointed to the wings of his cavernous cathedral. 'Bring forth the heretics!' he called, 'and let them bathe in the truth this day.'

The crowd intoned again on cue: 'It is the will. It is the way!'

Two groups of Cawdor gangers, resplendent in clean blue cloaks and gleaming orange armour, climbed onto the abutment, dragging captives up the rocky slope behind them. Where the gangers were freshly bathed and dressed in new or cleaned clothes, the captives were dirty, and what was left of their clothing was torn and bloody. Multiple bruises and cuts showed through the gaps in their clothes, and most were barely conscious.

One group struggled with an Escher woman who pulled at her chains and spat at her captors. 'You brainwashed sons of ratskins can all go straight to bottom of the sump and rot!' she screamed.

The bronze mohawk that swept over her head into a ponytail was matted with blood and large patches of hair had obviously been ripped out. The gang tattoos she wore across her forehead and above her ears were marred in several places by long gashes. Blood had pooled and dried around her ears and nose, while sweat and dirt streaked her bruised and battered arms, legs and torso.

Still, the thick-muscled woman towered over her captors. She glared at them as they pulled her across the raised outcrop and yanked on the chains shackled to her wrists, pulling over two of her captors. 'I will not burn for your enjoyment!' she yelled as she ran, half-stumbling, toward the edge of the flat, rocky dais.

The other gang members, holding their own captives, could only watch as she made a break for the wings of the cave. Before she could reach the edge, Cardinal Crimson leapt from his spot in the centre of the dais, landing between her and freedom.

'No,' he said, loud enough for the congregation to hear. 'You will burn for your own salvation.' With that, Crimson grabbed the tall, powerfully-built Escher by the neck and leg and lifted her over his head. He took two steps forward and tossed her off the edge of the rock like a sack of garbage. She soared, screaming and cursing, through the air, landing in the bubbling pool of acid. Her screams intensified into an incoherent wail as she sunk into the roiling mass. The acrid smell of charred flesh wafted over the crowd, who had resumed their chant of 'Burn, burn, burn!'

One by one, the other captives were given unto the cleansing pool, and with each redeemed soul the chanting grew more fervent until the words echoed throughout the cavern. After the last body had been consumed by the pools, Cardinal Crimson, now fully robed once again, stood alone on the rocky platform and raised his hands toward the heavens. The chanting ceased immediately.

'The souls of the wicked have been cleansed today and we have sent them to their final reward at the left hand of the Undying Emperor,' he intoned. 'Go forth and spread the word. Go forth and bring the heretics unto me and I will bathe them in the holy fire of Redemption.'

The enthralled masses replied as one: 'It is the will. It is the way.'

The service concluded, Cardinal Crimson bowed his head and left the dais. He was immediately surrounded by a retinue of gangers and robed deacons who escorted him through the teeming crowd. Parishioners surged forward, hoping to get near or even touch their leader, but the circle of bodyguards shoved back, forcing open a path through the masses, and sending more than one congregant into the acid pools as they guided the Cardinal to safety.

One of the deacons, a middle-aged man named Ralan with thin black hair slicked off to one side, a piercing look to his eyes, and an acid burn that wrapped around his neck in the rough shape of a hand, walked to the side but always just behind Crimson. He cleared his throat, as if trying to get the Cardinal's attention, but afraid to speak out of turn.

After a few minutes of coughing and clearing his throat, the deacon opened his mouth. 'Cardinal?' he asked. 'A message arrived for you during the service, and I knew you would want to read it as soon as possible.'

Crimson glanced at the deacon. 'You read the message?'

'Of course not, sir.' Ralan bowed his head in contrition. 'But it came from that special messenger. The one you hired recently, sir. I knew the matter to be urgent.'

Ralan held up an envelope. Crimson, galled at the impertinence and stupidity of the man to bring this matter to him in such a public place, snatched the envelope out of his hand. He glared at Ralan until he fell out of his customary position back into the crowd of deacons and bodyguards at the rear of the procession.

Crimson opened the message and read it quickly. It was only four lines, but he read it twice to make sure that it wasn't a mistake.

'May the Undying Emperor damn him to the depths of the Underhive,' he muttered under his breath. He looked back at Ralan. 'Did the messenger wait for a reply?' he asked.

The deacon nodded his head, his lips pursed tight together.

'Good. We shall have further need of him,' said Crimson. He continued on in silence for a few minutes, then asked, 'And what of that other matter?'

Ralan looked pained to have to answer verbally, but finally unpursed his lips and said 'It is being taken care of, sir.'

'Be sure that it is, Ralan. Be sure that it is.'

* * *

KAL SAT AT his regular table in the Sump Hole nursing a
Wild Snake. Normally, he would have gulped down the
entire bottle in a single shot, snake and all, mostly to
avoid actually tasting the vile stuff. But it *was* morning,
plus he had a lot on his mind. His pockets were empty,
his worst enemy was holding his best friend hostage
and even if he did find this Jobe Francks, that still
wouldn't get back the money he had lost at the tables.

All in all, it should have been a fairly normal morning for Kal Jerico, but he knew it was about to get
worse.

'Fry up some millisaur eggs, bud,' called a familiar
voice. 'And don't try to pass off giant spider eggs like
last time. And bring me a Snake to wash it down with.'

Yolanda dropped into the chair opposite Kal without
even looking at the bounty hunter. 'Nothing worse
than the taste of that man's eggs,' she said. 'Except the
aftertaste they leave behind.'

Kal took a long draught from his bottle and tried not
to make eye contact with his partner. But he could see
her looking at him now through the murk of the half-
filled bottle. She cocked her head to one side, regarding
him with a raised eyebrow.

'What in the hive is the matter with you, Jerico?' she
asked. 'It looks like you lost your best friend…'

Kal stared at his bottle.

'Oh, no!' she said. 'It's Scabbs isn't it? What happened?'

Kal broke his silence. 'It's not Scabbs, though I
haven't seen him yet this morning. It's worse.'

'Oh no!' said Yolanda. 'You lost our money, didn't
you?'

She slammed her fist down on the table so hard, it
knocked Kal's bottle over. Kal's hand whipped out and
caught the bottle by the neck and righted it without

spilling a drop. 'It's even worse than that,' said Kal. 'I lost Wotan.'

Yolanda had raised her hand up and pointed a finger at Kal, but stopped in mid-gesture. 'The dog?' she asked. 'That's why you're so bummed? You lost your stupid dog?'

Kal nodded, not even bothering to correct her. Wotan was a cyber-mastiff, no mere dog.

'But the money's okay, right?' she asked.

Kal shook his head.

'Kal Jerico! You scavving idiot!'

Yolanda jumped to her feet and slammed both fists onto the table. This time there was no saving the bottle. It bounced right off the edge and shattered on the floor.

'It still gets worse,' said Kal, figuring at this point, she couldn't get any madder.

'How?'

Kal snapped his fingers toward the bartender to get another bottle. 'Well, it's a long story that involves Nemo and Cardinal Crimson.'

'Holy, scavving Helmawr's rump!' she cried. Her face was now so red that the tattoos running across her forehead and temples practically pulsed and glowed.

'Yolanda, you'd better sit down and take a breath before your head explodes,' said Kal. 'And let me explain how this wasn't my fault.'

'That's not terribly likely,' she said. Just then her eggs and Snake showed up, so Yolanda sat.

With Yolanda glaring at him over a plate of runny, grey millisaur eggs and a bottle of foul-smelling homebrew, Kal described how he'd been tricked into losing the money and then forced by Nemo to take on a bounty to get his cyber-mastiff out of hock.

Yolanda pushed the empty plate away and downed the rest of her Snake. 'So, how does Crimson enter into all of this?' she asked.

'Well, this Francks character is some sort of Cawdor prophet who wandered into the hive from out of the Wastes,' said Kal. 'Crimson supposedly knows something about his history that might help us find him.'

'So what are we supposed to do?' asked Yolanda. 'Just walk up to Crimson and ask him to turn over his precious prophet?'

'That was pretty much my plan,' replied Kal.

'Are you scavving crazy?' she yelled. She slammed her bottle down on the table, rattling the dish dangerously close to the edge. Kal could see her tattoos begin to throb again. 'Every time we get mixed up with those two lunatics, we end up smelling worse than...'

Scabbs walked up, preceded by his odour. Yolanda gagged and it looked like she might toss her breakfast back onto the table. 'Well, worse than him after taking a bath in raw sewage.'

'Hey, I took a bath after that, I'll have you know,' snorted Scabbs. He plopped down into the last chair with an audible squish.

'Maybe next time you should use soap,' snapped Yolanda.

'And water,' added Kal.

'You just keep your trap shut, Jerico,' she snarled. 'You have no right to talk to him that way this morning.'

Scabbs scratched at a patch of skin hanging from his chin. 'Did I miss something?' he asked.

Yolanda jabbed her finger at Kal. 'Mr Lucky lost all our money and his dog last night *and* ran us afoul of both Nemo and Crimson.'

Scabbs glanced back and forth from Yolanda to Kal, with an odd expression on his scabby face that Kal couldn't quite read. 'Is that all?' he finally asked. 'That's a pretty normal day's work for Kal Jerico. Besides, I'm sure he's got a brilliant plan to get back Wotan and our money, don't you Kal?' He looked at Kal with a big smile on his face.

'Yes, Jerico,' purred Yolanda. 'Tell Scabbs your brilliant plan.'

Kal looked at the doting smile on Scabbs face and the sarcastic smirk on Yolanda's – and found inspiration. 'I did have a good plan,' he said, 'But in times of need, I think it's always best to turn to our friends and family, don't you?'

The smile and smirk disappeared from both of their faces, replaced by the furrowed brows of befuddlement. 'Yolanda, I want you to contact the Wildcats and find out anything you can about Cawdor gang activity that might point the way toward Francks.'

'That's actually a pretty good idea, Jerico,' she said. 'What are you going to do?'

'Scabbs and I are going to pay a visit to an old friend who can keep an eye on Crimson for us and let us know when Francks contacts our acidic Cardinal friend.'

Scabbs smiled again and clapped Yolanda on the shoulder. 'See Yolanda? What'd I tell you? Kal's on the job.'

JOBE FRANCKS CHECKED the information Bitten had given him and then looked at the building in front of him. It was always tough to locate anything in the Underhive. It wasn't like the buildings had addresses painted on the walls. Most didn't even have walls. But this had to be the place. The note said 'North corner of Glory Hole settlement, orange two storey building'.

Perhaps he was just tired. He had been up for twenty-four hours now, and he'd been travelling all night through the Underhive, which is tough for a juve let alone someone his age, but this two storey building didn't look like a Cawdor gang hideout.

For one thing, all of the walls, doors and windows were intact. For another thing, he'd seen no patrols or guards, and here he was supposedly standing outside the front door to – he checked the parchment Bitten had given him again – the Universal Saviours.

Lastly, there were no slogans painted on the side of the building, or anywhere along the street for that matter. No 'Death to the heretics' or 'Praise be to the Undying Emperor' anywhere to be seen. Not even a single 'Be Saved or Die' banner. It was refreshing to say the least. Even in his day, the hardliners were already in the majority. It seemed it was much easier to convert people to an absolute faith than one that depended too much on personal beliefs.

Still, Francks was sure even a moderate gang would have an extreme reaction to a stranger wandering into their hideout, so he knocked on the door first. A few moments later, a much too young voice behind the door asked, 'What's the password?'

Jerod had said nothing about a password. Jobe tried the simple approach. 'Bitten sent me!' he called through the door.

He could hear sounds of footsteps and hushed voices through the door. A moment later, the door opened a crack. A young pair of eyes just visible beneath long, straight hair peered out at him through the gap. 'Are you Mr Francks?'

Jobe almost laughed. He didn't think he'd ever been called mister before. 'Yeah,' he replied. 'Jobe Francks. Can I come in?'

The door closed again and he could hear more hushed voices. Then the door opened all the way and he walked in. As soon as the door closed, Francks slapped the young juve across the temple with the back of his hand.

'Don't you ever open the door again unless you hear the password,' he growled. 'Do you understand?'

'But Mr Bitten told us to expect you, Mr Francks,' he protested, his voice rising into a whine.

'And you have only my word that I am Jobe Francks,' he snapped back. 'What if I'd been some rival gang member, huh? You'd all be dead right now because you opened the door without authorization.' Francks looked around the room. There were maybe half-a-dozen juves sitting around tables. He couldn't tell what they had been doing; perhaps playing cards. There were no weapons and no upper echelon gang members in sight.

'Where is your leader?' he asked the long-haired juve. 'Where's the rest of the gang? And why aren't you juves cleaning weapons or at least guarding the hideout?'

The kid ran long fingers through his stringy hair, pushing the strands off his face for the moment. Francks could see the fear in his eyes – more fear than there should have been even given the browbeating he was currently undergoing.

'Every… everyone's out,' he stammered. 'They were… we've been called out by the Righteous Saviours. They all left hours ago.'

Tears welled up in the juve's eyes and Francks softened a bit, putting an arm around the kid's neck and leading him to one of the tables. 'It's been bad, hasn't it?'

The young juve plopped into the chair. Even without his cloudy-eyed sight, Francks could see the weight this kid was carrying. There was every chance he'd be the leader of the Universal Saviours by nightfall.

'They say we harbour heretics,' he began, 'but we don't. It's just that our leader, Breland, won't condemn every wyrd and unbeliever on sight. He says,

"We are all on separate paths to salvation, but the paths converge to a single point, like spokes on a wheel."'

'Breland sounds like a smart leader,' said Francks, adding to himself, 'perhaps a little too smart for his own good.' He looked around the room again. Like outside, there were no slogans painted on the walls, no altars of fire or sacred pools of acid. What he did see were books. Lots and lots of books. An expensive habit, thought Francks. Bound tomes were virtual relics, worth at least triple their number in weapons.

He now realised that the juves had all been reading when he came in. Francks looked at the books on the table in front of him and recognised a couple of titles: *The Universal Path* and *Questioning the Truth*. Bowdie had forced him to read these when he was just a juve. They had been sacrilegious works even then. One said that the Undying Emperor was more an ideal – a universal force – than a god, and that all would be saved if they just walked the path of a virtuous man. The other taught that reason and forgiveness were the supreme qualities of man, that intolerance and hatred were the hallmarks of a limited mind.

Francks could see now why the Universal Saviours had run afoul of other Cawdor. They were espousing heretical ideas. It was a wonder they had survived this long. 'Where is the meeting?' he asked.

The long-haired juve looked at Francks and then at his fellow Saviours. They all shrugged, leaving the decision up to him. 'At an abandoned factory not too far from here,' he said. 'I can show you the way.'

Francks shook his head. 'No. You stay here and keep your brothers safe until I return,' he said. 'Don't open that door unless you hear the password, and hide these books somewhere safe. They're worth more than your lives. Any of our lives.'

MARKEL BOBO WAS taking it easy. He'd been out of work for days, which suited him just fine. The life of an intelligence gatherer tended to be stressful and he'd been in dire need of some downtime. So, for the last few days, he'd hardly moved from the parlour of Madam Noritake's House of Fun – at least not until Jenn Strings finished her last client of the day. Then the two of them would retire to Bobo's room upstairs, which was paid up for another month at least.

Officially, Bobo was on the payroll of House Helmawr, but he'd just finished one job and was waiting for new orders. In the meantime, he had decided to forego freelance work and spend more time with Jenn.

So, Bobo sat in an overstuffed chair, drink at his elbow and cigar in his hand, watching the unending parade of flesh that passed back and forth through the parlour. None of the girls paid any attention to Bobo – they all knew he belonged to Jenn – and none of the clients even noticed him. A small, nondescript man, Bobo stood well short of two metres and weighed little more than the slightest of Madam Noritake's girls. He had a forgettable face topped by short, thinning hair of an unremarkable colour.

As always, Markel wore slightly rumpled, loose-fitting, beige and grey clothes. He blended into every background, an effect he worked quite hard to perfect. While there were no weapons visible on or near Bobo's body, he could disembowel a man in a second with any number of sharp implements secreted away within easy reach.

He didn't expect any trouble but, as a general rule, Bobo knew that was exactly when trouble sought you out. Right now, he was waiting for trouble, hopefully of the paying kind, but he wouldn't bet on it.

'Good morning, Markel,' said a familiar voice from the doorway.

'Morning, Kal,' replied Bobo between puffs on his cigar. 'Sit down. I've already ordered you a drink.'

Kal dropped into the chair opposite Bobo, picked up the glass, and downed its contents. 'How'd you know I was coming?'

'Word travels fast in the Underhive, Kal,' said Bobo. 'Plus, your friend there does tend to announce himself well before he arrives.' He pointed at Scabbs, who had sprawled on a couch, sending a cloud of dirt, dried skin, and noxious fumes into the air.

'I need your help,' said Kal. He waved at the bartender to get another drink.

'So I gathered,' said Bobo. 'You never come around just to drink.'

Kal smiled. 'I drank, and I'll drink again.' He took the glass from the bartender, downed it in a single gulp, and then slammed it on the table beside him. 'But, I also came to warn you that Nemo seems to be collecting on old debts.'

Bobo took a long drag on his cigar and puffed an intricate series of smoke rings that practically danced in and around each other. 'Hasn't forgiven you for beating him to Armand's stolen intel, eh?' he asked. 'Or is he still sore about what we did to his two thugs?'

'The twins?' asked Kal with a smirk. 'They were hardly thugs. More like clowns with guns. What did they call themselves?'

Bobo thought for a moment and then smiled as well. 'Seek and Destroy. I remember Wotan sat on one of them.'

'Good times,' said Kal with a chuckle, but his smile faded quickly. 'And now Wotan is paying for it.

Nemo's taken my cyber-mastiff hostage and is forcing me to bring in a bounty to trade for him. If I know Nemo, it won't be an even trade. We may be next.'

Bobo stamped his cigar out in the empty glass, leaned forward, and lowered his voice. 'That might explain some odd news I heard yesterday,' he said.

Kal leaned in as well. 'What was that?'

'Business first,' said Bobo. 'I assume you can pay for my services, right?' Bobo actually assumed just the opposite, but it was fun to watch Kal try to squirm out of paying his debts.

'Well, actually, I'm a bit tight at the moment,' said Kal with a sheepish green. 'You know how it is.'

'I do,' said Bobo. 'Probably better than most. So, what are you offering?'

Kal looked almost upset at Bobo's gruff, business-like manner. 'Do you talk to all members of the royal line of House Helmawr like that?' he asked.

Bobo took another long puff on his cigar. 'You're like, what? Forty-second in line?'

Kal looked almost completely deflated. Bobo could tell he was off his game today. Nemo must really have him worried. 'Look,' said the little spy, 'put in a good word with your cousin Valtin the next time you talk and I'm all yours.'

Kal smiled. 'You are too good to me,' he said.

'You're right,' said Bobo. 'But as you say, I do need to keep the royal line happy.' He handed Kal one of his cigars.

'So what was this odd news you heard?' said Kal as he took the cigar and lit it up.

'It seems someone is hiring assassins on the QT,' replied Bobo. 'I don't know who or why, or who's being targeted.'

Kal puffed on his cigar and pondered the news. 'What does that have to do with me?'

'Perhaps this bounty hunt is just an elaborate setup to get you killed,' said Bobo. 'It's just the kind of complex setup Nemo loves.'

'Great,' said Kal. 'Just what I need. Not only do I have to deal with Nemo and Crimson, but now assassins? This case just gets better and better.'

'Crimson?' said Bobo, his eyebrow arching. 'Cardinal Crimson?'

'That's the thing,' said Kal. 'Nemo's bounty is some sort of Cawdor prophet. One of Crimson's crew, I guess. Only we can't get close to his holiness... '

'Yeah,' said Scabbs. 'He wants Kal dead even more than Nemo. Probably because Kal dropped him in that pool of acid.'

Kal blew a cloud of smoked into Scabbs's face. '...so we were hoping you could watch his craziness for us.'

'You want me to get close to Crimson?' said Bobo. 'That rates more than just a mention to cousin Valtin,' but Bobo was smiling now. This actually sounded like fun and he was getting bored. 'But this goes into the debt column should you ever advance those forty-one steps up to the throne. I'll even put out some feelers to see if I track down who's hiring those assassins.'

'Great,' said Kal. 'Thanks. Yolanda's out checking her gang contacts to see if we can flush out this prophet. We'll follow up with her and contact you later.'

Bobo stared at Kal. 'She's out there alone? Isn't that kind of risky if Nemo's on the warpath?'

'Oh I wouldn't worry about Yolanda,' said Kal. 'She can take care of herself.'

'DAMN THAT JERICO,' grumbled Yolanda as she trudged through a tunnel connecting two domes. She hardly

looked where she was walking, letting her legs take her on the all-too-familiar path back to her roots – back to the lair of the Wildcats – while her mind wandered back to a life that was, but wasn't, her own.

Yolanda, daughter of House Catallus, had long ago given up the boring, phoney, political life of a Spire brat to go live downhive where she could enjoy life on the edge. There, her fiery temper found her on the wrong side of one too many arguments with the Underhive's male-dominated society, which led her to the Escher, a House of strong women and subjugated men.

But even the Hive City Houses were too tame for Yolanda Catallus, and so she pushed her way down into the dark places where only the strongest survive, where men and women are forced to fight to survive. The Wildcats took her in, nurtured her violent nature and eventually made her their leader. Yolanda had finally found her home. Until Kal Jerico came to take her back.

'That was the day you ruined my life, Jerico,' she called out to no one.

The Wildcats wouldn't take her back once they found out who she really was. A Spire brat had no place leading an Escher gang. Not even one as bloodthirsty as Yolanda Catallus. But life changes. It's the only constant in the Underhive.

'You either move when the acid comes pouring down or you get washed away as so much detritus,' said Yolanda, repeating an old, Underhive proverb.

So, Yolanda became a bounty hunter. It was really the only life left to her. Her main skills all involved violence and death, and this allowed her to stay at least a hair's breadth on the right side of legal. How she became partners with Kal Jerico, though, even Yolanda didn't truly understand and she bemoaned her fate nearly every day.

'Kal Jerico will be the death of me yet,' she grumbled.

'I think you're wrong about that,' replied a booming voice from behind her.

'Helmawr's rump!' said Yolanda, snapping out of her reverie. 'How could I have been so stupid?'

The tunnel she'd been walking through had long ago fallen into disrepair. I-beams, pipes and metal plates had been scavenged from the domes at both ends to shore up the walls and repair cave-ins. It was like walking though a metallic jungle. Yolanda had even had to push strands of tin piping out of her way several times as she walked through. She had done so automatically, without thinking – without keeping an eye out for the hidden dangers.

Now she would pay the price for her daydreaming. Two Goliaths stepped out from behind a sheet of steel ahead of her. Chains dangling from metallic shoulder pads stretched across their massive chests to thick, leather ammo belts at their waists. Other than bits of metal armour and chains, both were practically naked. Their muscles rippled, glistening with sweat in the dim light of the tunnel.

One pulled the ripcord on his chainsword and it screamed to life. The other raised an autocannon up to his hip, hardly even needing his second hand to steady the monstrous weapon.

'Maybe it's us Goliaths who are so smart, eh?' the booming voice behind her was still audible over the grinding metal-on-metal screech of the chainsword.

Yolanda turned her head just enough to look back down the tunnel without taking her eyes off the two gangers ahead of her. The speaker, a Goliath by the name of Gonth, stood with his massive hands on his hips. Yolanda saw what looked like a meltagun slung at his waist, just below one hand.

She recognised Gonth by his bright red mohawk and by the one missing ear. A nasty-looking gash ran from the scabbed-over wound all the way down and across his jaw line to his chin. Blood seeped from the wound, staining his iron shoulder armour with streaks of red. Gonth had been Grak's second-in-command until yesterday when she and Kal turned Grak's head in for the bounty.

Gonth was flanked by two more Goliaths. Both held shotguns ready and aimed at her. The three of them had apparently been standing behind a mass of beams and pipes waiting for her to pass. Now she was caught in the middle. Five on one, she thought. Hardly sporting odds. She decided to handle the situation in her normal manner – by turning up the heat.

'Sorry about the ear,' said Yolanda. She turned her body to the side to give both sides a smaller target and allow her to see all five without turning her head too far. As she turned, Yolanda moved her hands toward the pistols at her waist. 'I was aiming for your neck.'

THE FIREFIGHT HAD already started by the time Jobe got to the factory. He could hear laspistols and bolters blasting as he slipped inside. Most of the metal sheeting that formed the walls of the factory had been stripped off long ago, leaving just a maze of support beams at ground level.

Jobe darted from beam to beam, working his way ever closer to the action. He passed a makeshift ladder – pipes screwed into a beam – which led to a second level, and decided to climb up to gain the high ground. Of course, high ground usually also meant higher visibility to the enemy but Jobe felt a sudden urgency to find the Universal Saviours quickly.

The second level looked much like the first, only with less flooring. There were far fewer support beams to hide behind up top as well. Apparently, this had been a wide-open section of the factory. Perhaps an assembling room or mass storage. The bigger problem was the floor, or rather the lack of one. It was a patchwork metal grating and wide open areas criss-crossed by beams.

Jobe dropped to his hands and knees and crawled forward. He wasn't worried about falling so much as staying undetected, especially since all he brought to this gunfight was a knife. A stray slug whizzed overhead as he crouched and he could smell the acrid, electrical odour of burnt ozone. He was definitely getting close to the action. A little further along he began to hear voices.

'Quit hiding, you heretics,' yelled a nasally voice. 'Come out and accept your salvation like men.'

The taunt was answered by a hail of slugs, which was immediately silenced by the loud report of a laspistol.

'I got one, Tyler,' yelled another, higher pitched voice. 'I think I got one of those lousy Unies.'

Jobe had found the Righteous Saviours and they had the high ground. He could see at least five of them, crouching behind the few beams that extended through the second level to the roof above. Each had a patch of flooring behind them and an opening to fire through. They had chosen their spot well. It appeared the Universal Saviours had walked into a trap.

As his gang shot down into the dark, the one called Tyler kept slinging insults at the rival gang. 'You Unies are worse than wyrds and muties,' he called. 'They're abominations, sure. But you chose to live as a Uni. The Undying Emperor will see you all burn.'

The ganger with the high-pitched voice started to chant. 'Muties and Unies and Wyrds,' he began. 'Burn. Burn. Burn.'

Soon the entire gang, Tyler included, was chanting in between shots. 'Muties and Unies and Wyrds – Burn. Burn. Burn.'

The whole scene reminded Jobe of another place and time. Against his will, his eyes clouded over, turning the present-day world completely white. Then he could see again, but he was crouching next to Syris Bowdie, their backs pressed up against the crumbling wall of a burned out building!

'Syris!' he exclaimed. 'How…?'

'An ambush, that's how,' replied Syris. 'Ignus knew we couldn't turn our backs on a soul reaching out for salvation.'

Francks remembered now. They had learned that a witch-wyrd was in trouble, physically and spiritually. She wanted salvation, but had turned to the wrong set of Cawdor for help. Jules had her tied to a stake in the centre of Acid Hole and was preparing to light her up. When Syris and his gang showed up, they were immediately caught in a crossfire as Jules's men had taken up position on the surrounding rooftops.

'Come out, come out wherever you are,' called Ignus in his damnable sing-song voice. 'Come out and join your wyrd pal, Bowdie! We can have a twofer.'

Jobe tried to remember how they had got out of this ambush but his cloudy mind's eye forced him to live through it again with no foreknowledge.

'You're going to burn in the end anyway, you blasphemous abomination,' called Ignus. 'Save yourself today, and save us from starting a second fire.'

He laughed a long, cackling laugh, and Jobe turned and peered over the crumbling wall to try to take a shot at the arrogant ganger. At that moment, Ignus dropped a flaming torch onto the gas-soaked rags surrounding the bound wyrd. A huge gout of flame leaped up and engulfed her, sending Ignus running for cover.

The crackling of the fire mixed with the woman's screams to create an eerie howl. Jobe felt a tear rolling down his cheek as he witnessed the murder for a second time. The air sizzled near his head and he dropped back behind the wall as a laser blast slammed into the dirt next to him.

Jobe looked at Syris, about to ask him what they should do, when he noticed his mentor's eyes had clouded over like white smoke drifting across his blue orbs. A moment later, Jobe heard new screams and looked up to see several New Saviours on nearby rooftops fall to the dusty pavement.

He looked back at Syris with a furrowed brow, a question obviously on his lips. Bowdie's eyes had cleared and he was smiling. 'They must have lost their footing,' was all he said before running off.

'What about the witch?' asked Syris.

'She's with the Emperor now.'

As Jobe stood to follow Syris, he found himself back in the factory, standing in full view of the Righteous Saviours. The tear he'd shed for the burning wyrd dropped off his cheek onto his shoulder.

'Hey, old man,' called the high-pitched ganger. He pointed his laspistol at Francks. 'Move your shrivelled butt out of here before I frag you good.'

Francks stared at the young ganger. He was wearing the customary orange body armour and blue cloak of his gang, but his bright red hair gave away the fact that he'd been an Orlock ganger before being converted.

'We all follow a path, my son,' said Francks, and then pointed at Tyler. 'But that one is leading you in the wrong direction.'

'Great Undying Emperor,' exclaimed the ganger. 'He's another Uni.'

'Must be their dad come to take them home to mommy,' said Tyler. 'Shoot him, Miguel, and forget him.'

As Miguel aimed his weapon, Francks's eyes clouded over and he whispered a single word: 'Stagger.'

Before he could fire, Miguel crumpled to the ground, falling to the side as if something had slammed into his hips. He almost fell through the hole, but Tyler reached out and grabbed him by the belt and hauled him back onto the patch of metal flooring they had shared.

'Stagger. Righteous, stagger,' intoned Francks, and one by one the Righteous Saviours fell to the floor. Most fell through to the floor below. The rest were too dazed and confused by their sudden vertigo to move, but Francks knew this respite wouldn't last long.

He called out softly to the Universals with both his voice and his mind. 'Run, Universals. Run home. Run now!' He waited to hear the scrabbling of feet below and then stepped off the beam. Jobe Francks floated to the floor and followed the retreating Universals, disappearing into the maze of beams.

JEROD BITTEN FRETTED over an open ledger. Four more ledgers lay in a stack to his left and another two to his right. The columns of numbers in the open ledger were already making his old eyes blur but he knew he needed to balance the rest of the books before bed so he rubbed the heels of his closed fists into his eyes for a minute and tried to refocus.

After a while, satisfied that the numbers in the open ledger added up, he closed the oversized book and set it on top of the short stack to the right. He was just about to reach for the next ledger on his left – one labelled US – when he heard a staccato knock at his door.

Bitten cocked his head and counted the knocks. After listening to the rhythm twice, he rose from his desk and started for the door. Halfway there, he hesitated, shuffled back to the desk and dropped the ledgers into the bottom drawer, and then returned to the door. The knocking had continued the entire time and was getting much louder and faster by the time he reached for the handle.

When he opened the door, the light from Bitten's parlour spilled out onto the step, outlining a cowled figure standing there, poised to knock again.

'What took you so damn long?' demanded the voice from beneath the hood.

'I was…'

'Close the scavving door,' interrupted the visitor.

It was pitch black past the pool of light coming through his doorway. Britten stepped outside and closed the door behind him, plunging them both into darkness.

'Hold out your hand,' said the demanding voice.

Bitten was beginning to get worried, but complied. The stranger immediately grabbed his wrist, seemingly unaffected by the inky blackness, and then slapped something down into his palm.

'Here's the package you requested,' stated the voice in the dark. 'You understand your part in all of this?'

When Bitten didn't reply immediately, the pressure on his wrist began to increase. 'I understand,' he said at last. His wrist was freed as soon as he replied.

'Good. Don't fail in this or your past will finally come back to haunt you.'

Bitten opened his mouth to protest.

'Don't speak,' said the figure. 'He knows what you did, and you should have died long ago because of it.'

'I… I won't fail him this time,' said Bitten.

There was no reply.

'I… Hello?' Bitten reached out with one hand and pawed at the air in front of him. Nobody was there. He reached back and opened his door. The light hurt his eyes, which had just got used to the dark. The figure was gone. He stepped inside quickly and slammed the door. After a moment, he slid the locking bar down into place and walked back to his desk.

He looked at the package in his hand. It was a large envelope, thicker and heavier than he had expected. He opened it and peered inside. A low whistle escaped his lips. He dumped the huge wad of credits onto the desk. Even without counting it he knew this added up to more money than the bottom lines on any two of his ledgers.

4: IN THE TRENCHES

FOREMAN GRONDLE SCRATCHED at his neck, his fingers completely disappearing within the thick, black tangle of his beard. Work at the site had been slow this morning. No, that was an understatement. Not a single piece of rubble had been moved since the remnants of his crew had unburied their fellow workers the day before.

Now, he stood at the construction site alone. What workers he still had on payroll were out recruiting. Luckily, he didn't need skilled workers at this point. He just needed grunts who could move debris from one pile to another. Once they got that blasted rock pile cleaned out, he could get some skilled tradesmen in to shore up the wall of the dome, but some days it felt like he would never even get that far.

He heard a noise like a low rumbling back near the entrance. 'What now?' he asked. Grondle turned and groaned from the strain on his knees. They'd been aching all morning. The previous day's exertion after the rock slide was the first real work he'd done in years and he'd got painfully out of shape as a foreman. 'I'm gettin' too old and too fat for this,' he sighed.

But the next moment put a smile on the large, round foreman – not that anyone would be able to see it beneath the black forest covering his face. His new crew leader, an industrious ex-Orlock ganger named Ander, with thick arms and a thicker head, was leading his crew into the dome.

No, leading wasn't the right word. Dragged behind him in chains was more accurate. Ander and a few of the other paid workers held long lengths of chain attached to lines of manacled people, who staggered or were dragged along behind them.

Grondle hobbled over toward Ander and his crew. He moaned and grumbled with each step as his ponderous weight compressed his aching knees, but as bad as Grondle felt, he could tell the new workers felt worse. They were a sad mixture of scavvies, ratskins, muties and even some humans – at least what might once have been human. What little clothing the group wore was nothing more than filthy rags held together by string or worse. It was tough to tell where soiled clothing ended and dirt-encrusted limbs began. The grime was so thick that even the manacles attached to their ankles hadn't rubbed any of it off.

He wouldn't have been surprised if Ander had grabbed them all from the Ash Wastes, except he knew Ander didn't have the guts to venture outside the dome. As he neared the rag-tag group, Grondle noticed two more disturbing things about the crew. First, they stunk. A horrid mixture of urine, faeces and toxic waste radiated off them like a glowing, radioactive stench. Second, each member of the chain gang had nearly identical bloody bruises on their temples.

Grondle asked the question he knew he shouldn't ask. 'Where did you get your crew, Ander?'

Ander drew his hand down a stringy goatee and smirked. 'At the volunteer centre,' he said. 'And I'm sure I can find more volunteers as needed.'

Grondle looked at the chain gang and considered his options. He quickly realised he had none. 'Take them to the rock pile,' he said. 'I'll supervise them while you and your crew go recruit some more workers.'

'Not a problem, Grondle. The streets are filled with volunteers.' He turned to his companions. 'It's all in how you ask, right boys?' They laughed, and then handed the chains to Grondle before heading back toward the dome entrance.

YOLANDA DREW HER laspistols and fired to either side. One shot glanced off Gonth's shoulder pad, hardly even fazing the disfigured Goliath. The other hit the chainsword-wielder in the hand, burning off a finger. Yolanda didn't wait around to see their reactions. She dived forward into a tangle of pipes, beams and metal plates welded haphazardly into the side of the tunnel.

A stream of shells erupted from the autocannon and screamed through the tunnel behind her. She scrambled behind a loose piece of metal plating just as a shell exploded on the other side, spraying shrapnel into the rafters and across the floor. Above the din, she heard a somewhat more human scream of pain echoing down the tunnel. Apparently the overanxious Goliath had hit at least one of his comrades with the autocannon burst. Yolanda hoped it had been Gonth.

'Scavving idiot killed my brother!' said one of the Goliaths.

This was followed by two loud shotgun bangs and a dull 'Ooph.'

Yolanda knew from experience that a shotgun blast, even at close range, would do little more than enrage a Goliath, especially one large enough to handle an autocannon. She was right. The next sound she heard was the whine of the autocannon's cylinder revving up. She peeked out from behind the metal plate to see Gonth and the lone shotgun wielder diving for cover. The third Goliath lay on the ground, with a gaping bloody hole where his chest should have been.

A hail of shells screamed through the tunnel, slamming into beams, pipes, the floor and the ceiling. One hit the dead Goliath, spraying blood and limbs onto the walls. She was about to lean out a little farther to see what happened to Gonth when the screech of the chainsword impacting metal above her head made her pull back.

'That hurt!' said the Goliath, waving his four-fingered hand in the air as he came around the sheet of metal. He revved the motor of the whining chainsword and grinned at Yolanda, who had fallen into a squat in the cramped space behind the loose sheet of metal. The whine turned into a wail and then a screech as he raised the sword over his head and let it bite into Yolanda's metal shield. Sparks flew as it ground and sawed its way through the steel.

'This'll hurt more,' she said. Yolanda, her forearms braced on her knees, squinted as she aimed her pistols up high. Searing red energy spat from the end of her laspistols, slicing through the air and hitting the Goliath in the wrist. Both blasts impacted at a single point, cutting a neat hole through his wrist, bone and the mass of tendons that controlled the joint.

The Goliath looked up just in time to see his hand go limp and release the raging chainsword. It kicked off the wall and fell end-over-end in seeming slow motion toward his face. He tried to dive to the side, his mouth open in a soundless scream, but the chainsword caught him in the chin. It skipped against the jawbone and slid down to his shoulder.

Blood sprayed into the air as the whirling blade sliced into his flesh, ripping through tendons and muscles. The Goliath fell backward, still trying to get out of the path of the tumbling chainsword. It bit into his thigh, but must have hit bone and jammed. The extra weight and loss of muscle in his leg sent the Goliath crashing to the floor.

Yolanda sheathed her pistols and pulled herself to her feet. She stepped gingerly past the prone Goliath, who writhed in agony, the chainsword still whining and bucking as it strained against his femur.

'Don't say I never did anything for you,' she said as she yanked the sword free of his leg. Bits of red muscle and white bone sprayed out of the wound. She flicked the off switch and carried the weapon out into the tunnel, kicking the Goliath in the head as she left.

'That belongs to me,' said Gonth, pointing at the chainsword with his meltagun.

Gonth stood blocking Yolanda's exit from her hiding spot, meltagun levelled at her head. His armour had been scarred and blackened from autocannon shell explosions. She could also see streaks of red splattered across his chest and neck, but he seemed too calm for any of the blood to be his own.

Yolanda weighed her options. She did have the chainsword, but one shot from the meltagun would leave a wet spot on the floor where she stood. The other two Goliaths were nowhere to be seen, but judging from the shouting and shooting down the tunnel, at least one of them would be back soon. Plus, she could hear the injured Goliath scrambling around behind her. This was still too close to a fair fight for her liking.

'Fine,' she said as she pulled the ripcord. 'You can have it back.' The chainsword screamed to life, and

Yolanda revved the motor once before heaving it up into the air toward Gonth. As the new Goliath leader scrambled to get out from under the spinning weapon, Yolanda turned and sprinted down the tunnel.

The chainsword crashed to the floor behind her and the chain flew free, embedding into the wall next to her. The next moment, the wall burned red-hot, hissing and popping as the molecules became instantly super-heated. Yolanda kept running, weaving back and forth as parts of the tunnel burst into flame and melted around her.

She felt her back start to heat up and dived forward. The heat intensified and acrid smoke filled the air around her. She began to lose consciousness with the smell of burned flesh in her nostrils. Then a hail of bullets and laser blasts streaked down the tunnel above her and the heat stopped.

Yolanda looked up and tried to push the pain down and focus her tear-filled eyes. The tunnel was filled with Escher gangers. Several of them continued to fire down the hall, their long purple, red and yellow mohawks waving back and forth with every recoil.

'Looked like you needed some help,' said one of the women. She had bright blonde hair pulled up and over head into a ponytail. The sides of her head were shaved clean, showing the entire Wildcat tattoo that ran across her forehead and wrapped around both ears.

'Thanks, Themis,' said Yolanda to the Wildcat leader. 'But I had it under control.'

Well, we'll just leave you to it then,' said Themis, smiling.

That smile was the last thing Yolanda saw as she slipped into unconsciousness.

* * *

'WHAT ARE WE doing here?' asked Scabbs.

'I need to think,' said Kal. 'And the Breath of Fresh Air was the closest bar.' He pressed the tips of his fingers against his forehead. 'But it's too scavving quiet in here.'

Scabbs looked around. He and Kal were the only ones in the place other than Squatz, the dwarfish bartender, who was hobbling back behind the bar. He disappeared for a moment and then popped back up with an oomph, obviously having difficulty climbing onto his plank. 'This place used to be booming,' said Scabbs. 'What happened?'

'You two. That's what,' said Squatz. He spat on the bar and wiped it up with a dirty rag. 'You turned my doorstep into a battlefield against the blasted vampire, and my business has never been the same.'

'I thought your customers were eaten by the vampire well before we came along,' said Scabbs. He looked with suspicion at the bottle of House Special Brew that Squatz had placed in front of him. It had no snake in the bottom, which was a plus, but he didn't like the way it continued to bubble and froth.

'Or perhaps this stuff killed them,' he said. He took an experimental sip and gagged. It felt like his mouth was on fire. Scabbs scraped his tongue against the palm of his hand and gagged again as a wad of skin flaked off in his mouth.

'Careful,' called Squatz from the bar. 'That stuff'll stunt your growth,' he laughed. 'Looks like you've had too much already.'

Scabbs spat the dead skin into the bottle, where it fizzed and popped and shrunk as if being eaten away. 'You're one to talk,' he said. 'I don't need to stand on a plank to see over the bar.'

'Girls! Girls!' said Kal. 'Get to the part where you're pulling each other's hair, already, would you? A good brawl would at least help me think.'

'If it's a bar brawl you want,' said Squatz, 'Go back to your precious Sump Hole. This be Hive City. The Enforcers keep this place civilised.'

Kal snorted. 'Yeah. Thugs with power mauls roaming the city busting heads, that's civilised.'

'Besides,' added Scabbs. 'Kal's got debt collectors and assassins after him.'

Kal tried to shush him, but Scabbs kept talking. 'He had to duck out of the Sump Hole just last...' Kal jammed the still fizzing bottle of House Special into Scabbs mouth and tipped it up. The burning liquid scorched his throat as he was forced to chug it down.

'So,' said Squatz. 'That was you who dropped the assassin last night, then?'

Kal released his hold on the bottle. 'Assassin?' he asked. 'What assassin?'

Squatz dropped back down from his plank and waddled around the end of the bar. 'Maybe not, then,' he said. 'Whoever took down old Krellum was a hell of a skilled fighter. Shattered his knee and put two big holes in his chest. At close range too. Like someone got the drop on him.'

Scabbs grabbed the bottle from his mouth, spilling the rest down his shirt. He watched Squatz climb up onto the chair opposite Kal and stand looking at the bounty hunter in the eye, as if sizing him up.

'Couldn't have been you,' said Squatz. 'I don't think you're that good. Lucky, sure, but not skilled enough to get the drop on Krellum.'

Scabbs pushed his chair back, hoping to get out of the line of fire. Kal was never one to let an insult go unchallenged, but he almost dropped the empty bottle when his friend laughed.

'Heh. You're probably right,' said Kal. 'And I'd have taken him in for the reward. As I remember, Krellum has quite a healthy bounty on his head. Where'd you say he was found?'

'I didn't say,' replied Squatz. He stared hard at Kal, perhaps debating how much more he should divulge. 'And you don't get any more out of me for free.'

Kal looked at Scabbs. 'Pay him,' he said.

'Do what now?'

'We owe Squatz for letting us use his place as a base of operations last time,' said Kal. 'Pay him.'

Scabbs dug into his trousers and pulled out the few credits he had left along with a handful of ash grey detritus. He scowled at the smiling Squatz and dropped the whole dirty handful into the little man's pudgy hands. Squatz looked down at the wad of credits and crud in his palm and swore under his breath.

Then they both looked back at Kal, who had his pearl-handled pistols out and trained on Squatz. 'Now, you'll tell us what we want to know and maybe you live to spend that money.'

Scabbs's scowl turned into a smile. That was the Kal Jerico he remembered.

'I... I don't know much,' said Squatz. His face was the same ashen colour as the dirty credits in his hand. 'Krellum was found by the Enforcers this morning in an alley, just like I said – two blasts in his chest and a broken leg.'

'Where was this alley?'

'Just a few blocks from here.'

'Who was the target? Who ordered the hit?'

'I...' Squatz gulped. 'I don't know. Honestly. I don't.'

'Squatz?' Kal pushed the barrel of his weapon into Squatz's cheek. 'You know everything that goes on around your bar.'

'Really, Kal,' he said. 'I don't know. Whoever hired Krellum, did it quietly. I didn't even know he was in town. He always used to come by for a bottle of House Special before a job, but not last night. Maybe that crazy preacher scared him off. Did a number on the rest of my patrons.'

Kal holstered his laspistols and looked hard at Squatz. 'I'm only going to ask this once,' he said. 'And I don't want to have draw my guns again. What did this preacher look like?'

A GROUP OF Universal Saviours crowded around Jobe Francks in the hideout. The word had spread that the 'Prophet of the Body' was in their midst, had even saved the gang from a grisly death at the hands of the Righteous Saviours. Food and drink had been piled on the table next to Francks and he had to admit that it was pleasant to have a crowd listening to his every word and handing him food instead of throwing it at him.

After telling the gathered gangers the story of the factory battle – downplaying his role as simply the power of suggestion upon the weak-minded – Francks told them the tale of the Return of Bowdie. He described Bowdie's death at the hands of the intolerant Ignus and how Ignus had disposed of the body in the Acid Pools.

As he told the tale, Francks's eyes clouded over and he found himself transported back in time once again. 'I was on the run after that day,' he said, his voice seeming to echo as if it had to travel over a vast distance to reach his own ears. 'The New Saviours had eyes everywhere, and Ignus still wanted me dead.'

He heard a gasp, probably from one of the juves, but it barely registered as his subconscious mind had taken over. 'I found myself back at the acid pools again, a week after Bowdie's death,' he said.

And then he was there.

Francks looked about. The Universal Saviours' hideout had faded away, leaving him alone in the middle of the pools. He was scared. He'd been running. A couple of New Saviours had chased him through the settlement, but he'd given them the slip and run out into the middle of the pools.

The only people who came out this far were acid farmers, and it was too late in the day for even them. The encroaching darkness gave him some protection from prying eyes, but made it difficult to pick his way across the uneven pathways.

He stopped. An odd sound put him on edge again. He drew his laspistol and peered about, trying to find the source of the sound. There it was again.

Thump-plop. Thump-plop.

He whirled around, but there was nothing behind him.

Thump-plop.

He stood still and concentrated on the sound, but in the vast open field of pools, it was almost impossible to tell where the sound came from.

Thump-plop.

Francks scanned the nearest pools, looking for movement in the gathering darkness.

Thump-plop.

He moved slowly toward an intersection of two paths.

Thump-plop. There.

Ripples hitting the near bank of one of the pools. He crept around the pool, nearly tripping over a loose piece of masonry at the edge of the pool.

All of a sudden, a certain dread fell over him. This was the pool where Bowdie had been gunned down. *Thump-plop.* He moved to the spot where Ignus had stood, fearing what he would find there. And there it was. He gasped.

Bobbing up and down in the acid, periodically slapping into the bank of the pool was a large dark shape, the size of a human body. Francks fumbled in his pocket for a torch and, throwing caution to the wind, flicked on the beam. He aimed the torch down toward the pool and almost cried out loud when he saw the face of Syris Bowdie.

The body didn't have a mark on it; not from the attack and not from the acid. His skin and clothing glistened from the liquid, but had not been eaten away at all by the toxic pool. His hair floated around his head like a wreath and his cloak was wrapped around his body like a shroud.

Francks reached down to grab his leader by the arm and pull him free of the acid, but his hands began to burn as soon as he touched the wet clothes and he dropped the torch into the pool. It sizzled and popped as the acid ate its way through the casing. Francks grabbed his own cloak, wrapped it around his hands and reached down again.

'It was then I heard shouts and the sound of gunfire from behind me,' said Francks to the assembled Saviours. The vision began to fade as soon as his hands touched the acid. He was back in the hideout with his new parishioners. 'Ignus's men had seen me. I had no choice but to run. When they reached the body, I knew I hadn't imagined it because they all stopped and aimed their own torches down into the pool. I got away because they found him. His very presence saved my life.'

'A miracle,' gasped one of the juves.

Francks nodded. 'Yes, it was,' he said. 'But no one was to know about this miracle. I watched from a safe distance as

Ignus was called out to the pools. He screamed at his men and they weighted the body down with ropes and huge chunks of masonry then tossed it back into the acid.'

'But it came back, isn't that right?' This question came from the leader of the Universal Saviours. Francks looked at him with a furrowed brow. 'I have read accounts of the Return of the Body,' he explained.

Francks smiled. 'Yes. Bowdie returned once again two weeks later. This time he was seen by several acid farmers. They pulled him out and brought him into town. Unfortunately, the body disappeared that night and was never seen again.'

'Another miracle?'

Francks shook his head. 'No. I suspect his final disappearance was the handiwork of a somewhat less than divine being.'

CARDINAL CRIMSON LOUNGED in a soothing bath of hot oils mixed with a special elixir of vital essences. He had no idea what the medics put into the elixir, but the stench of the bath often brought to mind the scent of the sacrificial altar. He felt that not knowing was better for his soul. He was doing holy work on this world – in fact it was a miracle he was alive – so the pain and suffering of a few was a just cost for his continued good work. He knew the Undying Emperor understood it was all for the good of humanity.

The baths were a twice daily ritual to prevent the remnants of his skin from drying out and flaking away, to keep his exposed muscles supple and pliant so they wouldn't tear apart when he moved, and to stave off infections that now had ample opportunities to invade his scarred body.

It was a time of quiet reflection and, more importantly, a time of utter vulnerability. His inner circle knew not to disturb the Cardinal during his bath. It was drawn by the medics, who then left by a back entrance and returned only after Crimson dressed and returned to his duties.

And so, Crimson soaked and dozed and dreamed of sitting at the right hand of the Undying Emperor, where he passed judgement on the blasphemers. 'Down to the Abyss with you, witch-wyrd,' he called out. He looked out at the gathered throng of wyrds, mutants and heretics. 'Be gone,' he called. 'There is no place here for the damned or the deformed.'

One of the misshapen figures, a mutant with pink, fleshy growths on his bare head and shoulders, opened its mouth to protest. 'Excuse me, your eminence,' it said. 'I'm sorry to interrupt your bath, but there is an important matter…'

Crimson stared in disbelief at the mutant, trying to make sense of the creature's statement when he recognised the voice and opened his eyes. 'Ralan,' he said, staring at the officious man standing in the doorway. He fiddled with a piece of parchment, absent-mindedly pulling off bits and dropping them on the floor. 'If this is not as important as you think it is, I will hand you over to the medics and you will get a much more personal bathing experience during my next treatment.'

Ralan swallowed hard and passed his hand over his stringy hair, which was plastered to his head by the heat and humidity of the bathroom. 'I'm sure you would want this report as soon as possible, your grace,' he said. 'It concerns the heretic Kal Jerico.'

Crimson stood and exited the bath, the oils still glistening on his skin and exposed bones. 'Robe!' he commanded.

Ralan dashed across the room and grabbed the robe. He draped it around the Cardinal's dripping, skeletal frame and followed him out of the room.

'What has the heretic Jerico done now?' asked Crimson as he stormed down the hall, his robe billowing out behind him.

Ralan had to run to keep up, and the exertion made him wheeze. 'It seems the bounty hunter is on the trail of the prophet,' he said between huffs. 'He is out searching for Jobe Francks right now!'

Crimson slammed open the door to his office. 'Why must that man defile everything we try to do in this world?' he said. 'He is the hand of chaos reaching out of the void to thwart me at every turn.'

'But sir,' said Ralan, 'he is just looking for Francks. That doesn't mean he will find him.'

Crimson fell back into his chair and grabbed his head between both bony hands. 'But he will find him, Ralan,' he said. 'The man is relentless. He will find the prophet and he will ruin all that we have worked so hard to achieve.'

'Perhaps…' began Ralan, but then stopped.

The Cardinal pulled at his hair and began screaming. 'Damn Jerico! I want him dead, Ralan. Dead. Do you hear me?'

'Yes, Cardinal.'

'Put all of our gangs on the task,' said Crimson. He shook his hands in the air. Wisps of grey hair floated down toward the desk. 'Kal Jerico must be dead by the end of the day.'

'Yes, Cardinal.'

Ralan turned to leave, and Crimson smoothed his hair back down and took a breath. As his rage ebbed away, his mind cleared and a thought occurred to him. Crimson started to laugh. 'Wait, Ralan,' he said as his aid left the room. 'I have a better idea.'

Ralan turned at the door, and Crimson thought he detected a note of scorn on his face. Crimson waited for the obligatory 'Yes, Cardinal' but it did not come.

'I think we may be able to use this information to our advantage,' he said. 'I think we can use the chaos that the heretic Kal Jerico is bound to sow to help the cause of Redemption this time. Perhaps, just perhaps, if he plays his part right, I will have the chance to redeem Kal Jerico's soul in the pools of fire before this is all ended.'

'What would you have me do, your eminence?'

'Bring me Kal Jerico, alive!'

YOLANDA AWOKE IN the Wildcats' hideout. It was strange but familiar, like waking in your childhood bed after a long nightmare. She was warm, which reminded her of the melta that had been aimed at her back, but a quick hand check beneath her vest came up clean. Her skin seemed to be unharmed. No, the warmth was all over, which was odd. Underhive hideouts were not known for warmth.

Then she remembered. This had once been her room when she led the Wildcats. It was right above the kitchen in the back of a burned-out eatery. The Wildcats had found the kitchen intact, including all the old pots and pans. The dining room was more rubble than actual walls, but the kitchen and the apartment above were another matter. It had become the official bedroom for the leader of the 'Cats.

'Themis must be trying to butter me up,' said Yolanda, 'giving me her room to sleep it off. I wonder what this will cost me down the line.'

'Not a thing, if I know Themis,' said a voice in the dark. 'She thinks she still owes you for that Spyrer rig you gave us.'

Yolanda recognised the lilting, high-pitched voice. 'Evening, Lysanne,' she said. 'That wasn't a gift. It was a loan. I hope you haven't got it shot up.'

Lysanne opened the door to let some light in the room. The teenage Wildcat looked much the same as Yolanda remembered. She still wore loose, black trousers and the wrap-around robe that tied at the sides. She'd dyed her hair black with a streak of purple running down the parting. She'd also received her Wildcat tattoo, a series of whorls and interlacing lines of black, blue and purple across her forehead. As she rose in the gang hierarchy, the tattoo would grow past her temples and eventually over her ears.

'Not to worry,' said Lysanne. 'We've kept it safe. We never take it into battle. It would make us too big of a target. But it does have other uses.'

Yolanda remembered. It had been a Malcadon rig from the Spyrer unit sent down to hunt the Vampire. Not only could you climb sheer cliffs while wearing the rig, it also had web spinners. 'I'll bet you can get into some interesting spots with that rig,' she said.

Lysanne nodded. 'So, are you ready for some supper? The mavants are already serving downstairs.'

'I was out that long?' asked Yolanda. She got up and collected her weapons from the bedside table.

'All day,' said Lysanne. 'Some of the newer girls wondered if you'd ever wake up.'

'Hope I didn't disappoint anyone,' said Yolanda with a smirk. She fastened her weapon belt and followed Lysanne down the stairs.

'Well, I made fifty credits betting on you,' said Lysanne over her shoulder. 'So, I'm happy.'

Yolanda chuckled. 'You should cut me in for half. I think I earned it.'

'What, saving your life wasn't payment enough?'

'Fine, we'll call it even.'

Lysanne guided Yolanda through the kitchen. Three mavants, male slaves bound in service to the gang, toiled away in the kitchen. One stood over the burners stirring a steaming pot. Another was busy cutting bread and stacking it on large platters. The last one held a tray full of bottles and waited, head bowed, while the two women walked past and through the swinging door. All three wore nothing but dirty white shirts and shorts. Their heads looked like they'd been shaved with dull knives. Patches of hair remained in some places, while cuts and scabs could be seen in the bare spots.

'Themis has given the mavants trousers?' asked Yolanda, looking back as they went through the door.

'I am nothing if not compassionate,' said Themis.

'Well, you can take compassion too far when it comes to men,' said Yolanda. She sat down on a cinder block at the main table, a large block of petrified wood the Wildcats had found years earlier. It was their prized possession. 'Even a little starts to give them ideas, makes them think they own us... instead of the other way around.'

Themis smiled at the Wildcats' former leader. 'How is Kal Jerico?' she asked.

'Still getting me into more trouble than he's worth,' said Yolanda. 'That's why I came to see you.'

The drink mavant walked around the room distributing bottles of Wildsnake to the assembled Wildcats. He placed the last bottle in front of Yolanda and turned toward the kitchen. She kicked him in the rear as he passed, sending him tumbling through the door. 'Serve the guest first,' she called after him.

'Does it have anything to do with those Goliaths who attacked you?' asked Themis.

Yolanda upended the bottle and poured its contents down her throat, snake and all. 'Nah, that's old news.' She tipped her bottle toward Themis who nodded in return. It was all the two would say on the subject.

Gratitude was seen as a weakness by the Escher, but both women knew there was a blood bond between them now.

'Now we're looking for some crazy Cawdor prophet,' continued Yolanda after the exchange. 'We wondered if you had heard anything. Has there been any unusual Cawdor gang activity in the last few days?'

The bread mavant entered the room. His fellow slave must have explained the proper etiquette for serving guests because he shuffled immediately over to Yolanda with the tray. She grabbed a slice and pushed him on around the table.

He served Themis next. Themis ripped her bread apart and stuffed a large chunk into her mouth. She talked around the wad. 'There was something about a madman coming into Hive City the other day from the Ash Wastes. Wild hair and creepy eyes. Wearing rags that our mavants wouldn't be caught dead in. Looked more animal than human, but I guess that's normal for men, huh?' she laughed.

'That could have been anything,' said Yolanda. 'Scavvies try to break security all the time.'

'Ahh, but this one made it through security, supposedly someone found the guard wandering the docks later. And I heard the mystery man left with two Cawdor.'

She looked at Lysanne, who was last to get her bread and had just slapped the mavant on the butt. 'What's the name of that gang,' asked Themis. 'The Cawdor that hang around Madam Noritake's all the time.'

'The Soul Saviours?' said Lysanne, but it was more of a question than an answer. 'I think. Or maybe the Savers? All their names sound the same to me.'

'That can't be right,' said one of the other 'Cats, a juve with long mousey-brown hair that Yolanda had never met. 'Because we heard today that some wild-haired Cawdor helped the Unies – the Universal Saviours – escape from the Righteous Saviours down in Glory Hole.'

'Was it the same guy?' asked Yolanda. She chewed on her bread and tried to digest both the hard crust and the information about the travelling Wildman.

'Probably not,' said Lysanne. 'I heard that report as well. This guy was wearing the blue cape and orange armour of a Cawdor.'

'But one of the Righteous told me he had weird eyes,' said the juve. 'All cloudy and swirling. He said it was a wyrd. Used some kind of witch power on them. When they woke up, the Unies and the wyrd were gone.'

Themis gave the juve a stern look. 'What were you doing talking to a Cawdor?'

The juve blushed and stared at the crust of bread on the table in front of her. 'Nothing sacred, that's for sure.'

The Wildcats began laughing. Several of the girls slapped the juve on the back and congratulated her on such a brazen conquest. Yolanda just kept chewing her bread and thinking. Two reports in two days of a wild-eyed man connected with the Cawdor. That had to be more than mere coincidence. Kal would want to know about this.

The soup came out from the kitchen and the mavant Yolanda had kicked reappeared with another tray of Wild Snake. She looked around at her laughing sisters and at the amusing mavants. Jerico could wait, she thought. She needed a girls' night.

GRONDLE'S DAY HAD turned out far better than he could have hoped after his late-night meeting with Guilder Tavis the evening before. The chain gangs worked harder than the paid labourers ever did, and all they expected in return was an occasional drink of water and fewer beatings than they received on the street.

The mound of rubble was now half the size, and Ander, his Orlock goon of a crew chief, had rousted up two more gangs for the swing shift. With any luck, the debris pile that had haunted this construction job would be gone by morning.

'Need any more workers, boss?' asked Ander. 'Me and the boys could recruit plenty tonight. The great thing about street people is they all sleep in the same burned-out holes after hours.'

Grondle shook his head. 'No. I just need you to keep these new gangs working through the night,' he said. He pulled at a few stray hairs that had been sticking straight out from his bushy beard all afternoon and thought for a moment. 'Maybe tomorrow night, though,' he continued. 'We'll need a lot more workers for the next stage.'

The two of them worked out arrangements for transporting and housing the chain gangs that were going off shift as Ander's men supervised the shift change. A muffled boom made Grondle catch his breath and the flesh on the back of his neck tingle. 'Oh no,' he said and his attention snapped to the construction zone.

The wall of the dome above the rock slide had erupted outward and a cloud of white powder billowed out from the gaping hole. But Grondle knew that was just the beginning.

'Run!' he called. 'Get off the pile!'

Ander's men reacted immediately. They dropped the chains and sprinted down the hill amidst a sustained low rumble that grew louder and louder as they ran. One lurched forward and sprawled face first into the rubble. His mates ran past him. He rolled down the hill until he found his feet and stumbled on, well behind the others.

The chain gangs tried to follow but were hampered by the manacles around their ankles and the chains stringing them all together. They had to move in unison, which was impossible to do quickly.

As the cloud above the mound expanded, large chunks of debris emerged from the dust, raining down on the top of the rock slide. Several larger pieces, some as big as the men rushing down the pile, flew out the side of the cloud and plummeted toward the lower areas where the chain gangs had been standing – were still standing.

The incoming shift had to turn around before they could descend. They were still trying to reverse direction when the outgoing gangs ran into them, knocking several workers to the ground. The chains connecting them all went taut causing a cascading collapse of bodies.

Chunks of masonry and jagged pieces of metal crashed into the mass of bodies. Screams pierced the low rumble, echoing horribly in Grondle's ears. He stood rooted to the spot as the weight of the debris began an avalanche that swept down the pile of rubble, burying the chain gangs and threatening to overtake Ander's men.

The man who had stumbled screamed as rocks and chunks of metal began to fly past him. Soon the surge of the avalanche overtook the man and carried him, tumbling and rolling the rest of the way down the hill.

As the rumble began to die off, Ander and Grondle ran to the base of the rock slide. An arm and a leg stuck out at odd angles part way up. The two men yanked at the rubble and, with the help of the rest of Ander's men, soon had the half-buried worker free. Blood covered his face and chest and streaks of red ran down his arms and legs, but he was alive.

'You're usually more sure-footed, Rafe,' said Ander with a smile and a little laugh.

Both seemed a bit forced to Grondle, but the injured man returned the smile and tried to laugh as well, which turned into a hacking cough. After the spasm, Rafe looked at Grondle. 'Something hit me in the back of the head,' he said. 'While I was rolling I saw this and grabbed it.'

He opened his hand. In his palm sat the charred remains of a small metal box with wires protruding from two sides.

'That's a detonator,' said Grondle.

'Helmawr's rump,' muttered Ander. 'Sabotage?'

Grondle plucked the detonator from Rafe's hand. 'Looks like it,' he said, muttering a curse of his own under his breath. 'And all this time we thought we were cursed.'

'What do we do about it?'

Grondle glared at the enlarged mound of rubble that had swallowed all four chain gangs and ruined another day of work. His gaze rose to the new gaping hole in the side of the dome, which would have to be patched. 'Get more workers,' he said. 'I need to talk with our employer about providing some protection.'

THE ASSASSIN SLIPPED into Glory Hole through a tunnel few knew existed. He was in a basement surrounded by kegs and shelves filled with dusty bottles. A twisted knot of pipes criss-crossed the low ceiling above him, and beyond the stairs could be seen a maze of larger conduits in a crawlspace.

He shut the access panel behind him and moved a couple of empty kegs back in front of the secret entrance. The assassin cocked his head, as if listening to some faint or far away sound and then crept over to the corner at the foot of the stairs. A large, vertical conduit pipe set into the wall rose up through the ceiling and down through the floor. He reached out and released a hidden catch on the pipe, opening yet another secret hatch.

The assassin crept inside the conduit and pulled the hatch closed behind him. Pressing his legs and hands against the sides of the pipe, he scampered up the pipe, climbing as easily as a spider. At the top, the pipe turned ninety degrees and he was able to crawl on all fours to the other end. After emerging, the assassin looked across the street at the building he had just exited – a local bar called Hagen's Hole, usually populated by bounty hunters.

He smiled and loped noiselessly across the roof, away from Hagen's. As he ran, he pulled out a piece of parchment and read it. The note said simply 'North corner of Glory Hole settlement, orange two storey'.

After reading the note, the assassin popped it in his mouth, chewed it up, and…

JOBE FRANCKS AWOKE with a start, sitting straight up in bed. There was a terrible taste in his mouth, and he spat a wad of parchment into his hand. He'd seen it all – the assassin, the trip into Glory Hole, the note with the Universal Saviours' address on it – and he might have convinced himself that it had all been a dream, except for the doughy wad of wet parchment in his hand.

Another assassin had been sent to hunt him down, was probably inside the settlement already and coming his way. Jobe had no time to lose. It was time to move on again.

5: IN THE CROSSHAIRS

FRANCKS STEPPED ONTO the roof of the Universal Saviours' building. His hand shook as he closed the door. The vision of the assassin had been intense. He'd never experienced anything like that before. Sure, he sometimes relived the past through his cloudy eyes, but this was like seeing through someone else's eyes. He'd been inside the assassin looking out, had known who he was and what he was doing. For a time, Jobe Francks had been the assassin.

After the vision, he'd dressed, stopped to warn Breland and started to leave.

When he'd put his hand on the front door, a feeling of dread came over him. Death lay in wait outside that door. He'd backed away, his eyes wide in fear and confusion. It was happening too fast.

He wasn't ready for the next stage of the Universe's plan. Not yet. Not here. People would get hurt. Die. Perhaps not him. The Universe wasn't quite done with him yet. But Breland and his gang – the reading juves and the all-too-tolerant Universals – they would pay the price for his fear. They would die for him, for his cause – if he let them. He had to find another way.

And so, Jobe Francks found himself on the roof, skulking towards a gap between the buildings. It was important to be seen but not caught. The timing would be tricky. He ran toward the edge, trying to time his strides for the final leap but old age and the thick boots he'd only worn for a day tripped him up. He had to stutter step at the end and lost much of his momentum.

He jumped. He had no choice at this point. He sailed over the alley in a shallow arc. The brick wall came up at him fast. He wasn't going to make it. Jobe pumped his legs, trying to run through the air, but it didn't help. He reached out with his hands as he fell. His fingertips caught on the rough ledge. His body bounced against the wall. His fingers slid, scraping against the edge of the bricks. He could feel blood trickle down the inside of his palm to his wrist.

But he held on. Francks glanced down at the shadowy pavement below. He'd break a leg at least if he let go. His legs scrabbled against the wall, trying to find some purchase. His arms began to ache but his toes finally caught in the grout between bricks and, with the adrenaline now pumping through his veins, he climbed the wall and then dropped on the roof.

Francks lay there breathing for only a moment before pushing himself back to his feet and running across the roof. He kept low, trying not to be seen from below. He found the roof access and dropped into the building. It was dark, but his eyes adjusted quickly and he found his way down to the door.

Now he could exit from the wrong building, giving the Universals some protection, but he still needed to find a way to get out of the settlement alive. Francks tried to reach out with his mind to the assassin. He could sense him nearby, on a building across the street. He sent a silent command, as he had done with the Righteous gang, but the assassin's mind was too focused, too well trained. He'd have to find another way.

Francks opened the door and stepped out. He had to hope the assassin wouldn't shoot the first old man he saw. Professionals don't like to make mistakes, and he was coming out of the wrong building. He walked down the street toward the intersection. As he turned the corner, right before he would be out of sight of the assassin, Jobe opened his mouth.

'For I am the light and the way and the path to glory,' he called out, preaching loud enough for the assassin to hear. 'Hear the word of the Undying Emperor and be redeemed.'

Reaching out with his mind again, Jobe felt the assassin moving from his position. He'd heard. He would follow him, away from the Universals. Now he only had to worry about his own safety. So he ran. Down the street and around another corner he ran.

It would take the assassin a few moments to get out of the building. He didn't have to rush. One building. Two buildings. The third was bombed out. He dashed through a hole in the wall and kept running. He could feel the assassin getting closer, padding down the street, weapon in hand. Perhaps night vision goggles on. He had little time.

Jobe tripped over a loose pipe on the floor. He sprawled on the ground in a clatter. The assassin turned the corner. Had he heard? Francks couldn't tell. He rolled away from the debris and found his feet again. He ran out the back of the building and down the street. He knew where he had to go. Had a vague idea of how to get there. He just needed to keep one street ahead of the assassin.

He felt the assassin exit the burned-out building just as he turned another corner. His breath began to catch

in his throat. His old lungs and legs were no match for
the young assassin. He needed just a little more time.
He was almost there. He reached out with his mind
once again.

'Trip,' he commanded.

He heard a clatter and a muffled yelp from behind
him. 'Got you,' he said, and ran on.

A few minutes later, Jobe found the place he'd been
looking for. He turned one last corner and sprinted for
the door. It opened just as he got there and he barrelled
through, almost knocking down the armoured man
coming out.

'Watch it, old man,' snarled the bounty hunter as he
pushed Francks away and then continued out the door.

Francks fought down the adrenaline-inspired
impulse to punch the much bigger man, and simply
bowed his head and walked over to the bar. 'You must
be Hagen,' he said to the bartender, a large man with a
round stomach just barely covered by a stained, white
shirt.

'Yeah. What of it?' asked Hagen.

'Snake me,' said Francks, slamming a credit down on
the bar. He looked around Hagen's Hole and smiled.
The place was filled with ratskin guides, mercenaries
and bounty hunters – lots of bounty hunters. The back
wall was plastered with wanted posters showing
mutants, scavvies, renegade gangers and assassins. He
was safe, for now.

As he drank the Wildsnake Hagen handed him, Jobe
Francks reached out with his mind once more and
found the assassin, sitting on the roof of the building
across the street and wondered how long he'd wait out
there.

He finished his drink, swallowing the snake hole,
and headed for the back room. While the regulars

played cards and drank their foul brown drinks, Jobe
Francks slipped through the door to the basement. As
he moved the barrels away from the hidden door,
Francks thanked the Emperor for the vision of the
secret exit.

KAL TIPPED THE bottle up to his lips and took a long
draught of liquid breakfast. He looked at Scabbs sitting
across from him. His partner was poking at his eggs. He
lifted up the edge of the dull yellow mass with his knife
and peered underneath. Kal wasn't sure, but he thought
he saw something move beneath the eggs.

'I keep telling you,' said Kal, 'The only thing in the
Sump Hole that you can swallow is the booze, and
that's only because it's so vile it kills anything that
might crawl inside.'

Scabbs pushed the plate away and took a swig of his
own drink. 'Then why do we spend all our time here?'
he asked.

Kal finished his Wildsnake and spun the bottle on
the table. 'Because it's the best hole in the Underhive.'

Scabbs humphed. 'We need to find a better place to
live.'

'What and miss all this excitement?' Kal smiled.

'You mean like being ambushed by Goliaths who are
still out for our blood?' said Yolanda as he dropped
into a chair. 'Or do you mean dodging Crimson and
Nemo just so we can get back the money we already
earned? That the excitement you're looking for, Jerico?'

Kal's smile didn't diminish at all. 'Yeah. Something
like that,' he said. 'Have a bad day, honey?'

Yolanda glared at him. 'You call me "honey" again,'
she sneered, 'and you'll have to stand up to smile.'

Kal leaned forward and put a serious look on his face.
'I'm sorry, Yolanda,' he said as sincerely as he could. 'Here,

have the rest of my eggs.' He pushed Scabbs's plate toward his female partner. Scabbs opened his mouth to say something, but Kal shot him a look, and he sat back.

Yolanda dug into the eggs that Scabbs wouldn't eat and described how Gonth and several members of the Grak gang had attacked her in the tunnels. 'I don't think they're going to let this go, Jerico,' she said after a while.

Just then something black with lots of legs did crawl out from beneath the eggs and Yolanda skewered it with her knife. She pushed the plate away, grabbed Scabbs's bottle, and took a long drink. 'We'll have to kill every last one of those Goliaths before this ends.'

Kal waved her off. 'I can't worry about that now,' he said. 'We've got professional competition for our bounty. Seems someone is hiring assassins to go after this wandering prophet. One of them ended up dead near the Fresh Air.'

'Wandering is right,' said Yolanda. 'According to the 'Cats, this guy was seen on the docks with one set of Cawdor two days ago and then over in Glory Hole with a gang called the Universal Saviours yesterday.'

'Why is this guy so popular?' asked Scabbs. He scratched at his arm, sending a flurry of dried skin floating down to the table. 'You don't suppose he's the real deal, do you Kal? I mean why else would Nemo want him so bad?'

Yolanda spoke around the food in her mouth. 'The Wildcats did say that he'd used some weird powers in that battle and to get past a dock guard.'

Kal shook his head. 'Nah. He's just some wyrd. And Nemo's only interested in one thing – information. This guy must have some secrets.'

Neither Scabbs nor Yolanda looked convinced. Scabbs opened his mouth, but Kal shook his head again, trying to shut down this line of questioning. 'Look, it doesn't matter what this Jobe character is or isn't,' he said. 'He's a bounty, that's all that matters. Let's just bring him in and let our enemies worry about him.'

'Alright,' said Yolanda, reluctantly. 'I want to get our money back. What do we do next?'

'We could question the dock guards or that first gang, but I think those leads have gone cold,' said Kal. 'If that dead assassin was after our guy, that might explain him heading to Glory Hole. We should look for him there first. Maybe check Hagen's to see if anyone there has heard any…'

'Kal?' asked Scabbs.

But Kal wasn't listening. His attention had been drawn to the door of the Sump Hole. The debt collector in his shiny, pressed suit had just walked in. He pushed on the bridge of his glasses with a single finger to resettle them on his nose, and began scanning the room.

Kal slid off his chair and sidled up against the wall. He pressed a finger against his pursed lips and made a shushing noise. 'That little rodent of a debt collector is back,' he said. He opened the door to the bathroom and slipped inside. Through the crack, he said, 'Distract him while I get out of here. We'll meet at Hagen's Hole.' With that, he closed the door.

SCABBS TURNED AROUND and saw the officious little man at the bar. The bartender pointed back toward their table. He didn't know what to do. He wasn't the ideas man. That was Kal's job. Or Yolanda's in a pinch.

He looked to Yolanda, but she was still trying to wash the taste of bug out of her mouth with his bottle of Wild Snake. Then Scabbs got an idea. He grabbed the plate of half-eaten eggs and pulled the knife out of the table, making sure the dead bug stayed skewered on the tip. He turned and headed for the bar.

'What's the meaning of this?' he yelled, waving the knife around in his right hand. The bug flopped a little on the tip as he shook his hand. 'Snake in my bottle, okay. But bug in my eggs? That's just gross.'

One of the other early risers called out from another table, 'You mean you won't share breakfast with your brother, Scabbs?'

Scabbs turned to look at the speaker. It was Bear, a huge behemoth of a man with a stomach that rivalled Hagen's and arms as thick as rocket launcher tubes. Scabbs knew he could count on Bear's loud mouth. He took two more steps before he spoke.

'No, but I'll share them with you,' he said, and flung the plate of eggs toward Bear, making sure most of the runny, grey scramble splatted on the silk-covered chest of the debt collector.

Bear tossed his chair aside, ripping the legs right out of the floor, and advanced on Scabbs. Scabbs slipped around behind the debt collector and waved the bug-tipped knife in the air. The silk-suited man looked horrified by the bug whipping around by his eyes and ear, but the look of sur-prise on his face when Bear grabbed both of them and heaved them from the floor made Scabbs smile on the inside.

If this is a Van Saar debt collector, he thought, *they recruited him from the Spire. He has no business down here in the Underhive.*

Scabbs's smile was short-lived, though. Bear squeezed the two of them into a big hug, forcing both little men to exhale most of the air in their lungs.

The bartender, who'd been silent up until this point, simply said, 'Take it outside, Bear.'

And with that, the mountain-sized bounty hunter walked to the door, kicked it open and tossed the two men out into the street. 'Don't come back without your master, little man,' he said, pointing at Scabbs. 'You need to stay on Jerico's leash.'

Scabbs rolled over the debt collector, trying to kick as much dirt as he could onto the man's silk suit, and keep him from seeing Kal as he slipped out the door and then ducked into an alley. Kal smiled and winked at his partner before he disappeared.

'I'm so sorry,' said Scabbs as he helped the man up from the ground. He brushed at the man's jacket, but Scabbs's dirty hands and the egg still stuck to the debt collector's jacket combined into a fine pasty smudge on the soft material.

'Just leave me alone,' said the debt collector. He slapped at Scabbs's hands and walked toward the door. Just as he reached for the handle, the door opened up, hitting him and sending him flying into the dirt again. Yolanda stepped out as Scabbs went to offer his hand to the debt collector once more.

'Don't touch me, you vile person,' said the debt collector. He crawled away from Scabbs through the door, which Yolanda held open for him.

She smiled at Scabbs as she closed the door again. 'Well played,' she said. 'I didn't know you had that in you.'

'Neither did I,' said Scabbs. 'I thought Bear was going to kill me.'

'He would have,' said Yolanda, pulling Scabbs away from the bar. 'But I caught his eye and motioned for him to keep calm.'

'Thanks,' said Scabbs. They walked a little farther down the road. 'Well, I suppose we should catch up with Kal, huh?'

Yolanda walked a few more steps before answering. 'In good time,' she said. 'In good time. I could still use some breakfast.'

* * *

JOBE HAD BEEN running through the Underhive all night. At first he didn't know or care where he was headed. He just ran. He needed to stay ahead of the assassin. After a time, he couldn't sense the presence of his follower any longer and slowed down, but he never stopped moving. To sit was to die.

He just needed someplace safe to rest for a while and commune with the Universe. He needed to figure out where to go next. He needed to understand why he had returned to the Hive. He needed to determine where his destiny lay. He needed to sleep.

The morning began to hum in the Hive as he walked. Workers left their homes and headed out to factories or the mines or the docks. Faceless, nameless, futureless drones trudging back and forth through their lives. This was the monotonous existence the gangs rebelled against: the endless sameness, the senseless tedium of working for little or no reward, of moving forward but never getting anywhere.

Some turned to adventure, hooking their hopes on the one big score. Others sank into violence, wreaking vengeance for their tiresome lives on all they encountered. Still others, a dismal few, really, looked to a higher power to find some meaning in their lives. He thought it was unfortunate that so many Cawdor fell into the first two categories and never discovered the third possibility.

As he pondered these universal ailments, Jobe's feet kept walking, turning corners periodically and even climbing or descending stairs without any conscious effort. And then he stopped moving. Francks looked up, confused by his own lack of motion. He was standing in front of a door. He looked around to see where he was. Hive City. How had he got all the way into the middle of Hive City?

He looked at the door again. There was no name plaque above the frame. No number to signify an address. Just a brass knocker in the middle of the iron door. The Universe brought me here for a reason, he thought. So he knocked. A shuffling noise came from behind the door; not of feet but of paper and books. There was a bang, like a door closing or a drawer slamming shut. Then, finally, the sound of feet. The door opened.

'Good morning, Jerod,' said Jobe without even a hint of surprise in his voice. Jerod Bitten stood in the doorway, wearing a thick, red morning coat. The wall behind him was lined with bookshelves and a large desk occupied much of the room. Oil paintings hung on the walls and there were even a few sculptures on pedestals in the corners. Jerod Bitten had done quite well for himself in the past twenty years.

'What are you doing here?' asked Bitten. He looked completely bewildered by the visit.

But it made perfect sense to Francks. His body had guided him to the one place he could rest and meditate on the past. The one place in the entire Hive where he could be safe for a time. 'I just need a place to sleep,' he said. 'Can you put me up for a day?'

KAL STROLLED DOWN the road just inside the Glory Hole dome. He hadn't been down to this section of the Underhive since that whole vampire incident kicked off. He'd been drugged and kidnapped right outside of Hagen's Hole and things went downhill from there. Now he wasn't quite sure how to get back to Hagen's.

That's why he kept Scabbs around. The little man remembered every step he'd ever taken. Of course, he left a trail of dead skin wherever he went, so it couldn't be too hard to find his way back again. But now he was lost again, and he'd just stepped inside the dome. Every blasted-out building looked like the last, and it wasn't like he could just stop someone and ask. He was Kal Jerico. It wouldn't look good for the famous bounty hunter to ask for directions, especially to a bar.

He walked into the middle of an intersection and scanned all four streets, looking for some clue, some landmark to jog his memory. One of the streets was completely blocked off by a pile of debris. It looked odd, like it had been piled there instead of happening naturally – meaning from a grenade or a missile or perhaps a hive quake. Then it hit him. He'd created that pile himself; well he and Scabbs had while Yolanda watched and criticised.

They were going to try to trap a bounty up against the blockade, but Yolanda messed it up and Scabbs ended up blowing up the side of a building that fell on their quarry. Kal smiled. Looking back, that was a lot of fun – a lot more fun now than when it happened, of course.

He turned to look down the other way to see if the rubble from the explosion that killed their bounty was still there. What he saw instead was a group of Redemptionists walking toward him, weapons in hand. He looked back the way he had come. A second group of Redemptionists had appeared and now headed towards him. Kal hardly had to look to know what waited for him down the last street. A third group stepped out from a door, drew weapons, and fanned out across the street.

He had one exit and he knew it to be blocked. He had blocked it himself a few months back. 'Scav,' he said. 'I wish Yolanda was here. This is how you set a trap.' Kal drew his laspistols and fired into the first group. He then turned and ran toward the blockade, zigzagging down the street as las-blasts hit the ground around him.

SCABBS PUSHED AWAY the plate of food the mavants had served. 'That tasted pretty good,' he said. 'Like mom used to make.'

Yolanda tried not to imagine Scabbs as an ugly scab-covered boy sitting down to a meal with his ugly, scab-covered family, but the image popped into her head unbidden. She shivered and put it out of her mind.

She stared straight down the tunnel, not wanting to look at her companion at the moment for fear the image would return. 'Yeah,' she said. 'There are some places in the Underhive where you can get a decent meal, but Jerico insists on going from one hole to another.'

'He likes the barmaids,' said Scabbs. 'He says they help him think.'

Yolanda humphed. 'Only because his brains are in his pants.'

'What do you mean?'

Now Yolanda looked at Scabbs. There seemed to be an honest look of bewilderment on his face, although it was tough to tell underneath all the sores and flaky skin. 'Never mind,' she said. 'Let Jerico have his barmaids. I'll take an Escher-run restaurant any day. The mavants know how to cook.' Of course, one bad meal will get them ten beatings, she thought to herself.

'The food was good,' said Scabbs, 'but those waiters were awfully dirty.'

Yolanda stared at Scabbs as they walked. He had taken a bath a couple days earlier, but that had only washed off the top layer of crud. Still she had to admit that he was cleaner than most mavants she'd kicked

around. 'That's just part of the... décor,' she replied
after a moment. 'Like the barmaids in the Sump Hole.
Something to take your mind off how dirty and poor
you are.'

Scabbs nodded his head but Yolanda doubted he
truly understood. He seemed to revel in being dirty and
poor. It was the only thing that explained why he had
stayed with Jerico so long.

As she pondered why she stayed with the disgustingly
swarthy bounty hunter, Yolanda heard something rumbling behind them. 'Did you hear that?' she asked.

'Hear what?' said Scabbs. He picked at the sores on
his elbows as they walked, which made a scraping
sound. Glancing down at his arm, he said 'Sorry. Didn't
realise you could hear that.'

The rumbling continued and began to get louder.
Yolanda shook her head. 'Not that,' she said. 'But stop
it anyway.' She pointed back down the tunnel. 'I think
something is coming. Probably those scavving Goliaths
again.'

Yolanda scanned the tunnel, looking for somewhere
to hide. They were at least a mile from the entrance to
Glory Hole, and it was a pretty featureless tunnel. They
were trapped. The rumbling sound grew louder and
began echoing all around them. Yolanda wasn't sure,
but it sounded like engines.

'I hear it now,' said Scabbs. 'What is that?
Chainswords?'

Yolanda shook her head again. 'No,' she said. 'Bigger.
Much bigger. Run.'

Around a bend in the tunnel emerged three men on
motorcycles. They belched black smoke, leaving a roiling
dark cloud in their wake. Yolanda ran. She glanced over
at Scabbs. He was running as well, his short legs pumping twice as fast as hers, but he was still falling behind.

The motorcycles gained on them. Yolanda could now see the riders. They wore what looked like Orlock colours and waved chains over their heads. 'What's their problem,' she asked. 'We haven't ticked off the Orlocks... not lately.'

In a moment, they were on top of Scabbs. The lead biker swung his chain toward the little half-breed. It snapped out and caught him in the calf, wrapping around his legs with a clang and pulling his legs together. Scabbs pitched forward and hit the ground hard as the bikes zoomed past.

They'd be on her in a second. She stopped and drew her sword. The second biker tossed his chain at her. A large hook swung on the end as it flew. Yolanda side-stepped and slashed her sword down in front of her legs. The chain hit her sword and whipped around it several times before catching on the hook.

Yolanda braced herself as the biker drove by. When the chain went taut he yanked back hard. There was a moment of tension and Yolanda's sword bent danger-ously far over. Her bare biceps bulged as she fought against the biker's momentum.

With a snap, the tension eased and the biker flew back off his cycle. He hit the ground hard on his back and Yolanda heard a sharp crack. The riderless motor-bike wobbled and fell over, skidding down the tunnel until it came to a stop against the wall.

'That's one,' she said, but she knew the other two would be back to finish the job. Yolanda turned to see how Scabbs was doing, but he was nowhere to be seen. A pit formed in her stomach as she realised what had happened. She turned toward the departing bikers. Scabbs trailed behind them, bouncing and scraping against the ground as he clawed at the hooked chain wrapped around his ankles.

'Helmawr's rump,' yelled Yolanda as she ran toward the downed bike.

'You CAN'T STAY here,' said Bitten. 'It's not safe.'

'Another assassin tracked me down,' said Jobe Francks. He pushed his way inside and closed the door behind him.

Bitten stared at the closed door, unable to object, but unwilling to give in just yet either. He wondered how his life had got so complicated so quickly. Assassins. Jobe Francks. His own past with Ignus. It was karma, he decided. He was paying for the sins of his youth and now they'd come back threefold.

'Fine,' he said, resigning himself to the realities of the day, just as he had always done. 'But only for the day. We'll smuggle you out to another gang hideout tonight.'

Francks dropped into a chair and stretched his legs out in front of him. He looked exhausted. Bitten crossed to his desk and sat as well. He thought about the packet in his drawer, but decided it could wait for now.

'Who's after me?' asked Francks. He sat stretched out in the chair, rubbing his eyes with his fists. 'I can't see past the hate and the passion. I can't see the face.'

Bitten let the question and Francks's odd wyrd-talk hang in the air for a minute, as he considered his response. Perhaps it was time. He might never get another chance. 'It's Ignus,' he said. 'At least I think it's Ignus.'

'What?' asked Francks. He sat up in the chair, his face going flush. 'You said he was dead.'

'I said he was gone,' said Bitten. 'And even that was not quite true.'

'How do you mean?'

Bitten wiped a bead of sweat from his brow. 'He's not the man you knew. He's changed. Jules Ignus did die – he is gone, for good – but the man he became, the one who came after, that man is no more Jules Ignus than I am. He's more. More powerful. More influential. More righteous.'

'You're not making much sense,' said Francks.

Bitten laughed out loud. 'You. The prophet. Telling me I'm not making sense,' he said and laughed again. 'Now that's funny.'

Francks wasn't laughing. 'That's why I couldn't see him before,' he said. 'There's a thread of Ignus still woven into the plan. So I looked for him, but he wasn't here. But you say, it's not really Ignus anymore. I can use that. I can seek him out now.'

Bitten stopped laughing. 'You can't do that,' he said. 'You shouldn't do that. I told you I can't save you this time. He'll keep coming. You can't beat him.'

'I don't have to beat him,' said Francks. I just need to show him. I need to make him understand.'

'Understand what?' Bitten was starting to shake. He didn't like where this conversation was going anymore.

'His own mortality.'

With that, the conversation ended. There was nothing more Bitten could say. He couldn't help. He had to stay out of it if he had any chance of living through this. After a while, Francks fell asleep in the chair. Bitten opened the drawer and pulled the envelope full of credits out and walked across the room. He dropped the envelope in Jobe's pocket and then left the hab to run an errand.

KAL SHOT BLINDLY behind him, just trying to scatter his pursuers and give him a little more time. He scrambled up the pile of debris, desperately trying to reach the top before they regrouped and got a bead on him with their weapons.

So far, he'd been lucky. They were either terrible shots or he was just that good. As much as he wanted it to be the latter, he knew the odds of dodging that many blasts were pretty darn low.

He grabbed at the back of a chair lodged between a chunk of masonry and an overturned crate and tried to pull himself up another few feet. A laser blast screamed over his shoulder and obliterated the chair. 'Maybe they're better shots than I thought,' said Kal as he slid back a metre.

'Come down and you won't be hurt, Kal Jerico,' called one of the Redemptionists. 'We just want to talk.'

Kal caught himself on a table leg and turned around. There were about a dozen blue-robed gangers spread out in a loose group on the street. Kal wished Scabbs were here with his bandolier of grenades. That group just begged for a large explosion.

Behind the gangers stood a man wearing robes with a thin slick of hair pressed against the side of his head. One of Crimson's deacons. This was worse than Kal had thought. It wasn't some random gang of Cawdor trying to protect the prophet. Crimson had finally entered the hunt.

'We don't want to kill you,' said the deacon. He held his arms out wide in the universal greeting of friendship.

'Well that changes everything,' said Kal, who had no intention of becoming friends with a Redemptionist deacon. 'Because I have no problems killing you.' He aimed and fired both laspistols. One of the blasts caught the deacon in the shoulder, spinning him around and knocking him to the ground.

The gangers opened fire again. Blasts sizzled all around Kal, but none came close. They had orders not to hurt him. Kal wanted to wonder why, but he didn't have time. He fired back, dropping two of what he now assumed to be Crimson's personal guards.

The deacon, who had a much higher tolerance for pain than Kal had thought possible, pushed himself to his feet. 'We won't kill you, Kal Jerico,' he said again. 'But I have no problems causing you pain. Take him down.' This last was an order to his men.

'Oh scav!' said Kal. He shot a few more blasts and started to scramble back up the pile. Blasts ripped through chunks of metal and concrete all around him, sending plumes of dust and acrid smoke into the air.

Kal coughed as he inhaled a puff of powdered cement, doubling over and dropping another metre back down toward the base of the pile. Another blast screamed through the air, hitting the table he had just been clinging to.

'That was a little too close,' he muttered. 'Time to trust my luck.' He turned again, braced his feet against a metal door, and aimed at the approaching gang. He fired four shots in quick succession, dropping three guards and disarming the fourth. 'Damn, I'm good,' said Kal.

The next volley of shots all impacted below Kal, obliterating the door under his feet. Kal slid down the blockade. He grabbed at the debris around him, but couldn't stop himself. There was a large hole where the door had been, and he slipped right into it. Another round of blasts over his head started a small avalanche. Chunks of concrete, chairs, crates and other debris crashed down around Kal, burying him up to his neck in trash.

'Well,' said Kal. 'Those were pretty lucky shots.'

* * *

YOLANDA GRABBED THE handlebars and yanked the motorcycle upright. The engine was still running. She kicked a long leg over to straddle the thrumming machine, and pumped the throttle. The engine revved. She kicked it into gear and tore off down the tunnel, leaving the former driver moaning on the ground behind her.

Through the braids flapping around her face, Yolanda could see the other two bikers up ahead. Scabbs still tumbled along behind them. Thankfully they had slowed down, but it didn't look like the little man was struggling anymore either.

She didn't know if he was alive or dead, but figured it didn't matter. Either way, she had to kill the two gangers. Yolanda pulled out one of her weapons and gunned the bike, closing in on her quarry before she opened fire. She couldn't really aim while zooming along at top speed through a narrow tunnel, so she just fired a stream of blasts toward the bikers.

The first few shots went wide, but one hit the rear of the second bike, burning a hole through the frame. The rear wheel swerved and skidded, but the biker got his machine back under control just as it teetered danger-ously to the side. He turned in his seat, made a rude gesture at Yolanda and gunned his own bike, burning a long black mark into the floor.

Yolanda fired again, but misjudged the distance as he pulled away from her. She opened up her throttle all the way and crept closer. She fired a few shots at the chain holding Scabbs, but came dangerously close to his legs, so thought perhaps that wasn't such a good idea after all.

A loud bang brought Yolanda's attention back to the second biker, who now held a shotgun. Shrapnel flew off the wall beside her from the blast. She swerved as sharp bits of masonry rained down on her. The biker jerked his arm, pumping the shotgun, and aimed it at her again.

Yolanda hit the breaks and turned the handlebars sharply, putting the bike into a sideways skid. She dropped off to the side away from the shotgun, holding on with just one hand and her foot on top of the seat. The shotgun fired and the blast hit the side of the bike, sending sparks and bits of metal into the air.

After the blast, Yolanda pulled back on the handle, straightening her bike out. Staying low and off to the side, she steered with one hand while aiming her pistol. She had a better angle from there and fired several times, hitting the second biker's rear tyre with at least two shots.

The rubber shredded itself away from the rim in seconds. A steady stream of sparks began to spray out from the metal wheel. Without traction, the bike lost momentum and rear end began to skid back and forth. The biker dropped the shotgun to keep both hands on the handlebars, and kept it under control.

Yolanda pulled herself back upright and fired several more shots. Blasts hit all around the swerving biker. Chunks of metal and several gleaming pipes flew off the bike as her las-blasts rained down on him. Her last shot slammed into the biker's back, burning a hole through his leather coat. His hands flew up as he arched his back in pain. A moment later, he tumbled off the back of the motorcycle, bouncing and rolling right toward Yolanda's bike.

Yolanda tried to turn out of the way, but it was too late. Her front wheel struck the biker in the shoulder, spinning him about. His legs swung under her bike and hit her back wheel. She wasn't sure what happened next, but assumed his leather trousers got pulled up into the wheel because the back end of her machine bucked up into the air as she ran over him.

The next thing Yolanda knew, she was going over the handlebars. She tried to hold on to the seat with her powerful legs, but to no avail. She flew into the air and landed on her back in front of the bucking bike. With only a second to react, Yolanda fired two shots from her laspistol, hitting the handlebars with both.

The bike turned, tipped and skidded. The rear wheel slid right toward Yolanda. She rolled to the side, not even looking back. She didn't stop until she hit the side wall of the tunnel. The bike continued skidding down the tunnel until it slammed into the far wall.

Yolanda got up. Her back ached so hard she could hardly stand up straight, and she was bleeding from her knees and elbows. She looked down the tunnel. She could just see the last bike, with Scabbs, unconscious or dead, skipping along behind. She started to stagger down the tunnel as fast as she could.

Then her bike exploded.

JOBE FRANCKS DREAMED.

As usual, he looked down at himself to try to determine his age. For someone who could relive his own past, it helped to place the dreams in time. On this occasion, though, he didn't recognise his clothes or his body for that matter.

He was walking through a dark tunnel. Pools of light flashed over him as he walked. He was carrying something over his shoulder. He looked at it when he walked through a pool of light. It was a body.

The body had a blue cloak and he could see a patch of orange armour when the cloak flapped aside. A dull ache began to gnaw at his stomach. He tried to stop in the pool of light to look more closely at the body, but he had no control over his body. Another spot of light approached. He stared at the back of the body when he entered the light. It was there. A scorched hole in the cloak between the shoulders. His heart sunk.

He was carrying the dead body of Syris Bowdie.

He walked on, trapped in someone else's body, unable to alter the flow of time. He came to a round metal door. It curved slightly away at the top and sides. There was no handle in the door. Just a wheel sticking out from the middle. He spun the wheel and pulled. The door opened with a whoosh.

Francks noticed a small window in the door as it opened. He looked at the window as it came into the pool of light and saw a reflection there. It confirmed what he had begun to suspect. He was inside the body of Jules Ignus.

Ignus went through the door into the inky blackness beyond. He turned and pulled the door shut behind him. He switched on a torch and the beam hit the curved wall. They were inside a dome.

Even the poorest settlements had some power. Some lights would be burning somewhere, but this was pitch black. They were in an abandoned dome.

They walked through the dome for quite some time. Francks couldn't tell what Ignus was looking for. He was along for the ride but couldn't sense anything within Ignus. Perhaps there really was nothing there to sense.

After a time, Ignus stopped. He waved his light around. They were still near the wall of the dome, but had come quite a distance around from the door. They stood on the edge of a hole. The light hit crumbling walls around the hole. It was a bombed out building. The walls of the basement had crumbled in, leaving just a debris-filled hole.

Ignus pulled the body off his shoulder and dropped it down into the hole. Francks screamed, but no sound came out. Ignus turned around and flashed his torch on the wall of the dome behind him. He reached into his pocket and pulled out a metal box. There was a crude timer on the front. He set the timer to ten minutes and then taped the box to the wall as high as he could reach.

He then walked back toward the door, whistling as he went. When he reached the door, he opened it again and walked through, but then stood there waiting. The bomb exploded, lighting up the small dome with a flash. The dome shook and rumbled as the wall fell in and covered up Jules Ignus's murder. He closed the door and began to whistle again as he walked back down the tunnel.

Francks began to cry as the vision faded.

THE ASSASSIN HAD tramped around the Underhive all day, with no sign of his quarry. The old man had disappeared somehow from Hagen's Hole. It seemed inconceivable but he must have known about the secret exit. He'd left Glory Hole the same way, but the trail had long since gone cold.

Then he'd got lucky. A piece of news came his way that the old man had gone to see an old friend in Hive City. It was dangerous to do a job in the city, but not impossible, and he was being well paid.

And it had paid off. The information was good. He stood at a window, covered in a blanket of darkness and a special cloak he'd taken from a Delaque agent he'd taken down a few years back. The cloak soaked up the darkness and radiated nothing back, not even heat. He was all but invisible, even to infrared or night vision goggles.

In the room beyond were two old men, one asleep in a chair and the other sitting at a desk. One was the target and the other his friend. It didn't much matter which was which. He'd let the authorities sort out the bodies later. It was almost time to go to work.

6: THE CARDINAL RULE

A BLAST OF flame and heat hit Yolanda in the face, throwing her back down the tunnel. She flew five metres through the air and landed on her back.

'Ow!' she said. Yolanda was pretty sure nothing was broken, but felt she deserved a little rest after the second tunnel attack in two days. She lay there in a pool of light, staring at the roof of the tunnel and wondering how many more times this would happen this week. Then she rolled to the side. She crossed her arms and turned over and over.

A burning tyre landed behind her with a squelch. Yolanda stopped rolling when she hit the wall. She looked back to see the wheel roll down the tunnel, leaving a trail of smouldering tar and black smoke. 'I just don't need this,' she muttered as she pushed herself back to her feet.

Yolanda walked gingerly toward the burning bike. Smoke billowed toward the ceiling as a flaming puddle of fuel spread across the tunnel. She held her breath and darted past the puddle before it cut her off. On the other side, she searched for the trail of the final bike. It wasn't hard to find. Apparently, the motorcycle had been leaking oil, which mingled with drops of blood and bits and pieces of Scabbs's clothes and flesh.

As she jogged down the tunnel, following the trail of blood and oil, the black smoke behind her must have reached the ceiling. A decrepit sprinkler system cut in and stale-smelling water rained down on Yolanda, drenching her in seconds. Her dreadlocks soaked up the water and stuck to her face like thick, doughy strands. Rivulets of water ran down into her ears and eyes, and the ridge of her nose became a waterfall. Her leather vest and loin cloth became heavy with water and began slapping her bare skin.

Worst of all, a few minutes after the sprinklers started, the water all but washed away the trail.

'Helmawr's rump!' she yelled.

THE ASSASSIN CREPT across the roof of the old man's hab, searching for a way inside. The hab backed up to the wall of the dome, so there was no back door and the buildings on the block had been built side-by-side, so there were no alleys. The only door led right into the room where the two men had been sitting, and the windows were all barred, even those on the second floor.

Whoever lived here was highly security conscious. The home was secure from anything but a frontal assault and that would surely bring the enforcers, probably preventing a quick and quiet escape. But if there was one thing the assassin knew, it was that no hab in the hive was totally secure.

The roof yielded only one possible entrance. A metal, box-shaped ventilation unit ran across the roof and down the entire block of buildings. A small pipe dropped from the metal box into each building to push air in, while a larger shaft allowed the recycled air to re-enter the ventilation unit from the building.

All he had to do was crawl into the unit and climb down the shaft. He found an access panel to the unit three buildings down, but it had been welded shut. This guy is pretty good, he thought, but he was better. He pulled out a welding torch, set the flame to a blue-white pinpoint, and went to work on the welds.

A while later, after using his torch again on the attic vent, the assassin climbed out of the shaft, switched to nightvision on his goggles, and tiptoed across the rafters. He found the attic access panel, but then sighed when he realised it was screwed into place from the other side. He checked the small gas tank for his welding torch. It felt light. 'Should be enough,' he said.

He cut around the screws, leaving a small sliver of metal to hold each one. He then attached a suction cup and pushed the panel out. After pulling the panel up into the attic, he dropped down into what looked like a bedroom. He slipped out the door and down the steps.

At last, he peeked around the doorway into the main room. Both men were right where he had left them. If his luck held, this would be over in a minute and he could slip back out the way he came in. These two could rot for days before anyone found them.

Sliding a long, thin dagger out from a fold inside his light-drinking cloak, he slipped in behind the man at the desk. He reached around and clasped his free hand around the man's mouth as he jabbed the dagger through his neck from the other side.

The old man stiffened under his grip and kicked at the desk twice before going limp. The assassin looked up at the man sleeping in the chair. He hadn't stirred. He pulled the dagger out of the wound and leaned the dying man's head back against the top of the chair. Blood sprayed out the hole in his neck and pooled on the floor.

Being careful to avoid the growing puddle of blood, the assassin crept over toward the other victim. 'One down, one to go,' he said to himself as he prepared to strike.

'GET UP!' SCREAMED a voice in Scabbs's head. In his semi-conscious state, he couldn't tell if the voice was his own or Kal's, or perhaps someone else entirely. But the little half-ratskin had been so conditioned to respond to loud commands through his years of working with Kal and Yolanda, that he reacted out of pure instinct.

He stood without opening his eyes, snapping to attention before the voice spoke again and, more importantly, before the subsequent smack hit the back of his head. In retrospect, he probably should have opened his eyes first, for as soon as Scabbs got to his feet, he pitched over forward, hitting the ground hard enough to knock the wind out of his gut.

'Get up!' came the command again, quickly followed by a sharp rap on his back. This time it was definitely audible and definitely not Kal. Scabbs opened his eyes, and immediately wished he hadn't. A bright light pierced his skull, bringing the splitting headache that he'd only dully been aware of before into sharp focus.

In fact, his body ached from his feet to his teeth and beyond.

A hand holding a short length of pipe emerged out of the light and hit him between the shoulder blades again. Scabbs scrambled to his feet, trying to ignore the aches and sharp pains that wracked his body. He looked at his feet and saw the reason he had fallen earlier. His ankles, red, raw and swollen, were shackled together.

He started to remember. The motorbikes. The chain. Being dragged down the tunnel.

'Ow,' he said.

'Shut up and get moving,' said the Orlock ganger connected to the pipe-holding hand. He wore a red bandana around his melon-shaped head, a leather vest over a thin shirt and thick steel-bound boots, which probably explained the pains Scabbs felt in his ribs. But he had no visible weapons beyond the pipe. As Scabbs looked at him, the ganger raised the pipe for another blow, but Scabbs shuffled his feet forward, complying before the blow fell.

As he walked, Scabbs checked his injuries. He probably had some cracked ribs and a concussion. He rubbed the back of his head, and checked his hand; no blood, but there was a thick knot at the base of his skull. His grimy grey clothes were stained brown and red, but even though his shirt was mostly tattered fabric now, he was no longer bleeding from being dragged along by his captors. His swollen ankles ached and chafed against the manacles, but he felt no sharp pains as he walked, so the bones were likely intact. He felt lucky to be alive.

'Start over there,' commanded the Orlock, pointing at a large pile of debris.

Scabbs looked up. A couple of dozen other dirty, bloody, manacled people carried rocks, chunks of metal and other bits of unrecognizable objects down the hill and dropped them in bins. Other slaves – there really was no other word for the manacled workers – pushed full bins away from the hill while others brought empty bins back. Those had dropped their loads climbed back up the hill.

The Orlock guard shoved Scabbs in the back with his pipe. He stumbled a few feet before gaining his balance.

Taking a shallow breath so his ribs wouldn't hurt so much, Scabbs followed the slaves up the hill and grabbed a crumpled piece of pipe.

Yeah. Lucky. That's what he was.

SNAP!

Kal Jerico hadn't thought his life could get any worse after spending an afternoon trudging through raw sewage.

Snap!

He'd even spent a moment during his meeting with Nemo later that night musing. Now I've definitely hit bottom and things have to start to get better, he'd thought back then.

Snap!

Now, he realised those moments of his life were all just prelude to this one. This was definitely the lowest of the low.

Snap!

The whip hit Kal just below his knees on that tender piece of flesh above the calf. He marvelled at the precision. He had also just about bitten through his lower lip trying not to scream.

'Stop,' said a familiar voice.

Kal exhaled slowly through pursed lips, trying to force the pain out of his body with the air. It worked only slightly. His inhale was slightly harder. He'd always found it tough to breathe in while suspended above the ground by his wrists.

Cardinal Crimson walked around in front of Kal. He had a gruesome, toothy smile on his lipless face. His eyes practically danced in their open sockets. The look on the Cardinal's face was one of holy contentment. Ecstasy even.

'Looks like you just had an epiphany in your pants,' said Kal with a smirk.

Crimson raised a bony finger in the air. *Snap!* The whip hit the spot again. 'You will speak only when spoken to, heretic,' said Crimson.

'So, now would be okay, then?' asked Kal. He was pleased his voice only cracked a little.

Snap!

'You will answer questions, Kal Jerico, and keep your heretical comments to yourself.'

Kal kept several heretical comments to himself while he waited for the first question.

'What is your interest in the heretic known as "the Prophet of the Body?"'

Kal was so stunned by the question that he almost blurted out the truth. So, the prophet was a heretic in Crimson's eyes as well. That was an interesting piece to add to the puzzle. Kal wondered how much more information he could get out of Crimson while the Cardinal interrogated him.

'Why do you want to know?' he asked, and was immediately sorry he hadn't thought that out a little more.

Snap!

'I'm asking the questions, heretic,' said Crimson. He circled back around Kal. 'What is your interest in Jobe Francks?'

'He's a bounty, that's all,' said Kal.

'Who's paying you for this bounty?'

Kal considered his options. Nemo wouldn't be happy if Kal sold him out, but his legs were on fire and his shoulders and arms were shooting pains all the way down to his hips. Plus, the truth might actually be beneficial here. He heard the whoosh of the whip being pulled back for another strike.

'Nemo!' he cried out.

Crimson muttered something. Kal held his breath and strained his ears to listen, but he only got fragments.

'...lousy spy... can't let him get... what does he know... can't take any chances...'

After a while, Crimson stopped muttering and walked back into view. He smiled again. Kal tried not to shiver at the sight. 'Kal,' he started. 'Kal, we've not always seen eye-to-eye on things. But I think we can both agree that we hate Nemo more than we hate each other, right?'

Kal considered his answer quickly and carefully. 'Okay,' he said.

'Right,' said Crimson. 'That man is a no good spy. A heretic of the first order.' He held out his bony hand and placed it on Kal's flexed and aching shoulder. 'Let me burn my way to the point, shall I?'

Kal nodded. Anything to get Crimson's hand off his body.

'I will pay you twice what Nemo is paying to bring Francks to me.'

'Four times,' said Kal automatically, and then cringed. Still, he'd have to pay Nemo at least double just to get out from underneath his thumb.

The whip didn't come.

'Done,' said Crimson. 'We have a deal then?'

'That's dead or alive, right?' asked Kal. 'Same price either way.'

'Actually,' said Crimson, 'just dead.' His floating eyes bored into Kal.

'No deal,' said Kal defiantly. 'I'm a bounty hunter. Not an assassin.' He'd blurted the response before he could even think about it.

The fire returned to Nemo's eyes and his lipless smile shifted into a horrible sneer. 'Jobe Francks must die!' he screamed. 'He will die and you will die beside him. Two heretics sent to fiery redemption. It is the will of the Undying Emperor.'

'It's the will of an undead lunatic,' said Kal.

Snap! Snap! Snap!

It dawned on Kal that his lowest moment was still yet to come. When and if he got out of this chamber and back to Yolanda and Scabbs, he would have to admit they were right. Going to Crimson would have been a very bad idea. Probably just as bad as getting caught by Crimson.

Snap!

JOBE FRANCKS'S HAND flashed out and grabbed the assassin's wrist. He opened his eyes to see a bloody blade quivering a few centimetres from his chest.

'How in the…?' said the assassin, his eyes wide with shock.

Francks didn't hesitate to try to understand the moment. He acted. One leg whipped up, his booted toes slapping into the assassin's groin. He cocked the other leg and kicked the man in the gut, propelling him away from the chair where Jobe had been sleeping just moments before.

The knife flipped into the air as the man slammed into the desk. Jobe rose to his feet and snatched the tumbling dagger in one fluid movement.

'You were asleep,' gasped the assassin. He held his stomach and tried to catch his breath. 'How did you…?'

Jobe levelled a cloudy-eyed glare at the killer. 'Bad dreams,' he said as he advanced.

The assassin retreated around the desk as he fumbled in his billowing, dark cloak. He pulled out what looked like a gun with an attached gas canister. He snapped the trigger and Jobe dived to the side. Nothing more than a thin blue-white flame emerged from the tip. It was a welding torch. He twisted a knob and the flame lengthened, and then waved the torch back and forth in front of his body.

Jobe moved in on the assassin again. He flipped the dagger over in his hand to be able to parry. He didn't need it to kill, just to get past the flame. He made a feint with the knife, thrusting its tip toward the assassin's torch hand. Instead of flinching, the assassin dropped his arm under the attack and twisted his wrist, altering the angle of the flame.

The torch lanced across Jobe's arm. Pain shot through his body. The smell of burnt skin and hair wafted into the air. He pushed the pain down and disregarded the urge to grab his arm and look at the wound. Time enough for that later. Jobe pulled back a step to regroup.

It was then he happened to glance over at the desk and saw Bitten slumped in his chair. A trickle of blood leaked out of a hole in his neck. 'Oh my Emperor,' he exclaimed. 'What have I wrought?'

'Your own demise,' said the assassin.

Jobe looked back too late. The killer was on top of him. He slapped the dagger hand aside and drove Francks to the ground. With a deft move, the assassin scissored Jobe's legs together as he lay on top of chest and hand. He held Francks's free hand down and shoved the torch into his neck.

Nothing happened. He could feel his neck burning, but the searing pain he expected never arrived. The assassin lifted the torch up, obviously also wondering why Francks wasn't dead or dying, or even in pain. The torch had gone out.

Francks wanted to laugh at his luck, but the image of his dying friend drove everything else out of his mind. He looked into the befuddled face of the killer and the pain and anger and frustration of decades in the Wastes boiled over inside.

The killer reared back with the torch, but he never got the chance to smack him in the head. With nothing but the will of his mind, Jobe Francks tossed the assassin into the air. The killer flew up into the ceiling and stuck as if bolted through the hands and feet.

The assassin squirmed, but Francks held him in place with his mind. Jobe rose from the floor to his feet without bending his body or using his hands. He raised one hand and clutched at the air above him. He could feel the killer's neck in his grip even though he held nothing at all. The man gasped and choked as if unable to get his breath.

'What… what are you?' he gasped.

'I am the prophet,' replied Francks. 'And here is my message.' With a jerk, he twisted his wrist in the air. The assassin's head snapped to the side and a loud crack echoed through the room. Francks let his arm drop to the side and the killer fell to the ground in a crumpled mass.

As he looked at the dead assassin, Francks's mind cleared and he felt himself begin breathing again. He looked over at Bitten. Through his cloudy eyes, he could see breath escaping his friend's lips. He rushed to the chair. Hesitating for just a moment, he reached out and laid his hand on Bitten's shoulder.

At his touch, Bitten stirred. He tried to raise his head, but apparently didn't have the strength left for even that. 'You're alive,' he said, his voice raspy and barely audible. 'Good… idiot killed the wrong… old man.' Bitten coughed. A gurgle of blood spat out of the hole in his neck and bubbled through his lips, moistening his mouth with red liquid.

Jerod Bitten's eyes fell closed and his head lolled to the side. Jobe held his head in his hands and then leaned down and kissed his old enemy on the forehead.

Blood trickled down Bitten's cheek and ran through Jobe's fingers, staining his hand.

Bitten's eyes snapped open wide as if in terror or pain. 'The truth,' he whispered, 'is here. Find it.' And then he was gone. Jobe Francks sat cradling the head of his only friend in his lap and cried.

AFTER SEVERAL HOURS of tramping through the lower reaches of the Underhive, Yolanda was dry, but by no means happy. 'Scavving Jerico,' she said. 'This is his fault as usual.' She kicked a loose rock, sending it skittering down the dusty tunnel.

She'd picked up the motorcycle's trail just inside Glory Hole. After waiting for Jerico at the rendezvous point for an hour, Yolanda followed the trail deeper and deeper into the Underhive until it ended at a blank wall in the middle of a dark tunnel. In her torch light, Yolanda saw the last few drops of oil near the wall had been smeared. Something had scraped them to the side. It took her ten minutes to find the seam in the wall and pry it open.

Now she trudged down a corridor that had probably not seen regular traffic in decades, perhaps even centuries. Yet it bore marks of recent activity. The dust-covered walls were shored up with clean braces and the thick layer of sediment on the floor had been scuffed almost completely down the centre.

Someone lived or worked down here, and that someone had kidnapped Scabbs. 'And it's all Jerico's fault,' she said again. 'Him and his scavving debts. You should have been with us, Jerico.'

As she was about to continue her tirade, Yolanda saw a light ahead. She flicked off her torch and crept forward. The tunnel ended in the normal circular hatchway of early domes. A small window at eye level let out light from within. Yolanda stepped to the side of the window and craned her head around to peer inside.

Dozens of men and women in rags and chains worked under the watchful eyes of Orlock gangers. A burly man yelled at the gangers, who whipped a few straggling workers. It looked like the Orlocks were mining this abandoned dome for materials or tech, but she'd never known a gang to use slave labour – kidnapped slave labour at that. That was a sure way to get the Guilders after you.

Something moved past the window and Yolanda ducked back. When she looked again, her jaw dropped open. The shadow had been a couple of Guilder guards. They paced on around the area, as if they were guarding the work site.

What in the Spire is going on here, thought Yolanda? An abandoned dome in a deep crevice of the Under-hive filled with slave labour and Orlock gangers, all being protected by Guilder guards. What had Scabbs fallen into this time?

Whatever it was, she couldn't barge in alone. Then she got an idea. The Orlocks all wore bandanas, one of which could easily would hide her Escher tats; and dirty shirts one of which would hide her… other Escher assets. She just might be able to infiltrate the site, if she stayed in the shadows. With Jerico missing in action – again – she just might be Scabbs's only hope for rescue. She had to chance it.

Yolanda ran back down the dark tunnel. She knew where she could find her disguise. She just hoped the fire and sprinklers hadn't got to the two bodies she'd left behind.

THE DAY LIGHTS in Hive City flickered to life outside Jerod Bitten's hab, sending a beam through the window

onto the macabre scene inside. Jobe Francks sat on the
floor behind the large desk, with Bitten's bloody head
in his lap. He'd stopped crying hours earlier, more due
to his tear ducts drying up then to any sense of closure
to his grief.

The Universe had asked so much of him, and this
latest death had been one cost too many. His will to
push on in the name of the almighty plan had drained
away with his tears. He felt empty and lost, more so
than at any time during his years of wandering the Ash
Wastes. He now had no friends, nowhere to turn for
help, no idea where to go next.

As he sat, the light from the street shone on his face,
outlining his head in a soft, white glow. He raised his
head and gazed into the light being reflected down
upon him through an odd pattern of reflections from
the framed paintings on the walls. He could see the
path the beam traversed across the room. It bounced
from an image of Dust Falls to a rendering of the Spire
and then to an eerily familiar painting of the Acid
Pools before shining into his eyes.

The pools. Bitten had known then what was happening, but couldn't or wouldn't do anything to stop
it. He'd been too afraid of Ignus. But he'd known.
What did he say before he died?

'The idiot killed the wrong old man.'

Bitten had known what was coming. He had to. But
he was still too afraid to act. And this time that fear
cost him his life. Bitten's last words echoed in Jobe's
mind.

'The truth is here.'

Something stirred inside Jobe Francks. A new sense
of purpose. A newfound desire. Ignus was still alive,
still killing his friends. It was time for the killing to
end. Time for the plan to move forward.

Francks laid Jerod Bitten's body gently on the floor and climbed into the chair. He opened the drawers and combed through their contents, looking for something – anything – that might point to Ignus's current whereabouts.

The bottom drawer was filled with ledgers. He flipped through them. They contained accounts for all of Bitten's business dealings. After a while, it became obvious that Jerod had been funding a number of Cawdor gangs in the Underhive. He pulled out the note Jerod had given him. A fat envelope fell out of his pocket as well. He opened it to find a wad of credits.

'No time to wonder on that,' he said, and laid the envelope aside. Unfolding the note, he checked the gang names against the records in the ledger. The names and places matched. Jerod had helped each of those gangs financially and took a portion of their earnings in return.

Francks wondered if they were all like the Universal Saviours or if any of them were hardline fanatics like the Righteous Saviours. He wanted to believe that Bitten had been doing some small part in promoting truth over fear. It might be the former fanatic's only lasting legacy.

There was one last ledger. This one listed the names of several Guilders; investors perhaps. It seemed Bitten had become quite the manipulator of money. There was a healthy flow of funds between all of the accounts. Where it all came from and the paths it took would take weeks to follow through the books. But it didn't matter. There was nothing here that overtly linked Bitten to his past with Ignus or to the current location of that murderer.

He looked into the drawer again. It was empty, but images swirled in his cloudy eye. He saw a hand reach into the empty drawer and press down on the bottom close to the back corner. A small section depressed allowing the fingers to grab the bottom and pull it out.

Then the image was gone. Francks shook his head to clear the vision and reached into the drawer. He pressed the spot and pulled out the false bottom. Inside was nothing but a small brown key, almost invisible in the dark drawer. He pulled out the key and held it up to the light to look at it.

'What do you open?' he asked. Jobe's eye refocused from the key to the painting of the Acid Pools on the wall. Somehow he knew he was right. He walked over to the painting and pulled it off the wall. Behind it was another false panel like the one in the desk drawer. He never would have noticed it before finding the false bottom.

A moment later, Francks located the button that freed the panel. Behind it was a wall safe. He inserted the key and unlocked it. Inside he found what looked like another ledger with some loose paper sticking out from the pages.

He opened the ledger and pulled out the loose parchment. As he opened it up, a smaller, folded sheet fell to the floor. On the large piece was an odd drawing full of lines and arrows and notes written in small, fine handwriting. Francks looked down at the other sheet, which had opened up when it landed. It was a wanted poster with the name and image of Jules Ignus. At the bottom, in large print, it read '10,000 credits – Dead or Alive'.

He picked up the wanted poster and headed to the desk to look through the ledger. Instead of columns showing credits owed and earned, inside was a listing of dates, places and descriptions, written in the same tiny handwriting. Transactions? No. He took the ledger back to the desk and read a few of the passages at random. They were gang activities – the New Saviours' gang activities.

Francks scanned the entries. He found a description of the burning murder of the Wyrd girl. A few pages later he found a detailed account of the death of Syris Bowdie and the ambush and mass murder of the Saviours of Humanity. He flipped through the book. Every evil deed Jules Ignus ever performed was described in the ledger, complete with dates, places and names.

A thought occurred to Francks. He flipped through and found what he needed. The date Ignus buried Syris's body. As he read the sketchy account, which he'd witnessed in greater detail through his cloudy visions just that night, Francks felt his mind transported away once again.

He stood in the dome where Ignus had left Bowdie, but it was no longer dark. Lights blazed from the tops of poles spaced throughout the small dome. Around him he saw Guilder guards and some Orlock gangers, who all seemed to be standing around watching a large group of slaves hauling stone and chunks of metal.

Francks recognised the spot and moved his consciousness to the wall. He could feel the presence of Bowdie beneath the rubble. It was close. He extended his will into the mind of a large, hairy man who seemed to be directing the workers. The man scratched at his temple for a moment and then called to one of the gangers and pointed toward Jobe. The ganger whipped the slaves, driving them to the spot, where they began clawing at the rubble.

As his vision cleared, Jobe wondered what had just happened. Was it past, present, or future? Did he truly interact with the workers? He didn't know, but he needed to find that dome. Jobe checked the account in Bitten's journal. It described how Ignus had found the dome years earlier and had been siphoning archeotech from it slowly so as to not arouse suspicion from rival gangs or the local Guilders. It mentioned a map.

Francks opened up the drawing again and read the notes. It was the map, or a copy of it. Directions were scrawled in the margin in a different colour. He gathered up the journal, re-pocketed the envelope full of credits and headed for the door. Looking back at the bodies of the assassin and his dead friend, Jobe Francks mentally thanked them for renewing his faith in the plan and said a short prayer to speed them on to their ultimate rewards, whatever they might be.

SCABBS CRINGED AND bit his lip to hold back a scream as the whip stung his back. His shredded shirt provided little protection from the intermittent lashes, so each one ripped across his scarred and bleeding back. He dared not scream, though, because that merely brought more beatings.

'Get a move on,' said the ganger behind him. It was the same one who'd captured Scabbs – a gangly young man with a thin goatee and stringy black hair sticking out from beneath his bandana. He'd heard the foreman call him Ander.

'All you crew move to the back corner,' said Ander. The whip came down again, but this time it hit a scrawny girl ahead of Scabbs.

She fell to her knees and began to cry. Scabbs stepped forward and bent over her, catching the follow-up smack on his own, raw back. He cringed again and almost bit through his lip as the pain shot up his spine.

He pulled the girl back to her feet. 'Thank you,' she mouthed to him. 'My name is Arliana. I...' Scabbs heard the crack of the whip, but was too late. It slammed into her back again. He pushed her forward before she could scream, hoping to get away from Ander, who seemed to enjoy his work a little too much.

'Don't speak,' he whispered once Ander found a new target. 'Just work. My friends will get us out of here.'

'My friends are all in here,' said Arliana.

Scabbs put his finger to his lips and handed her a piece of pipe from the pile. He then dug out a chunk of debris of his own and followed her to the cart. The chain gang worked at the new location for an hour or so, clawing at debris and hauling chunks to the carts.

Ander's whip came down more often than Scabbs thought was needed. He helped Arliana as best he could, grabbing larger pieces that she struggled with and catching her when she stumbled. She smiled each time, but Scabbs had to admit to himself that his deeds were far from selfless. He simply hoped to keep Ander's attention away from his area.

After dropping a particularly large chunk of masonry into the cart, Scabbs turned to follow Arliana back to the pile. She'd got ahead of him as he had struggled with the concrete block. Halfway back to the pile, Scabbs heard Arliana scream. He looked up, but Ander was nowhere near her.

She stood by the pile, hands on her cheeks, screaming incoherently. Scabbs shuffled forward as fast as he could, but Ander got to her first. He raised his whip, but it never fell. Arliana was now pointing down at the pile. Ander turned and yelled at the foreman.

'Grondle,' he called. 'We got another body.'

Scabbs came up beside Arliana. She'd stopped screaming, but he heard her whimper. A hand stuck out from beneath the pile in front of her, palm up. Something seemed odd about it. The rest of the chain gang crowded around to get a look, pushing Scabbs and Arliana back.

'Don't just stand there,' said Ander. 'Get back to work. Dig it out.' He snapped the whip, hitting an old man standing next to Scabbs.

With each trip after that, more and more of the body came into view. The strangeness that Scabbs noticed became clear after a while, even to the weary eyes of the chain gang.

'There's not a scratch on it anywhere,' said Arliana under her breath as they worked together to lift an iron beam off the legs.

The body was not just perfectly preserved, it didn't have a mark on it anywhere. The tons of debris that had come off the pile that night hadn't left a single scratch or bruise on the exposed flesh and the clothes were neither torn nor even dirty.

By the time Scabbs and Arliana returned after dropping the beam in the cart, the rest of the gang had pulled the body free from the pile and laid it flat on the ground. Wild, frizzy hair topped a drawn, lined face. The clothes were definitely gang-issue, consisting of a leather coat and trousers and large boots.

'Hmmph, said Ander, for the moment forgetting that his slaves had stopped working. 'Not one of my men.' He called for Grondle to come over. 'This one of your workers from the earlier accidents?'

Grondle scratched his beard as he stared at the body. He looked over at the hole from where the workers had pulled the body, and shook his head. 'No. Never seen this one before,' he said. 'And we never worked in this area before this morning. Gotta be old. Really old.'

Ander shook his head. 'It's got to be recent,' he said. 'It's not even decomposed. I've seen old bodies. They look bad. They smell worse.'

Scabbs snapped his fingers. 'That's it,' he said before his mind stopped his mouth.

The whip didn't come though. 'That's what?' asked Grondle. He grabbed Ander's arm, which had raised up with the whip.

Scabbs looked at the two of them, trying to figure out which one was really in charge. He shrugged and said, 'The smell. It's all wrong. He's dead alright. I'd guess ten maybe twenty years based on the staleness of the clothes.'

He picked up steam as Grondle and Ander leaned in to listen. 'But the body itself has no odour,' continued Scabbs. 'No decay. No rot. It's perfectly preserved, like it's been kept in a vacuum all this time. But space would have done other things, bad things, to the body. It would be a mess. I can't explain it. It's weird. It's…'

'A miracle,' whispered Arliana. She dropped to her knees and bowed in front of the body.

The word spread across the entire gang like a wave. Soon, the entire chain gang had bowed in a ring around the body. Some muttered prayers. Others reached out to touch the miracle body. Scabbs looked at Ander, wondering how the nasty Orlock would react. Ander looked at Grondle, perhaps seeking guidance.

Grondle slapped his hand against his forehead. 'Helmawr's rump,' he muttered. 'Guilder Tavis won't like this.'

KAL'S TORTURE HAD gone on for hours with precious few breaks. His mouth was dry and his tongue felt so swollen that he kept gagging on it. He had vomited twice as far as he could remember, and his lips had cracked from the stomach acid he'd expelled. He could no longer feel his shoulders, which was a blessing. His back and legs, on the other hand, felt like someone had built a fire on him, using his skin as kindling.

Crimson had returned every so often to pace around him and preach at him. He would step out of the dark into the pool of light around where Kal hung, and smile his gruesome smile. He would then pace around, preaching. Crimson had given up asking questions once he realised that Kal knew little about the whereabouts of Jobe Francks.

Kal had eventually promised to kill Francks for Crimson, but somehow the crazy preacher realised Kal was lying. 'That is your problem, Kal Jerico,' said Crimson at the time. 'You kill for profit, but never for principle. Heretic.'

'I kill… only when needed,' said Kal. 'Only when my life… depends upon it.' He found the strength to raise his head and looked Crimson in the eye. 'I'd kill you now… if I thought it would… shut you up.'

Snap.

And the beatings continued. The torturer was quite skilled. He only worked an area as long as the body could handle and then moved on. Kal's pain radiated from head to toe, but he had only passed out twice – at least as far as he could remember.

And so the night wore on, with Crimson pacing around the pool of light, extolling the virtues of fiery redemption. Kal almost wished for that release or failing that the chance to kill Crimson and stop his incessant sermon. Anything had to be better than listening to this madman for another minute.

'Your body and soul will burn away,' intoned Cardinal Crimson. 'The heretic Kal Jerico will be consumed, but only in consumption can a soul find redemption…'

Lights blazed on all around Kal and Crimson, bringing the sermon to a halt – for the moment.

'What is the meaning of this?' screamed Crimson. His head turned back and forth as he scanned the chamber. 'Who intrudes on this holy inquisition?'

'I am terribly sorry, your eminence,' came the reply from behind Kal. He thought he recognised the slightly nasal voice.

'What is it, Ralan?' asked Crimson. A look that Kal could only guess was a scowl crossed the Cardinal's face. It was hard to tell without lips, but the patches of skin on his cheeks and forehead wrinkled and his teeth grated together.

'There has been some news on that, ahem, that other matter. Bad news, I'm afraid.'

Crimson snapped his fingers, which sounded like rocks breaking, and then curled his bony finger to motion the speaker over. The deacon who had commanded Crimson's guards during Kal's capture walked into view. The two of them huddled together and began talking in low voices.

Kal tried to listen, but only heard a few whispered words: 'body... dome... Tavis.' As Ralan gave his hushed report, Crimson's face got redder and redder. It was an odd sight as the patches of skin stood out like velvet against the white teeth and exposed skull.

'What am I paying these people for?' he screamed at last and stormed off. The last thing Kal heard was, 'Check back with Bitten...'

With Crimson gone, the torturer must have decided to take a break, because Kal heard him move off as well, leaving Kal alone – with the lights on. He scanned his surroundings, looking for a way out. He was hanging above a rocky dais in a huge cavern. Bubbling pools of acid or waste or something worse dotted the chamber below. To one side, a path led from the floor of the chamber up along the wall to an exit high above. He could also see other exits in the far wall beyond the pools.

There must be at least one more way out behind him, Kal reasoned, as Crimson and Ralan had just left in that direction. As he glanced around the room, something metallic glinted in the light, catching his eye. He searched for the source and saw it again, near the upper exit.

He turned to get a better look and saw Bobo stick his head out of a shadow and wave. Then he was gone. Kal smiled to himself. He might get out of this alive after all.

7: UNEARTHLY TROUBLE

'MOVE IT ALONG, slave.' A hand grabbed Scabbs by the arm and pulled him away from the miracle body. 'Come with me. Now!'

The voice sounded familiar yet strange. As he stumbled away from the crowd of worshippers, Scabbs looked into the face of the guard. Then he looked again. 'Yolanda?' he asked.

'Shush, stupid,' hissed Yolanda. Then, louder, 'Back to work.'

She pulled him toward the carts, which had been abandoned as soon as the body was discovered. 'Move that cart,' she commanded.

Scabbs looked at the cart. It was full of debris and had the iron beam he and Arliana had hauled off the body. 'Can't I move that one instead?' he whined, pointing at a half-full cart behind it.

Yolanda slapped him across the face. 'Move it!'

Scabbs rubbed his cheek and then grabbed the handles of the full cart. Leaning into it, he shoved with all his strength and the cart moved a few centimetres. 'Don't get lost in the part,' he said with a grunt.

Yolanda smiled. 'Good to see you, too,' she replied softly. 'Follow me,' she commanded out loud.

Scabbs put his head down and strained against the cart. The cart rolled forward, gaining a little momentum.

It was tough going, but he was okay as long as he kept it going. He followed Yolanda, who headed toward the dome entrance, and the Guilder guards.

'Taking this cart out to dump,' she said to the guards as they approached.

'Slaves don't leave,' said one of the guards. 'Grondle's orders.'

Scabbs's heart sank, but Yolanda replied quickly.

'Grondle told me to get this cart out of the dome.'

The guards looked at each other. One shrugged, but the one who had spoken wasn't so easily swayed. 'Then have Grondle come tell me that,' he said. 'Otherwise he stays.'

Scabbs looked at Yolanda to see what she would try next. Her hands strayed toward her holsters. He decided to duck under the cart if she started shooting, It wouldn't be necessary; Yolanda turned and grabbed Scabbs by the arm. 'Come with me,' she said. 'We'll go get Grondle.'

Scabbs gave a pleading look to Yolanda. He wanted to get out of there. Why didn't she fight? His unasked question was answered as Yolanda pulled him away from the door and they passed four more Guilder guards marching toward the door.

As they walked back toward the carts, Yolanda said, 'We're going to need a diversion. There are just too many guards, and I don't relish taking on Guilders. They have a bad habit of putting people in slaver camps.'

'Tell me about it,' said Scabbs.

She ignored his remark. 'And I'm going to need help to get you out of here,' she said.

'Where's Kal?' asked Scabbs.

'Jerico is MIA,' she replied. 'We're on our own again.' They stopped walking halfway between the entrance guards and the carts. 'Look, you stay here while I go find help. Start a diversion if you can.'

Scabbs didn't like this plan and said so. 'I've been chained, whipped and driven to exhaustion. Get me out of here.'

Yolanda slapped him again. 'Do as I say, slave,' she said.

He looked up into Yolanda's fiery eyes. She didn't seem to be role acting anymore. 'What kind of diversion?' he asked.

'I don't know,' she said. 'Start a slave revolt.'

Scabbs glanced back at the crowd around the miracle body. It had grown substantially larger since they had left for the carts. 'I can do that,' he said.

Yolanda gave him a kick in the rump and headed back toward the entrance. Scabbs watched her go. She spoke to the guards for a moment and then one of them spun the wheel to open the door. Yolanda grabbed the cart and shoved it forward. Scabbs got an odd feeling of satisfaction watching her strain to move it through the door.

'Hey,' said Kal. It came out as barely more than a whisper. He coughed and spit some bloody phlegm onto the cavern floor. 'Hey,' he called a little louder this time. 'Come here. I'm ready to talk.'

He heard the torturer scramble to his feet behind him and then the sound of footsteps. The man came around in front of Kal. He was tall and lanky, not the squat, thick-armed brute Kal had expected. His close-cropped hair made his head look like a fuzzy melon. A half-smoked tox stick hung from his lips. He was almost comical looking, but the welts and cuts on Kal's backs and legs kept him from laughing.

'Whaddaya want?' asked the torturer. The tox stick bobbed up and down as he spoke.

Kal forced himself to stare directly at the man's eyes as he spoke. 'Drink of water?' he asked.

'Only if Crimson orders it,' he replied. The torturer turned to leave.

'How about...' Kal coughed a few times and then spat another wad of phlegm on the floor, just barely missing the man's boots. 'Tox stick?' he finished. 'Crimson can't argue... with putting fire in... my mouth.'

He tried to give the torturer his best puppy eyes but with only Wotan as a guide, he wasn't sure how effective it would be.

The torturer shrugged and pulled the stick from his lips and put it between Kal's. The ash on the end was longer than the stick, but Kal hadn't really wanted it anyway. He just needed to buy a little more time.

'One more thing,' said Kal.

'What is it?'

'Goodbye.'

Kal wrapped his numb hands around the chain holding his wrists and pulled himself up. At the same time, he lifted his knees and kicked out. His feet struck the man in the stomach, doubling him over and sending him stumbling back toward the edge of the dais.

Before he could regain his balance, the tall man's legs were swept out from underneath him by a smooth roundhouse kick. He fell over backwards, screaming, right into the bubbling pool below the dais.

'Nice kick,' said Kal.

'You too,' replied Bobo. 'Didn't think you still had it in you.'

'I'm stronger than I look,' said Kal.

They looked at each other for a moment. 'Want to get me down from here?' asked Kal.

'Huh,' said Bobo. 'I thought you could do it yourself.'

He walked behind Kal and a moment later, Kal felt himself falling to the floor. He crumpled to his knees and hugged his shoulders, kneading them with his fingers to massage some feeling back into them.

'Found these,' said Bobo. 'Thought you might want them back.' He dropped a pile of clothes and weapons on the floor next to Kal. 'Can you walk?'

'If not, I'll crawl,' he said as he grabbed his trousers.

'And if you can't crawl, I'll carry you,' said Bobo with a laugh. 'Yeah, I know that old adage.'

Kal looked up at the small and wiry spy as he pulled on his clothes. Bobo was maybe a metre-and-half tall and his arms looked like twigs. 'You'll carry me?' said Kal. 'That I'd like to see.'

'Okay, maybe drag is a better word,' said Bobo with a smirk. 'Up to you. Walk or drag. But do it quick.' He glanced around the chamber.

Kal winced as he slipped his arms into the sleeves of his leather coat. He then picked up his pearl-handled laspistols and tested the weight in his hands. The muscles ached with the strain, but it would do. He twirled them both once and slipped them into the holster.

Next came the real test, though. He pulled one foot under him and tried to stand. The leather trousers rasped against his raw legs, but the muscles responded just fine. Kal gritted his teeth against the pain and rose to his feet. Standing with one foot slightly in front of the other, he flipped his collar with a flourish.

'I'm ready,' he said.

'HE HAS RETURNED,' called Jobe Francks as he strode through Hive City. 'The Bowdie has returned. Come rejoice in the great renewal of spirit.'

At least one person's spirit had been renewed already. Francks felt alive again. His purpose had returned, and his mission, after so many years lost in the wastes, his mission was nearing completion.

As he walked, Jobe felt like he had become one with the Universe. His senses extended out from his body in all directions. He could feel the air moving through every strand of his wild tangle of hair as he moved. The light from roof of the dome warmed his skin. He felt connected to all the people around him, as they scurried to and fro on their way to jobs and homes.

He could feel their eyes upon him, hear their whispers and know their hearts. Hemma was late for work and worried about losing her job, but was amused by the odd man talking to the wind. Zubriski felt guilty because he got a promotion by stealing his friend's idea and was intrigued by the thought of renewing his spirit. Darnell was simply trying to get through another day of drudgery and wanted to avoid eye contact. Ritto wondered about the strange man who seemed to leave no footprints.

Francks looked down at his feet. Everything seemed normal until he realised he could see his shadow moving beneath his feet as he walked. His feet were no longer touching the ground. 'Come see the miracle body,' he called to those around him. 'Come find the meaning that your lives have been lacking for too long. Follow me to the promise of a better future.'

Their stares gave him power. Their fears and strife and pain drained away as he passed. He felt that energy surge through his body. He glowed from within, basking in their lightened souls. Most went about their days afterward feeling a little lighter, a little better about their lot in life; perhaps simply amused by the strange spectacle. He could feel the word spreading out around him, infusing the consciousness of the Hive.

Some even fell in step behind him, hoping and wishing to find that better world he promised. Jobe Francks hoped and wished he had the strength to give it to them.

'How LONG HAD you been watching?' asked Kal. He found it helped to talk while walking as it kept his mind off the searing pain in his legs and shoulders. They hadn't stopped moving since they left the cavern and every stride sent a new wave of pain through his body. The two had walked almost all the way up to Dust Falls, a deep settlement perched on the edge of a huge chasm. Once back in even that piece of forlorn civilization, they should be safe from Crimson's men.

Bobo didn't answer right away and Kal glanced down at him. The little spy gave him a sheepish smile. 'All night, huh?' said Kal.

'I tried to get your attention every time Crimson left,' said Bobo. 'But that guy never stopped whipping you until that last time.'

'Tell me about it,' said Kal.

'Are you in a lot of pain?' asked Bobo.

Kal's glare was his answer.

'Sorry,' said Bobo. 'Of course you are. Once we get to safety, I can put something on your skin to help it heal – and to dull the pain.'

'That'll be good,' said Kal through clenched teeth. They walked in silence for a while as Kal mastered his pain once again. 'What have you found out?' he asked at last. 'Did Crimson let anything slip about Jobe Francks?'

Bobo screwed up his face. 'He's very tight-lipped, that one,' he said. 'At least when he wasn't preaching at you or his followers.'

'Scav,' said Kal. 'Nothing at all?'

'A few snippets, that's all,' said Bobo. 'I'd say he's got at least two covert ops going on. One seems to have something to do with a body in a dome. I'm not sure if he's trying to retrieve a body or hide a body.'

They entered the Dust Falls dome as Bobo gave his report and Kal breathed a sigh of relief. He needed to sit, drink a bottle of Wild Snake and figure out his next move. All those things could be achieved at the Dust Hole, a beaten and battered saloon at the edge of the chasm.

Bobo continued his report. 'I'm fairly certain Crimson's other operation involves getting rid of Francks. He may be the one behind the two assassins sent after the prophet.'

Kal stared at him. 'Two assassins?'

Bobo nodded. 'Yeah. After the first one was found dead in that alley, I heard reports of a second assassin being dispatched.'

'Dispatched where?' Kal looked around and found the entrance to Dust Hole. He moved off in a different direction.

'That's the thing,' said Bobo as he jogged to keep up. 'He was sent to Glory Hole, but then the last report I got had him heading into Hive City. Something about his target getting bitten or going to get bit? Didn't make a lot of sense.'

Kal stopped just outside the saloon. 'Bitten?' he asked. 'Could it have been a name? I heard Crimson say something about someone named Bitten.'

'Could be,' said Bobo as they entered Dust Hole. 'My informants say the assassin was last seen in Old Town near the dome wall if that's any help.'

Kal sat at a table and cringed as he pressed his sore flesh against the chair. 'Looks like I'm going to Hive City next.'

Bobo grabbed a couple Snakes and sat across from Kal. 'You want I should come along to keep you out of trouble?'

Kal grabbed the bottle and drained it before answering, letting the snake that gave the drink its name slide down his throat. 'No,' he said, spinning the bottle idly on the table. 'Go back and keep on eye on Crimson. Let me know if you find out anything else.'

Bobo sipped at his own drink and fished in his trousers. He dropped what looked like a small rounded piece of rubber on the table. 'Then you'd better take this,' he said.

Kal picked it up and rolled it around between his fingers. 'What is it?'

'Latest thing from the Spire,' said Bobo, smiling. It's a communication device. Fits in your ear. With it we can talk no matter how far apart we get. It's similar to the vox units Nemo uses, but less invasive.'

'Where'd you get this?' asked Kal. 'Looks military.'

'Better you don't know,' replied Bobo.

Kal put the communicator in his ear. It fitted snugly, but felt a little strange. 'Great. Now, get back to Crimson. I need to know what he's up to.'

Bobo pulled out a small tube. 'What about the balm?' he asked. 'Don't you want me to apply it to your back and legs?'

Kal took the tube and scanned the Dust Hole, checking out the local scenery: barmaids in low cut blouses and short skirts. 'I think I can find someone to do that for me,' he said.

AS HE WALKED back toward the crowd surrounding the miracle body, Scabbs had no idea what he was going to do. Kal made the plans. Scabbs just messed them up. That was his normal contribution anyway.

But Kal wasn't here, so it was up to Scabbs. If he wanted to get out of this alive, he had to come up with something. It shouldn't be too hard. He already had a mob. He just needed to turn up the heat.

He came up behind Grondle and Ander, who were both yelling at the workers huddled around the body. Scabbs was taken by how comical the two men looked from behind. Grondle's large head was bright red, making him look like a bearded beet. Sweat flew off the loose hair poking out from Ander's bandana, spraying his short boss with a sweat shower.

'Back to work, ye worthless scavvies,' said Grondle. 'It's just a dead body.' He turned to Ander, with a pleading look on his face.

Ander snapped his whip a few times, lashing the nearest prostrate slaves. 'Move it,' he screamed. 'I'll whip you to death if you don't move.'

They still had the whips, but the men had lost their power. The praying slaves completely ignored the men and the whip. They seemed almost trancelike on the ground.

Ander raised his hand again. Scabbs stepped in and grabbed his forearm on its way up. The tall ganger's head snapped around and their eyes locked together. Ander's eyes went wide in surprise. Scabbs tried to look determined, but down deep inside he was as surprised as Ander.

Before the Orlock crew chief could react, Scabbs reached in with his other hand and snatched the whip out of Ander's hand. 'You will not whip these people again,' he said and strode past into the sea of kneeling slaves.

'What the–' started Ander.

Scabbs stopped, turned and raised his hands into the air. The barbed end of the whip trailed on the ground at his feet. 'Hear me, slaves,' he called out. 'This is a great day. We are witness to a miracle. Come and bow before the miracle body unearthed here today. 'Come bask in the glow of its salvation.'

As he faltered for words, Scabbs stole a glance at Ander and Grondle. The round foreman simply stared, his mouth slack and his eyes unfocused. Ander seethed and fumbled with the catch on his holster. Scabbs hurried on, getting an idea on the spur of the moment, a la Kal Jerico.

'Rise up,' he yelled. 'Rise up and stand against the hand of tyranny and the fist of oppression. Rise up now. The miracle body will deliver us from evil. Rise up!'

The prostrate slaves looked up at Scabbs. Several scrambled to their feet. Scabbs walked among them, keeping bodies between him and Ander as he continued to preach. 'They wish to keep us from the miracle body,' he said, pointing at Ander and Grondle.

Several of the other Orlock guards had joined them. Ander talked and pointed at Scabbs, but he pressed on as the slaves continued to stand up around him. He noticed that the group had grown larger. Slaves from the other chain gangs had pushed their way down the hill to see the body.

'This is our time now,' said Scabbs. 'We have freed the miracle body from its earthly prison and brought it into the light for all to see.'

The Orlocks advanced with whips, chains and pistols in their hands. 'Get that scabby little man,' called Ander.

'But we must act now, my friends,' called Scabbs. He backed up as the whips snapped into the crowd. Several gangers rushed toward him. 'Seize your freedom and secure the path for the miracle so we might share it with all the hive.'

The slaves stood their ground, but Scabbs could tell they still harboured too much fear of the whips, so he decided to use his. His arm flipped back and flew forward. The barbed tail of the whip snapped in the air behind him and slashed past him, slicing his cheek along the way but at the other end of its flight, the whip connected with Ander's face as well. When Scabbs pulled his arm back, the whip snapped again, tearing off a chunk of the Orlock's tiny goatee.

It was like a shot of adrenaline through the crowd. The slaves erupted into action. Those nearest Scabbs clawed at the gangers trying to grab him, pulling them away and driving them to the ground. Others rushed forward, toward Ander and Grondle. The foreman turned to run, but he couldn't get his girth moving fast enough and the first few slaves caught him from behind.

Ander backed up, firing into the crowd as he tried to retreat. Slave after slave dropped to the ground, with scorch marks on their chests, shoulders and faces. Scabbs's eyes went wide in horror as he saw the price of his brilliant plan. Those Ander shot writhed in pain on the ground if they were lucky. Their wounds looked like ground up, broiled meat.

Ander levelled his pistol at Arliana, who rushed forward like a mad woman. Scabbs screamed, 'No!' and ran forward. His foot caught on a power cable attached to one of the light poles. He tripped and pitched forward into the dirt.

He heard a loud crack and a strange creaking noise, and looked up to see the pole tipping over. The mob scattered as it plummeted to the ground. The lights popped and flared with one last gasp of illumination before going dark.

Everything became quiet but Scabbs had no idea why. It wasn't pitch black. There were other light poles, just none near the body. He glanced around to see slaves and Orlocks alike staring back at the body.

Scabbs pushed himself back to his feet and turned around. The miracle body shimmered in the shadowy twilight, casting a soft bluish-white glow on the faces of all those gathered around.

YOLANDA WAS TIRED. It felt like she'd been running back and forth through the Underhive all night and most of the morning, which was, of course, exactly what she'd done. At least during this trip she hadn't been attacked by Goliaths or kidnapped by Orlocks. That was a refreshing change from recent events.

'Damn you, Jerico,' she muttered for at least the tenth time this trip. 'Right now, I'd be counting my share of the last three bounties you squandered, if it hadn't been for you and your stupid dog.'

She ran past the spot where Gonth's gang had ambushed her the day before, being careful to check the nooks and crannies amongst all the extra supports for any hiding Goliaths. 'At least the return trip will be quicker and easier on the legs,' she said, once she was satisfied there was no ambush this time.

The plan was simple. She'd borrow the Malcadon rig from the Wildcats and use its web spinners to immobilise the Guilder guards. Then she could snatch Scabbs and get out with no fuss, or messy Guilder deaths. Yolanda didn't want to cross them. She'd had a bounty on her head before and didn't relish having to run from the likes of Jerico again.

Her brilliant plans all came crashing to a halt as she made the last turn before the Wildcats hideout. She jumped back around the corner and pulled out her laspistols. The street looked like a war zone. Peering around the edge of the building, Yolanda counted at least ten dead 'Cats strewn about and a couple Goliaths.

Yolanda slipped around the corner and edged down the street, hugging the wall. There were 'Cat bodies lying in the gutter and hanging out of windows. The stench of blood filled the air, but the red pools beneath the bodies were still. The last drops had drained from them some time before she arrived.

The two Goliaths had fallen in a heap just outside the door to the Wildcats hideout. She could see a shotgun and a heavy stubber sticking out from beneath the bodies as she approached. Both dead Goliaths had bandoliers of frag grenades wrapped around their bodies as well.

With all the carnage and unclaimed weaponry lying out in the open, Yolanda despaired of finding any 'Cats alive inside. She inched toward the door, weapons trained on the opening. One of the Goliath bodies moved and she fired two blasts into its side.

A voice cried out from inside. 'Keep on coming. We can keep piling up your bodies.'

'Themis?' Yolanda called back. 'You're alive in there?'

'Yolanda,' came the reply. 'Thank the Emperor. Did you see any Goliaths on your way in?'

Yolanda peered over the half-wall at the edge of the hideout. Themis and a few other 'Cats hunkered down behind overturned tables, their weapons trained on the door. Two other 'Cats knelt by the dead Goliaths. When they saw Yolanda, they went back to work, trying to remove the behemoths from the doorway.

'It's clear out here,' said Yolanda. 'You can come out and clear your dead.' She holstered her weapons and moved to the door to help the girls heave the Goliaths out of the way.

Yolanda and Themis talked as they cleaned up after the battle. 'What happened?' asked Yolanda. She stripped the bandoliers off one of the Goliath bodies. They'd have to drag the huge gangers out of the dome eventually, as the rival gang might return to claim the corpses, but any gear left behind belonged to the victors – a victory being any battle you didn't run away from.

'Gonth and his gang arrived just before morning,' said Themis. She sliced through the bandolier to get it off, sawing into the Goliath's thick skin as she cut. 'We tried to take them in the street, but nothing stopped them until we retreated into the diner and concentrated our fire.'

Yolanda glanced around at the carnage. The remaining girls were hauling bodies to the Wildcat graveyard. She searched the faces of each dead Wildcat as they were carried past. 'Where's Lysanne?' she asked. 'She didn't...'

Themis shook her head causing her cascade of golden hair to shimmer around her head. 'She's shook up, but okay,' she said. 'She's resting. I sent her out in the rig to slow them down. It's the only thing that saved us. Otherwise they would have overrun the diner.'

Yolanda realised the implication immediately. 'What happened to her?'

'They must have had a grenade launcher,' said Themis. She wiped her dagger on the Goliath's back. 'We heard a huge explosion. The whole dome shook. The rig crashed into my apartment above the diner's kitchen.'

'And she survived?'

Themis nodded. 'That rig is tough. Saved her life. Of course, it won't be much use unless we can scavenge some parts somehow.'

Yolanda felt a knot forming in her stomach. 'This is all my fault, isn't it?' she asked. She wanted to blame it on Jerico again. It was his gambling that started the ball rolling, but *she* had brought the Grak gang down on the Wildcats.

'We're not pointing any fingers,' said Themis. She began stripping the gear from the second Goliath. 'They may have been looking for you. Or maybe they just wanted some payback for that fight in the tunnel. Whatever started this, we plan to end it. If it will ease your guilty conscience, you can help us take down Gonth and his gang.'

Yolanda nodded, but then stopped. 'I… I can't,' she said. 'At least not yet. You see, that's why I returned. I've got a problem of my own. Scabbs is in trouble and I needed to borrow the rig. But I guess I'll just have to do it myself now.'

Themis grabbed Yolanda by the shoulders and looked her in the eyes. 'You're a Wildcat, Yolanda,' she said. 'We stick together. And I know Lysanne would force me to help you anyway, once she heard Scabbs was in trouble. I don't understand it, but that girl is sweet on him.'

'He does grow on you,' said Yolanda, and a smile almost flitted over her lips as the follow-up joke went through her mind. 'But no, I can't ask you to help. It's Guilders and you don't want any part of that.'

Themis stood and pulled Yolanda to her feet. 'Come on in and tell me all about it,' she said. 'We'll help you and then you can help us take on Gonth.'

Yolanda shook her off. 'Did you hear me?' she asked, a note of hysteria entering her voice. 'We'll be fighting Guilder guards. We'll all be marked afterwards. I can't ask you to do that, not you and not the Wildcats.'

Themis hooked her arm through Yolanda's and walked into the diner. 'Not to worry,' she said. 'We probably won't survive the attack on Gonth's hideout anyway.'

KAL LOOKED AT the open door with suspicion. In the underhive, an open door was commonplace. Actually, open walls were commonplace. No door whatsoever was more the norm than an open door, but when it came to Hive City, doors with numerous locks and barred windows were just common sense.

After all, thought Kal, they had to keep out the Underhive riff-raff out, didn't they?

So, when he'd finally found Jerod Bitten's hab, the open door had stopped him short. Something was amiss inside.

It had actually been all too easy to find the place. If he'd had Bobo with him, Kal was certain they would have spent the day sneaking around alleys to listen at windows, or distracting clerks at the post office to check mail records, or perhaps sitting in a dark room, watching the streets through the curtains. Kal had simply asked around.

Now, with the door ajar, and him on record with several locals as a stranger asking after Mr Bitten, Kal wished he'd gone the more circuitous, more devious route. Well, there was nothing for it but to continue on in his own unique style.

Kal drew his laspistols, kicked the door open the rest of the way and dived through. He rolled on the ground and popped to his feet. With his arms out wide, pointing his pistols to either side, he did a quick pirouette to scan the room. It appeared empty.

He was certain the move had looked impressive, but it had probably been a big mistake. First of all, there was nobody here to impress. Second, while Bobo's balm had done wonders for the pain, the skin on his back and legs was still raw, and the nerves painfully close to the surface.

Making a mental note not to move so quickly for a while, Kal took a step toward the rear door and tripped over the body in the middle of the floor.

'Aw scav!' he said as he fell. His laspistols flew from his hands as he clawed at the air. When he hit the floor, Kal bounced and then rolled away from the body, coming face to pale face with another corpse behind the desk.

Kal sat up and glanced back and forth at the two bodies. One was covered in a Delaque shadow cape, which made it tough to see in the dim light. He was young and athletic looking, but his head was turned a little too far around toward his back to be considered normal. 'You would be our second assassin,' said Kal.

The other was an older man with short-cropped, grey hair wearing a thick, luxurious robe which had been ruined by the pool of blood surrounding the body. 'And I certainly hope you are not Jobe Francks,' he said, 'for both our sakes.'

Kal stood and walked to the door, cringing at several new pains in his legs. He noticed a trail of bloody footprints heading from the body to the door that he had missed during his grand entrance. He closed and bolted the door and then drew the blinds across the barred windows.

'So, three people were in the room and one left after blood was spilled,' he said, turning to face the deadly tableau. 'Let's figure out who you two are.'

Kal took his time searching the bodies and the rest of the hab. The cloaked man was obviously the assassin. He had no identification on his body, but the array of tools and weapons was a dead giveaway. Not to mention he was too young to be Francks. He assumed the old guy was Bitten. He was wearing bed clothes, which matched clothes Kal found in the closets upstairs. Plus, judging from the blood splatters, he had been sitting at the desk when he got stabbed.

'So, our Mr Francks survived,' said Kal. He breathed a sigh of relief. 'Now I just need to figure out where you went. Again.'

The books and ledgers on the desk were of little use. Kal had no head for numbers and the columns of tiny handwriting blurred together and made his head hurt after a while. He closed the ledgers and stacked them on one side of the desk.

Underneath one of the books he found a folded piece of parchment. Inside was a list of names and places written in the same small handwriting. Kal scanned the list. He recognised two names as the Cawdor gangs Francks had visited. Something about the other names sounded familiar as well. He'd just seen them in the ledgers.

Kal opened up the books one by one again. Each one held accounts for one of the gangs on the list. Yet there was one more book after he got through the list. 'What's in here?' he wondered out loud.

He opened the book and looked through it. Kal recognised a name here and there as Guilders he had done bounty work for in the past. One name appeared over and over that Kal recognised but couldn't place. That name was Tavis. 'Where do I know that name from?' he asked himself.

He noticed another piece of paper sticking out from underneath the open book. He pulled it out. It was an old, yellowed wanted poster. 'Jules Ignus?' asked Kal. 'What's the significance of this?'

He turned it over and noticed what at first looked like a small smudge in the corner. Looking closer, he saw it was more of the same tiny handwriting. Just two words, but they brought much of the past few days into clearer focus for Kal.

Written in tiny letters, almost too small to see, was a name: Cardinal Crimson.

RALAN DESPISED HIS role in the organization. As Crimson's personal attaché, he'd had to do a lot of horrible and disgusting things over the years, from the daily applications of oil to the Cardinal's body to the running of petty errands such as fetching the holy foot-wrappings. His life was at best degrading, and all too often it became agonisingly painful.

The worst task though, was delivering bad news. That was how he had earned the hand-shaped acid brand on his neck and cheek. He touched the scar tissue as he walked toward the Cardinal's office. That piece of news had also involved the heretic Kal Jerico, as he remembered.

He reached the door but hesitated before knocking. Ralan always went through this battle with himself. To wait gave him some small respite before the coming tirade. To wait *too* long ran the risk of delivering the news too late, which could be worse and brought a worse punishment. He touched the scar again and knocked.

'What is it now?' screamed Crimson through the door.

Ralan opened the door. 'I have news about the heretics, your eminence.'

The Cardinal looked up from his lounge chair. 'It had better be good news,' he said. Crimson's robe hung open, showing his leathery skin and protruding ribs.

Ralan swallowed hard and pressed on. Best to do it quickly, like removing a bandage from a pus-covered wound. 'It is not, your eminence,' he said, and then pressed on quickly. 'The second assassin has failed and Jobe Francks is on the move once again.'

'The Emperor damn him to the abyss!' screamed Crimson.

'I'm afraid there is more,' said Ralan after the outburst. 'The heretic Kal Jerico was seen entering Bitten's hab.'

Crimson unleashed a chilling scream that rattled the door against its frame. 'I hate that man!' he said. 'How did you let him escape?'

Ralan wanted to protest that it had not been his decision to leave the heretic unguarded, but that statement would have been rewarded with an instant trip to the pools of redemption. 'I am sorry, sir,' he said instead. 'I have men ready to retake Jerico.'

Crimson paused from his ranting to consider the idea. 'Are the two heretics together?' he asked.

Ralan shook his head. 'Many people saw Francks leave Hive City, sir,' he said. 'The heretic Kal Jerico has not caught up with him yet.'

'Then watch him closely, but do not interfere,' said Crimson. He had calmed down considerably and a toothy smile actually flashed across his lipless face as he drummed his bony fingers together. 'He can lead us to Francks and we can take care of both problems at once.'

Ralan started to deliver the last piece of news, but reconsidered and turned to leave. He almost made it to the door before Crimson spoke again.

'You said many people saw Francks leave the City?' he asked. 'Why was that?'

Ralan's heart fell. He turned. 'Ah yes,' he said, trying to paste an innocent smile on his own, scarred face. 'I almost forgot. It seems Francks was preaching about

the return of the body again, and this time people were
listening.'

'Listening?' said Crimson. 'Was that all?'

'And following, I was about to say.'

Crimson now had a low, deliberate tone to his voice,
which Ralan found more frightening than the screaming 'Why this sudden interest in the ramblings of a
crazy prophet?'

Ralan put his hand on the door handle, hoping to
make a quick exit once he was finished. 'They say he
was floating, and even glowing, sir.' He swallowed hard
one more time and gave the last piece of news. 'He
claimed that the body had returned and promised to
take them to it.'

'Hold!' screamed Crimson. He stormed across the
room, his open cloak billowing out behind him as if
battered by a stiff wind. He grabbed Ralan by the
throat, his fingers digging into the scar tissue. 'Forget
Jerico,' he said, his lipless mouth mere centimetres
from Ralan's face. 'Get your men and follow me.'

'Where?' asked Ralan, wheezing to get the air to
speak.

'To kill Jobe Francks. I know where he's headed.'

8: ON THE RUN AGAIN

SCABBS STOOD WATCHING his people, quite pleased with himself. He even struck a pose, a la Kal, as the chain gang continued to move rocks – only this time they were using the rubble to build an altar and a bier for the miracle body to lie upon.

Of course, his pose probably wasn't quite as majestic as one of Kal's many stances. His tattered shirt and the ripped trousers that barely covered his bloody body weren't as awe inspiring as Kal's leather coat. Plus he kept taking his hands off his hips to scratch at loose patches of skin.

Still, he was fairly happy with what he'd accomplished in the last few hours. The glowing body had ended the riot. The guards pulled back, either afraid of the possibly radioactive corpse or simply not willing to engage its fanatical worshippers.

The slaves had turned to Scabbs for direction. Arliana had given him a pleading look and he found it impossible to let her down, but had no idea what to do. He looked around at the bodies lit by the glow of the miracle body. 'We should get the wounded, don't you think?' he asked.

They acted like it had been an order and began working. Flush with power, Scabbs ordered some of the slaves to fortify their position. Arliana had suggested they build the bier, and Scabbs agreed. The body was the focal point of the revolt and needed to be seen. Plus, it was now the only source of illumination in the area. He didn't mention that part, though.

They now had a low wall between them and the guards and a supply of heavy, hand-sized rocks to hurl. Those slaves not working bowed in front of the bier, praying for salvation. Scabbs stood surveying his work, or rather their work. He had never felt so strong and vowed to never run from danger again; to stop relying on Kal and Yolanda to save him all the time.

But they were still prisoners and it was only a matter of time before Grondle got reinforcements. As the lord of the slaves pondered these problems, he heard a commotion in the distance. This was it. Either more guards had arrived or Yolanda had brought help. He needed to be ready for either.

'People,' he called. 'Something is happening. We need to… what's the phrase? Oh right. Get to battle stations!' Scabbs felt he needed to end with some sort of flourish, so he set his legs apart and struck his arm into the air and pointed.

The slaves looked at him quizzically and then turned their gaze upward to see what he was pointing at. 'No.' he said. 'Get behind the wall and grab a rock.'

As the workers moved toward the wall, Scabbs backed up and took position behind the body. From there, he saw the guards, who had been standing outside rock-throwing range, pull weapons and prepare for battle.

Inexplicably, they lined up facing away from the slaves.

The commotion behind the guards grew louder. He heard shouts and weapons fire. The guards began to back up toward the slave compound, as if pressed from the front. It's Yolanda, thought Scabbs. Time for the diversion.

'Fire!' he called. Nothing happened. A few of the slaves turned to stare at Scabbs, and he realised a little of what it must be like to be Kal Jerico. 'Throw your rocks at the guards while they aren't looking.'

A moment later, rocks and small chunks of metal soared into the air from behind the wall. Most thudded harmlessly on the ground, but a few connected and while the damage was minimal, the effect was devastating.

As more and more rocks rained down on the guards, many of the Orlock gangers in the group dropped their weapons to cover their heads. Others ducked or broke ranks and ran. In a moment, only the Guilder guards were left to face the commotion, and they were quickly overrun.

But instead of Yolanda and the Wildcats, or Kal and his blazing laspistols, or Bobo, or anyone else that Scabbs might have expected, the group that broke through the guards' ranks consisted of Hive townsfolk led by a wild-haired man wearing a blue Cawdor cape.

They rushed forward, pelted by rocks as Scabbs was too dumbfounded to order a ceasefire, and jumped the wall. 'Stop,' screamed Scabbs, and even he wasn't sure if he meant his people or the newcomers.

Most of the rock throwers turned their attention back to the Guilder guards, who were too few to force their way through constant barrage. The townsfolk rushed to the bier and fell to their knees.

'Behold, the body of Bowdie, our saviour!' said the wild-haired man. 'He has been delivered unto us once again. May his message of hope never again be buried by the deceiver.'

Scabbs looked at the old, grey-haired Cawdor. As he turned, Scabbs saw swirling cloud of white drifting through the man's eyes and felt himself falling into them. He shook his head and looked away. 'You must be Jobe Francks,' said Scabbs, focusing his attention somewhere just below the man's chin. 'My friends and I have been looking for you.'

STARING AT THE ledgers, Kal had figured some of it out. Crimson and Francks and Bitten were all intertwined somehow. Most likely Crimson had hired the assassins to kill Francks. He must know something about the Cardinal's past; something to do with a body. Crimson had muttered something about a body while torturing Kal.

Bitten was the link between the two. He'd obviously been helping Francks ever since he arrived, setting him up with places to stay. He looked at the wanted poster with Crimson's name written on the back. It seemed Bitten knew something of Crimson's past as well. But why had the Cardinal left Bitten alone until now if he knew so much?

'Tavis!' said Kal out loud. Crimson had also mentioned the Guilder's name. That's where he'd heard it before. Bitten's dealings with Guilders over the years must have provided him some protection. They were a powerful force in Hive City and the Underhive. Powerful enough to give even Crimson pause. Powerful enough that Bitten had been able to set up his own Cawdor gangs – gangs so loyal they were willing to harbour a fugitive from Crimson.

'But none of that tells me where Francks has gone now,' muttered Kal, looking at the list. 'He left this behind. Why? Bitten's death? Maybe, but I think it's something else. It has something to do with Tavis and the body, I'm sure. But what? Where? Damn, I need a break.'

There was a knock at the door. Kal pocketed the list and the wanted poster and crept across the room, avoiding the trail of bloody footprints as he walked. 'Yes?' he said.

'It's Jann,' came the reply. 'Is that you, Jerrod?'

Kal needed to deal with this quickly. He opened the door and slipped through, closing it behind him. There was a quite attractive older woman on the doorstep.

'Hi,' he said. 'I'm a… *business acquaintance* of Jerrod's.'

'Oh, are you two in a meeting?' asked Jann. 'I just need a moment.'

'He's not here,' said Kal. 'That is to say he's, um, gone.'

Jann's eyebrows furrowed. She was either confused or suspicious. Neither was good for Kal. 'I'm his new… bookkeeper. Jerrod just stepped out while I was going through the books.' Best to keep the lies as close to the truth as possible; that's what Kal always figured.

This seemed to ease her mind as the smile returned. 'Well tell him to come over when he gets back,' she said. 'I simply must tell him about that strange prophet who went through the streets a while ago.'

Kal's mind raced, but he kept his face calm. 'Prophet?' he asked.

'Oh didn't you hear him?' said Jann. She reached out and touched his arm, as if to bring him into the fold. 'This odd man with wild hair and strange eyes walked right through here this morning, preaching about the return of the body or some such nonsense.'

'Oh?' said Kal. He patted her hand and smiled. 'How interesting. Where did you say he went?'

Jann smiled. 'I don't know,' she said. 'I joined the crowd for a while, but when he left Hive City, I stopped. He wasn't that interesting. I don't know why so many people were following him. But I know Jerrod takes an interest in that religious stuff, so I wanted to let him know. You'll tell him, won't you?'

Kal's smile broadened. 'I certainly will,' he said, 'just as soon as he returns. Thank you so much for coming by.' He took her hand and brought it up to his lips before releasing it. 'Really. Thank you so much.'

As Jann left, Kal turned and slipped back through the door. He waited a minute before leaving, but left and ran down the road toward the nearest dome exit. A crazy prophet trailing a mob of townspeople shouldn't be too hard to locate. That was strange even by Underhive standards.

'YOU NEED MORE guards?' screamed Tavis. 'What in Helmawr's name is going on doing down there, Grondle?'

The foreman scratched at his beard and stared at the floor. 'I don't rightly know, Mr Tavis,' he said. 'The slaves found a dead body and revolted. Several of my men got hurt in the riot.'

'If they can't defend themselves against unarmed slaves, why am I even paying them?' Tavis once again questioned the choice of Grondle as foreman. He'd come highly recommended, but the man was obviously incompetent. Perhaps his information had been tainted by jealousy. Not every guilder had could afford his own dome and his rivals would love to see him fail.

'They did defend themselves, sir,' said Grondle. He began to stammer. 'They... they killed many of the slaves. It was horrible.'

'Why did they stop?' asked Tavis.

'Sir?'

Tavis drummed his fingers on the desk. 'Why did your men stop killing the slaves?' Grondle's face showed Tavis the answer. His eyes went wide and his mouth opened in astonishment. The fat man obviously didn't have the stomach for it.

Tavis rolled his eyes and sighed. 'You ordered them to cease fire, didn't you?' he asked.

Surprisingly, Grondle shook his head. 'No, sir,' he said. 'No. Mr Tavis.' Grondle wrung his hands together. His discomfort was more pronounced than usual. 'It was the body,' he continued. 'Everyone just stopped when it started to glow.'

Tavis stared at Grondle, unsure he had heard that last bit correctly. 'Which body did what?'

Grondle started talking very fast, as if Tavis had pulled a cork from his mouth, and the whole story of the miracle body and the riot came pouring out. 'After that,' he said, wringing his hands again, 'I told Ander to just keep an eye on the slaves while I come talk to you. I figure with a show of force, we can get the slaves working again. They have us outnumbered right now and seem willing to fight to the death over this miracle body.'

Tavis nodded and smiled. 'I'm glad you came here personally to bring this to my attention,' he said.

Grondle wiped one meaty paw across his forehead and Tavis watched in dismay as sweat trickled off the large man's palm onto the recently-cleaned rug. 'This gives me a chance to tell you two things,' continued Tavis. 'First, you're an idiot. And second, you're fired.'

Tavis stood and looked at the door. 'Meru?' he called. 'Come in here!'

His assistant entered. 'Escort this poor excuse for a human being from the premises, and then contact the captain of my guards. I will need several squads at my disposal within the quarter hour.'

Grondle looked at him with a furrowed brow, as if to say, 'That was my idea.'

Tavis shook his head. 'Your problem, Grondle, is thinking you can fix the problem by simply adding more guards to the site. That so-called miracle body has ruined the slaves, given them hope. You can never crush that out of them. No. We must kill them all – wipe the slate clean – and start over.'

As Grondle left the room, Tavis called after him, 'And don't come around looking for severance pay. If I see you again, you'll be the one slaving away in chains.'

BOBO HALTED IN the dark and waited. He'd been following Crimson and his men for quite some time and it was getting tougher to stay close enough to see them without giving himself away. Long dark tunnels were great when you had to hide; not so great when you had to follow someone through them.

It seemed like his steps echoed for miles like claps of thunder. He didn't dare light his torch in the unfamiliar tunnel, so he had to pick his way through, keeping a hand on the tunnel wall, with only the bobbing torches up ahead to guide him.

It had been easier at first. When Crimson stormed out of his office and ordered his personal guard to follow, Bobo had retreated into a side tunnel and found a hidey hole. Crimson and the gang marched by moments later with all the stealth of a Scaly.

He'd followed from a safe distance through the tunnel, comfortable that there was only one exit they were likely to use, as all others in the area led to the wilds – and the mutants who lived there – or back to Redemptionist holdings. Crimson was on the warpath, which meant heading into or through Dust Falls.

Tailing through a settlement was even easier. With people around, Bobo always disappeared into the background. He was so nondescript as to be nearly invisible in any group larger than two.

From there, Crimson headed into a tunnel that Bobo had heard was abandoned. After a while he realised why. The walls even near the settlement were badly cracked. Dust – jarred loose from his passing – dropped from cracks and settled on his head and shoulders. After the first ten metres, the tunnel got so dark he had to slow to a crawl.

He'd pressed on for a while, through twists and turns, stumbling on fallen debris and once running into a wall. After a moment, he realised the tunnel must have slid to the side about a metre during a hivequake.

So, now he waited. It was time to use the torch. The dust was still falling. He had to shake it out of his hair every few minutes or it mixed with his sweat and got into his eyes. He figured he could wait for Crimson's gang to get out of torch sight and then follow their trail through the dust.

The light ahead finally winked out, so Bobo flicked a switch and his torch flared to life. The cracks in the walls were far worse in this section. In fact the cracks had become gaping holes where the concrete had failed completely, leaving nothing but a lattice of reinforced iron bars running through metal beams. Beyond that was a black emptiness that even his torch couldn't penetrate.

'This is fun,' said Bobo, feeling less secure about his situation now than he did with the lights off. 'Sure, Kal, I'll help. No problem.' Bobo shook off the feeling of dread and moved forward, following the scuffling trail through the dust. He kept one eye on the floor and the other off in the distance, watching for Crimson's light.

Bobo made good time for a while until the trail disappeared. He flashed his torch ahead of him, but the tunnel simply ended in a huge, gaping hole. The floor fell away, leaving a jagged line of concrete and twisted rebar bent down into the inky blackness.

He inched his way to the edge and aimed his light all around. Past the walls and the shredded ends of reinforced bars, he couldn't see anything within the range of his light. If Crimson and his gang had descended into the gaping blackness, Bobo couldn't tell how.

Bobo decided it was time to call Kal. In fact, he probably should have let him know Crimson was on the move long ago. He tapped his ear to activate the communication device. 'Um... Kal?' he said. 'Kal? Do you hear me? Tap your ear to respond.'

'Bobo,' said Kal in his ear. 'What's going on?'

'I don't know how to tell you this,' said Bobo. 'But I just lost Crimson.'

KAL FOUND IT disconcerting to hear a voice inside his head and walk through the Underhive at the same time, so he stepped behind a pile of collapsed masonry as they talked. Bobo told him how Crimson and his goon squad had left the Redemptionist caverns and trudged halfway through the Underhive, and how he'd come to a dead end somewhere past Dust Falls.

'Well, I'm in Glory Hole now,' said Kal. 'It seems our Mr Francks was also on the move this morning, which may explain Crimson's march. I suspect Crimson hired your two assassin friends to kill Francks. I found the second one dead, by the way.'

'Why does Crimson want Francks dead?' asked Bobo, 'And why is Nemo so interested in keeping him alive?'

'I think the answer to both questions is information,' said Kal. 'This all has something to do with a body from Crimson's past. The Cardinal wants to keep the past dead and Nemo wants to dig it up.'

'Where does Francks come in?'

'I don't have all the pieces yet,' said Kal. He thought he heard a commotion from down the street, but it might have come from Bobo's side of the conversation. It was difficult to discern internal from external. 'I need to get to Francks before Crimson, though.'

'Do you need some help?' asked Bobo. 'I can probably get to Glory Hole in thirty minutes.'

'No. Francks is leaving quite a trail, so I doubt I'll have much trouble finding him.'

'There he is!'

'Did you find Crimson?' asked Kal. 'Or Francks?'

'What?' said Bobo.

'You just said there he is,' replied Kal.

'No I didn't,' said Bobo.

'Get him!'

'Helmawr's rump,' said Kal. 'Gotta run!'

Kal glanced down the street to see a dozen Goliaths heading straight toward him. They were armed with everything from laspistols and shotguns to what he swore was his grenade launcher.

'How in the Spire did they get that?' he cried as he bolted out of the alley and down the street away from them.

'What's going on?' asked Bobo in his head. 'How did who get what?'

Kal panted as he ran. 'Can't talk,' he said. 'Goliaths.' Kal tapped his ear, hoping that would turn off the stupid device.

The sound of weapons fire behind him made Kal dive to the side. Bullets pinged the ground at his feet while dirt and concrete shards flew into the air where the las-blasts hit. He rolled to his feet and darted around a corner.

About halfway down the next street Kal skidded to a stop. The well-dressed debt collector was walking right toward him.

'Mr Jerico,' he called. 'You are Mr Kal Jerico, are you not?'

Kal thought the man had an oddly formal accent for a Van Saar but he didn't have time to ponder that right now. 'Sorry bub,' he said as he ran past. 'Don't have time to talk right now. Tell the Re-Engineers I'll have their money soon.'

The man raised a finger. 'But I don't understand…' he began. The rest of his sentence was cut off by the explosion.

Kal glanced back as he ran. Part of the street behind the debt collector had become a crater. Large chunks of debris rained down all around the poor little guy. He dropped to his knees and covered his head with his hands. Kal was pretty sure he heard the man whimper.

'Bit of a sissy for a debt collector,' said Kal. 'You'd think he'd have some muscle with him.'

And that, Kal realised, was exactly what he needed. It wasn't too far. He just might make it if his luck held. The weapons fire had stopped after the explosion, and Kal risked another glance over his shoulder.

The Goliaths tromped past the debt collector, making the little man look like a rag doll lying on the street beneath the giant gangers. 'They do have some sense,' said Kal as he turned back to concentrate on running. 'They're not willing to risk a murder charge on a civilian.'

Kal turned another corner and pulled out his laspistols. He needed to slow them down a little more for this to work, and this was the perfect chance; the only chance. About halfway down the block, Kal leapt into the air, spinning around as he soared. He fired four quick shots at the apex of his leap. They all hit within centimetres of each other.

The corner building he had just passed had an odd front you didn't often see in the hive; mostly because all the older ones had fallen during hivequakes. The corner of the building was supported by a single column providing a covered entryway underneath.

The four shots chipped away at a cracked rock slab Kal noticed near the base of the column. His spin took him back around to face down the street. He hit the ground running, but heard no building-shattering boom.

'Scav,' said Kal. 'Now what?'

Laspistols and shotguns blasted behind him again, and he knew it was only a matter of time before they tossed more grenades. Then he heard a rumble. Kal glanced back. One of the Goliaths must have tried to cut the corner, because he had smacked into the column, which now lay in a pile of dust at the giant's feet.

A crack appeared in the wall above the Goliath and started to spread upwards at an alarming rate. The rest of the gang scattered as large chunks of masonry plummeted. Kal ran on. Only a few of the Goliaths had got past the chaos.

Now he had enough time. Two more turns and he was there. Up ahead was Hagen's Hole, best and only bar in the settlement, home to more bounty hunters than any other spot in the Underhive.

Kal still had his laspistols in hand. As he ran past Hagen's, he shot twice at the front door. He counted under his breath as he ran. 'Five. Four. Three. Two. One.'

The door flew open just as the remaining Goliaths ran past. Four burly men charged out, weapons in hand 'Nobody attacks Hagen's!' yelled one of the men. All four opened fire on the Goliaths.

Kal ran on, never looking back. He could no longer stop to ask directions from people who might have seen the mad prophet and his flock of body

worshippers, but Kal thought he had a good idea which
direction to go.

Bobo lost Crimson in an unused tunnel somewhere
past Dust Falls. Before the Goliaths started chasing
him, Kal had been following Francks's trail toward an
unused tunnel heading out of Glory Hole. From what
Kal remembered, that tunnel used to lead to Dust
Falls. It seemed like too much of a coincidence.

'I'm close,' said Kal. 'I can feel it. I just hope I get
there in time.'

Behind him, Kal heard a huge explosion. 'Oh scav,'
he said. 'Those stupid Goliaths blew up Hagen's.'

'Do I KNOW you?' asked Jobe Francks. The little man
didn't look like much with his shredded shirt and
pockmarked skin. Perhaps he'd been in some sort of
accident. But Francks had lived most of his life trying
not to pre-judge people by their appearance. Truly,
after decades in the Wastes, could he do any less?

'My name is Scabbs,' replied the scab-covered man.
'I'm a bounty hunter. Well, tracker actually. Kal is the
real bounty hunter. Kal Jerico. I'm sure you've heard
of him. We're partners.'

As Scabbs continued talking, Francks looked past
him to the glowing body of his dead friend. Bowdie
had been placed on a pile of stone and metal with his
arms crossed over his chest. His face looked peaceful,
serene. He looked just as Francks remembered.
Twenty years or more had gone by and Francks had
become an old, wild-haired man, but in death, Syris
Bowdie had remained young, vibrant and somehow
alive.

'Wait until I tell Kal that I found you,' continued
Scabbs. 'Well, I guess, technically, *you* found *me*. But
that can be our little secret, right?'

There was a pause in the little man's constant stream of words. Francks looked back at Scabbs, who was now staring at him and the body.

'Why are you here?' he asked. 'I mean I'm glad I found you. Kal will be happy because we need you to help get Wotan back. Wotan is Kal's dog, you see. Well, a cyber-mastiff. But...'

Francks placed a hand on Scabbs's shoulder, and the talkative fellow immediately went quiet. Francks looked deeply into Scabbs's eyes and absorbed his pain and fear. The fatigue and tension of a stressful night drained away from his face, and his tired eyes cleared and brightened.

When he released Scabbs from his grip and his gaze, Francks could tell he was at peace. 'To answer your question,' he said. 'I am here for my friend. I am here to bring his message to the world. I am but the messenger of hope. Syris Bowdie is that hope. His is the hope of the Universe.'

'But he's dead,' said a young girl standing next to Scabbs.

'Death is but one stage of life,' said Francks. 'There are others. There is more life than simply living until you die.'

'What do we do next?' asked Scabbs.

Jobe Francks knelt in the dirt beside his friend, basking in the warmth of the friendship he had lost so many years before. 'For now,' he said. 'We wait.'

He looked at Scabbs and saw the fear and doubt returning. 'But we have to get out of here,' he said, a note of hysteria creeping into his words. 'More guards will come and then we will all join your friend in the next stage.'

Francks smiled. He could see the strength inside the little man, but knew that Scabbs still needed others to bolster that strength. 'All will happen as it happens,' he said. 'Do not fear. The Universe has a plan for us all. You will not die this day, of this I am certain.'

Scabbs smiled and heaved a sigh of relief. He began talking again as his nerves got the better of him. Francks didn't hear a word of it. His eyes had fallen back upon Syris. The clouds began to swirl around his pupils as the glowing body filled his gaze.

In a moment, the scene in front of Francks transformed. Syris's body lay in a crumpled heap. The bier and altar had disappeared, as had the crowd of slaves and townspeople. The pile of debris had been replaced by a steep-sided hole.

Francks looked up. He was in the basement of a blasted-out building. A light shone down upon him from the edge of the basement wall above. He squinted to look past the light. At last he could make out the shadowy face of Jules Ignus. He was smiling as he placed the explosive charge.

But when Ignus turned back to look down into the hole one last time, he transformed as well. His skin began to burn away. Huge patches across his body dissolved before Francks eyes, revealing scarred and reddened muscles and pitted bones beneath. His smiling face changed into a gruesome, lipless visage, and the skin around his eyes melted away, leaving the orbs to bob around in an empty space.

Francks felt like he was looking at the ugly spectre of death itself, but knew, somehow, that this was no dream, no metaphor for deeds from the past or visions of the future. This was the present. This was the here and now. The Universe had called him to action. This was his time to shine.

Jobe Francks stood and looked at Scabbs, who stopped talking again as he became caught in the cloudy gaze. 'I must leave now,' he said. Scabbs nodded his understanding. 'We shall not meet again, but I give you this. Keep it safe until it is time.'

He pulled a leather-bound book from beneath his cloak and handed it to Scabbs.

'Where are you going?' asked Scabbs.

'To meet my destiny,' said Francks. 'To look into the face of evil and bring it my message.'

With that, Francks walked up the pile of debris, leaving no tracks or trace of his passing.

CRIMSON PEERED THROUGH the window of the dome hatch, and then spun the wheel. As he pulled the round door open, he motioned Ralan inside. The deacon's eyes flitted back and forth, peering into the darkness as he crept forward.

'Now,' said Crimson, and he reached out to give Ralan a shove in the back.

The deacon stumbled through the door, slipping on some loose rocks and pitching forward onto the ground.

'Be quiet,' hissed Crimson through his bared teeth. As Ralan got to his feet, Crimson motioned for the guards to follow.

The eight men saluted as one and marched through the door in double file, making twice as much noise as Ralan had falling down.

'Why am I surrounded by incompetents?' said Crimson. He stared up at the ceiling, not so much appealing to a higher power as defying it to provide him with a reasonable answer to his query. He followed his men inside.

He could see the lights of the worksite in the distance, but little illumination found its way to this back door – and for good reason, he knew. As far as anyone in the universe knew, that door opened onto a large void in the hive. Whatever had been there dropped away in a hivequake long ago. Or perhaps it was just one of those odd empty pockets the ancient builders simply forgot about or built around.

Whatever the case, only he knew the secret to reaching this door – a narrow ledge ran around the void just below torch light range. Crimson had used this access point in his early days to amass a small fortune in artefacts that he then used to escape detection and start a new life when things heated up for Jules Ignus.

More recently, the back door had allowed access to his saboteurs, who would now face the pools of redemption for failing to keep the construction crews from uncovering that abominable body.

'Blast that Tavis,' he said. 'This is all his fault. Him and his dome-sized ego.'

Ralan and Crimson's guards picked their way across the shadowy dome toward the lights. It became clear as they got closer that there were far more people in the dome than a simple construction site would account for.

Crimson caught up with his men when they came to a sudden halt. They stood above the construction site on a higher level of the dome. Below them, Crimson saw an odd assortment of people. Guilder guards stood at attention near the main dome entrance and walked in pairs around the perimeter of the lights. A small group of gangers dressed in chains and leather milled around between the guards and the work site.

But it was the worksite itself that got Crimson's attention. A large group of people, some well-dressed, others who looked like refugees from an Underhive bar, and a set of half-dressed slaves all knelt in a circle, their heads bowed in prayer. In the centre of the worshippers was a body lying in state on a crude altar, a body Cardinal Crimson had once vowed would never see the light of day again. He intended to keep that vow no matter the cost.

'Is that body glowing?' asked one of Crimson's guards.

The cardinal glared at him. 'It's just a trick of the lights,' he growled. 'Go get that abomination, and kill any of the heretics who try to stop you.'

Ralan opened his mouth as if he wanted to say something. 'They worship a false prophet,' said the Cardinal. 'They have been judged and will face the pools of redemption. Go!'

As he watched Ralan lead the guards around and down to the construction site, Crimson heard the snap of a stone crunching underfoot behind him. He turned and looked into the swirling, cloud-filled eyes of Jobe Francks. 'Still quick to judge and even quicker to send others to do your dirty work, eh Ignus?' he said.

'You will address me as Cardinal or your eminence,' said Crimson. 'Whatever you think you know about me, I am the leader of your faith. I would think you of all people – someone who claims to be touched by the Undying Emperor – would show some respect for my authority.'

'Respect for you?' said Francks. 'How can I respect someone who shows no respect for any living creature but himself? You are nothing more than a rat eating away at the edges of civilization. I should give you the respect reserved for such vermin – a quick and painless death. That is more than you deserve.'

Crimson took a step closer to Francks, turning slightly as he moved to hide his hand. 'What do you know about respect, wyrd?' he said. 'You've manifested abominable powers, just like your dead friend down there. It is an affront to nature. You are the ones who should be exterminated for the betterment of society.'

'But then who would you rail against?' asked Francks. If he had noticed Crimson's furtive hand motions beneath his robe, he didn't show any sign of it in his face, and he stood as still as a rock. 'Without the wyrds and the mutants and the heretics, you would be out of business. Your only power comes from picking and tearing at the fringes of society to bolster the beliefs of the faithful.'

'They betray the natural order,' said Crimson. What little skin he had left on his face flushed with anger at the heretic's lack of understanding. 'They betray the strictures of Redemption.'

'You are the true traitor to the cause of Redemption, Ignus,' said Francks. 'You always have been, and your stringent interpretation of the words of the Undying Emperor will only lead you and your flock to ruin, never to the ultimate reward the Universe has in store for the rest of us.'

Francks's calm, almost placid face mixed with his heretical words enraged the Cardinal even further. 'The abominations must be cleansed from the universe if the faithful are to live in the grace of the Undying Emperor,' screamed Crimson. 'It is the word. Redemption is the fire. I am its crucible.'

He pulled a meltagun from beneath his robes and pointed it at Francks. 'This wicked world will be cleansed, beginning with you.'

Francks simply frowned and shook his head. 'I don't know what saddens me more,' he said. 'That you believe every word you say or that you think you can create a better world through murder.'

Crimson glared at Francks as he squeezed the trigger.

9: REDEMPTION

'WELL, THIS SHOULD be interesting,' said Kal. He'd followed his instincts, and a fairly obvious trail, down a supposedly dead end tunnel. Luckily, the secret passage through the fake wall at the end lay open, and he'd been able to slip into the side tunnel with ease.

Now he'd come upon a round dome portal. Looking through, Kal could see a crowd inside including a large group of people on their knees bowed around what looked like a dead body.

Jobe Francks must be inside. That was the good news. The bad news was there were at least a dozen Guilder guards between Kal and the body.

He gave the wheel a spin and pushed open the portal. Stepping through, he was amused to find he had to tap the nearest guard on the shoulder to get his attention. Perhaps he should have simply slipped around the guards, but then that wouldn't be Kal's style.

'Kal Jerico, bounty hunter,' said Kal when the confused guard turned and stared at him. He gave the guard his biggest, most disarming smile. 'I'm here to help. What's the situation?'

The guard's eyebrows wrinkled as his confusion deepened. Then he must have come to a decision, because he sighed and placed a hand on Kal's shoulder.

'Well, it's the oddest thing,' he said. 'Since the workers found that miracle body, everything's got totally scavved. Then this new group barges in and starts worshipping as well. We're just waiting for word from Tavis…'

'Seldon!' yelled another guard, who stepped in between Kal and his new friend. 'Who is this man and why are you talking to him?'

'He's…'

'Kal Jerico,' said Kal. He extended his hand as the other guard turned toward him. 'Bounty hunter. I think I can help. Just let me take my bounty out of here and I'm sure everything will return to normal.'

The second guard stared at Kal from under a furrowed brow. He glanced down at Kal's hand before returning his gaze to his eyes. 'Leave now, bounty hunter, and you won't get hurt. This is a private guild matter and does not concern you.'

Kal flashed his smile again. 'Listen,' he said. 'I haven't slept. My entire body is one big welt, and all I want is my bounty. He just came in here with a crowd of followers. Let me take him and I'm sure the others will follow.'

Neither the smile nor the story seemed to work. 'Seldon, escort him out of here.'

Seldon grasped Kal below the elbow. With a quick twist, he turned Kal around and wrenched his arm into an extremely uncomfortable position. With a little more pressure, Seldon pushed Kal forward toward the open portal.

'Scav,' said Kal. 'They got here fast.' He ducked.

'Who got here fa–' asked Seldon.

The laser blast streaked over Kal's head. Seldon's body slumped to the ground with a dull thud. Kal dived to the floor by side of the door and kept rolling, figuring the next blast might encompass a larger area.

Behind him, he heard guards shouting and weapons firing. Several shotgun blasts replied from the Goliaths in the tunnel. By the time the first frag grenade exploded, Kal was back on his feet and running along the edge of the dome away from the door.

Several Orlock gangers stood between Kal and the body but after the explosion they moved toward the guards, the ends of their bandanas flapping behind their heads as they ran. Kal cut across toward the gathered worshippers as the battle heated up by the entrance.

Kal scanned the crowd for the wild-haired man, but didn't see anyone even close to that description. He did see a familiar face, though. 'Scabbs, you son of a rat,' he said. 'What in Helmawr's name are you doing here?'

'Kal,' said Scabbs. 'Great diversion. Did Yolanda send you?'

The immediate detour in the conversation made Kal pause a moment. 'Um,' he said. 'Yolanda?'

'Well, I was kidnapped and Yolanda tried to follow, but–'

Another explosion by the door made Kal turn. The Goliaths had pushed their way into the dome and now outnumbered the remaining guards.

'Whatever,' said Kal. 'We'll catch up later. That diversion will be on top of us soon. Did you see Francks? I'm sure he came in here.'

'He was here just a few minutes ago,' said Scabbs. He brought all these people to worship before the glowing miracle body.' Scabbs pointed at the bier in the middle of the circling crowd.

Kal glanced at the bier and did a double take, finally taking a good look at it. The body not only glowed, the light coming from it seemed to pulse. 'Okay,' he said, 'Now that's just strange.'

He shook his head, trying to get the image out of his brain. The sounds of the battle by the door were getting closer. He looked at Scabbs. 'Where is Francks now?'

Scabbs pointed toward the top of the pile of debris. 'He went to face his destiny.'

'Great,' said Kal. 'That can't be good.'

A las-blast hit the ground between them. Kal thought it was a stray shot from the Goliath battle but then he glanced where Scabbs was pointing. Ralan and his Redemptionists scrambled down the debris pile. Ralan had a laspistol in his hand.

'I'm really starting to hate that guy,' said Kal, pulling out his own laspistols. He fired twice, pulverising two chunks of rock on the pile below Ralan. He glanced at Scabbs. 'Crimson's men are here,' he said. 'So Crimson can't be far behind. I need to get to Francks now. I need a diversion… I mean another diversion.'

Scabbs smiled, which was somewhat disconcerting because Kal couldn't remember ever seeing the half-ratskin smile before. Plus two large flakes of skin at the corners of his mouth fell away when he did it.

'I have an idea,' said Scabbs. He turned and ran through the crowd of worshippers. Kal took cover behind one of the townspeople, hoping Ralan wouldn't chance hitting a citizen while Guilder guards were nearby.

Scabbs reached the bier and raised his hands. 'My people,' he called out, and Kal was amazed when the slaves raised their heads and stared at Scabbs. He pointed up the hill toward the Redemptionists. 'Behold, the unbelievers,' he called. 'They come to desecrate the shrine. They come to remove the miracle body.'

A murmur ran through the entire crowd. Kal stared at Scabbs. The pulsating light limned his head and arms, making him look almost angelic. He shook away that image as well. This was Scabbs after all, about as far removed from an angel as a rat is from a human.

'Rise up, my people,' called Scabbs. 'Rise up and fight the unbelievers. Do not let them near the miracle body,'

'This can't possibly work,' muttered Kal. He watched in amazement as the bare-fisted townsfolk and slaves ran toward the heavily-armed Redemptionist guards. One of the Redemptionists raised a rifle and took aim, but Ralan slapped the weapon out of his hands. He barked a command and they all holstered their weapons just before the crowd reached them.

Kal worked his way to the side and tried to climb up the pile, but it was too steep and the debris too loose. He needed to find another way. 'Scabbs,' he called. 'We need to get to the top.' He couldn't believe he was even thinking about asking this next question. 'Any suggestions?'

THE AIR AROUND Jobe Francks sizzled and blurred like mirages he'd seen in the Wastes. He felt his face and chest heat up. His nostrils filled with the smoky odour of charred hair. A ringing echoed inside his ears.

What an odd sensation it is to be burned alive, he thought. He felt that boils would soon erupt on his skin and then his organs would begin to cook. Francks felt himself drowning in the experience. It was almost welcome. Almost soothing. Life had been so hard in the Wastes. He'd lost everything years ago. Perhaps being burned to death was the fitting end.

Crimson's screams penetrated his mind – something about needing more power or a malfunction. Was it supposed to take this long? Why wasn't there more pain? A voice in Francks's mind told him to fight, reminded him that the Universe wasn't ready for him to die just yet. The thought seemed odd, almost amusing. 'We all die, don't we Syris?' he asked the voice. 'Why does it matter when?'

The answer came to him in a moment of absolute clarity. Death is no more than a single moment in time, a tiny blip on the fabric of the Universe. But the fabric is made up of all those blips. Each life adds to the tapestry, touching other blips and sparking new patterns to emerge and spread across the fabric like ripples in a pool. To cut a life short would tear a hole in the fabric. Redemption came only once the last stitch was sewn, the last pattern was woven.

'You must endure,' said the voice. 'A while longer. You must finish the pattern.'

Suddenly, the heat intensified. Pain lashed through Francks's body, screaming for attention from his brain. He reached out toward Crimson with his mind as he stretched his arm into the shimmering air. With a flick of his wrist, he knocked the weapon from the Cardinal's hand. The air returned to normal around him and the heat in his skin began to dissipate.

'You'll find me harder to murder than your sacrifices, Ignus,' said Francks.

'If you're so special,' cried Crimson, 'then why was your master so easy?'

'Was he, Ignus?' asked Francks. He looked down at the body of his friend. 'Then why did you have so much trouble removing his body? He's special, Ignus. Even you have to admit that now. Don't you Ignus?'

'Stop calling me that!' screamed Crimson. He rushed forward and leapt at Francks.

The two men tumbled to the ground in a heap. Crimson landed on top of Francks and straddled his chest, his robe pushed up around his knobbly knees. Francks tried to roll to the side, but was amazed at the strength in Crimson's skeletal frame. He was pinned and forced to stare up into the deathly apparition of Crimson's face.

SCABBS LED KAL around the outskirts of the battle between the Redemptionists and the body-worshippers. They stayed low, lest a stray shot from Goliath-Guilder battle catch them from behind.

'I'm sure I saw it over here,' said Scabbs. He glanced around for the ladder he'd seen Ander carrying earlier, but every scream from his left made him jump and turn toward the battle. Those were his people, and he had sent them against Crimson's guards. He knew what those animals were capable of. He'd almost been sent to the bottom of the acid pits himself once. He wouldn't forgive himself if the worshippers lost and got rounded up for redemption.

'You sure you didn't see it in a dream?' asked Kal. 'You did say you'd been knocked out last night.' Kal carried his laspistols in his hands and periodically shot into one melee or the other. 'Damn!' exclaimed the bounty hunter.

Scabbs whipped his head around to look at the worshipper battle, expecting to see one of the slaves fall to Kal's friendly fire. 'What is it?' he asked as he scanned the fight.

'I lost sight of Ralan,' said Kal. He waved his pistols back and forth in front of him as he searched for the missing Redemptionist. 'That scavving deacon has been a pain in my backside all night.'

Scabbs watched the battle a moment longer. Many of Crimson's guards had succumbed to the pressure of the riot. All Scabbs could see were worshippers beating on something at their feet. The guards still on their feet had pulled out their weapons again. They backed into a group and fired at any worshippers who came close.

'Ah, found it,' said Kal. He pulled the ladder out from beneath the wreckage of the light pole and set it up against a wall of concrete blocks; the last remnants of what used to be a building or perhaps just a basement.

Another shot rang out from the debris mound behind Scabbs. He turned to order his people to hold back, but found the barrel of Ralan's pistol poking him in the eye instead. The deacon grabbed Scabbs by the neck and twisted him around into a choke hold. He pressed the gun into Scabbs's temple and whispered 'shush' into his ear.

Scabbs tried to call out to Kal, who was now halfway up the ladder, but couldn't do more than gurgle. Perhaps it was the sound. Perhaps Kal was psychic when it came to Scabbs. Or perhaps he just expected the sidekick to get into trouble. Whichever the case, Kal turned on the ladder and looked down.

'Ralan,' he said. 'I see you finally made it. How've things been since I left?'

'No jokes this time, heretic,' said Ralan. He tightened his hold around Scabbs's neck. 'Come down now or I kill your friend.'

'I don't think you want to do that,' said Kal. 'He won't be much of a shield when he's dead. You kill him then I kill you.'

'Then we just stay here while the Cardinal handles his business and then go our separate ways.'

Kal seemed to consider the words. He twisted around on the ladder and hooked one arm through a rung. His other hand brushed away the strands of hair that dangled around his face. 'I don't have time for this,' he said. 'Foot or groin?'

Scabbs could feel the arm around his neck slacken a little and Ralan pulled the weapon away from his head to point it at Kal. 'I don't understand,' said the deacon.

'Fine,' said Kal. 'I'll let Scabbs choose.' He stared right into Scabbs's eyes and nodded. 'Now!'

Scabbs pounded the soft arch of Ralan's foot with his heel and slammed his elbow into the deacon's groin. The deacon's gun erupted as Scabbs dropped to the side. At the same time, he heard a laspistol blast whip past his ear.

After he hit the ground, Scabbs looked up to see Ralan crumpled on the ground with a neat, round hole burned through his forehead. He glanced at Kal, who simply holstered his weapon and shrugged.

'Him or us,' said Kal. 'Not a tough choice, really.' He began climbing again, adding over his shoulder, 'Get his weapon. Go help your people.'

Scabbs picked up the weapon, but was thrown from his feet by a massive explosion. Worried about Kal, he looked at the ladder. It cracked in half and fell to the ground. Kal was nowhere to be seen.

He turned back toward the miracle body and saw Arliana's still form draped over it. He didn't know what had happened. Perhaps Ralan had got her. Maybe the explosion. Either way, it was obvious she had died protecting the miracle. Now it was Scabbs's turn. He screamed a guttural, primal cry and ran back into the fray.

'THERE'S WEAPONS FIRE coming from the dome, Mr Tavis, sir,' said the sergeant.

'Well don't just stand there,' said Tavis. 'Deploy your men. I want that dome cleared by nightfall. If it moves, kill it.'

'But we have men in there as well, sir.'

'You heard my orders, sergeant.' Tavis grabbed the guard by the shoulders and twisted him around. 'I want my dome cleansed, top to bottom!' He gave the guard a shove down the tunnel and followed a few moments later once the squad had moved through the hatch.

Inside was bedlam. Tavis had expected a minor uprising between guards and slaves. What he saw was a war – a war with several armies and at least two fronts. And were those Goliaths in his dome? 'What in Helmawr's name is going on here?' called Tavis. Nobody answered.

'Secure this area,' called the sergeant. 'Form a phalanx and drive a wedge through those Goliaths. Cut their forces in half and surround them.'

Tavis was impressed with the sergeant. It was too bad he'd probably have to ship him off to the slave mines after this. He couldn't afford to have anyone left who had seen the supposed miracle body.

The squad dropped several grenades into the middle of the Goliaths, creating a huge explosion that rocked the ground. Those Goliaths not blown off their feet were staggered by the concussive force. The sergeant led the charge into the middle of the gang, shooting in a cross pattern to drive those left standing to the sides.

In a matter of minutes, the Goliaths had been separated into two groups, and once the squad linked up with the remaining Guilder guards on the other side, both groups were bound on two sides with the dome wall pressed up against their flanks.

Tavis jogged down the widening corridor. 'Excellent work, sergeant,' he called as he ran past. 'Now to see what can be done about those blasted slaves. Ander, bring your men. I will need your help.'

'Yes sir,' said the Orlock ganger. 'Time to cut the tail off that little rat for good.'

* * *

CRIMSON SLAPPED A bony hand on Francks's chest to hold him down. He balled the other hand into a fist and smacked Francks in the face. It felt like getting hit by stack of razors. The sharp edges of Crimson's knuckles cut into his cheek. He pulled his hand back and punched again. Francks could feel trickles of blood run down his face into his ear.

Crimson struck again. Francks's head rocked to the side into the dirt. Another blow followed and another. It was like a constant barrage of rocks falling during a hivequake, but there was no pain. Just a dull thud ringing in his ears as blow after blow rained down on him. Francks smiled.

'What are you smiling at?' asked Crimson as he continued pounding Francks. 'You enjoying this, you sick pervert? You like pain?' The sharp edge to his voice bordered on shrill as he shrieked at Francks.

'You can't hurt me anymore,' said Francks in between punches. 'You've caused a lot of pain in your life, Ignus. But your time is coming. The Universe knows what you are, and soon the world will know, too.'

Crimson grabbed Francks around the neck with both hands and squeezed. The skeletal fingers dug into his flesh like a knotted rope. Crimson's face was a patchwork of bright red skin stretched across bleached white bones and teeth. Francks felt like he was looking into the face of death. He laughed at the image, which enraged the Cardinal even further.

'No one laughs at me,' he screamed. 'Least of all a heretical witch. Prepare for your redemption, wyrd. Your laughter will echo all the way to the bottom of the acid pools.'

'I am ready for redemption,' said Francks. He could draw no breath, but could still speak. 'I am at peace with the Universe. It is you who must prepare. Your trials are just beginning.'

'Shut up. Shut up. Shut up!' screamed Crimson.

'Look at those people down there, Ignus,' said Francks. They have seen the miracle of the body. They will soon see you for the murdering little gangster you really are. Are you prepared for your own redemption? Because it is coming and now there is no way for you to stop it. You can't kill everyone.'

'Oh, can't I?' said Crimson. The Cardinal stood while holding onto his neck, dragging Francks to his feet. With surprising strength, Crimson lifted him off the ground. Francks let his feet dangle in the air. His moment was near. There was no stopping it now. No use fighting anymore. His pattern was nearing completion.

Crimson glared up into Francks's milky-white eyes as he held the taller man in the air. 'At the end of the day, I will still be Cardinal Crimson, and you will have joined Bowdie in death. Then we'll see who is laughing.'

Francks smiled again. He could feel the light of Bowdie warming his back and limning his head. 'I won't argue with you, Ignus,' he said. 'Syris always said, "Never argue with a crazy person." But you couldn't bury Bowdie and you can't bury the truth. We will rise up to defeat you. The truth will be my redemption and your downfall.'

Crimson moved one hand to Francks's groin and lifted him over his head. He turned toward the edge of the pit. 'You pathetic old man,' he said. 'The truth is over-rated. People don't want truth. They want carnage. They crave excitement to give their miserable lives some meaning. They want death... as long as it's someone else's and they can watch it happen. I will win in the end for I am Cardinal Crimson, and I can give them exactly what they want. You can't stop me. Nobody can.'

'I believe I can,' said Kal Jerico.

* * *

'WHAT IN THE Spire has happened here?' asked Yolanda. She came to a screeching halt as soon as she entered the dome, and then backed up to the dome portal to get a better look.

Themis stood next to her in the doorway. 'I thought you said it was just a few Guilder guards and some Orlocks.'

'It was,' she said. 'Just a few hours ago. Now it's a war zone.' She scanned the worksite, looking for Scabbs, but there was simply too much confusion. 'Look,' she said. 'All I needed was to get the Guilder's men out of the way long enough to get my friend. Well, mission accomplished. Take the 'Cats and get out now before we all get drawn into this war. I think I can make my way through the chaos.'

Themis pointed to the group fighting to their right. 'Isn't that our friend, Gonth?' she asked.

Yolanda wiped her dreadlocks away from her eye to take a closer look. 'I think it is,' she said.

An evil smirk played across Themis's face as her eyes lit up. 'You go get your friend. We've got a score to settle with that Goliath.'

Yolanda returned her friend's smile. 'Go get 'em, girl,' she said. 'But keep your back to the door and don't get squeezed.'

As Themis and the Wildcats moved off to flank the Goliaths, Yolanda took a deep breath and ran through the lane between the two battles. She'd almost made it to the far end of the Guilder line when the leader stepped in front of her.

'What are you doing here?' he demanded.

This situation required skills Yolanda loathed to use, and yet she knew it would work all too well. She rolled her shoulders back slightly and turned and tilted her head to the side. The effect of which was to accentuate her long neck and raise her breasts up just slightly in her skin-tight vest. She curled one lip up to give the guard a sly smile.

'Me and my girls are here to help,' she said. Yolanda turned her head to glance back toward the three-way battle, making sure her hair flipped around her face as she moved. When she looked back at the guard, she wet her lips. 'Do you suppose there might be a reward?'

'There, um, might be,' said the guard. He was totally mesmerised. His eyes had focused well below Yolanda's face and his mouth hung open slightly. Yolanda felt herself hating men for being so easily manipulated and hating herself for sinking to the level of one of Kal's barmaids.

'Well, why don't you go help them,' suggested Yolanda, 'and then we can discuss my reward later.' With this last line, Yolanda reached out and stroked the guard's cheek with a finger.

'Um, okay,' said the guard and he moved off, somewhat reluctantly, glancing back at Yolanda several times as he walked down the line.

She waved at him. 'You might want to help Themis,' called Yolanda. 'She just loves a man in uniform.' Yolanda watched the guard for a moment longer, realising that even if Themis didn't kill him, she'd probably just lost any chance at that reward.

'Oh well,' she said. 'It was worth the price.' She jogged off to find Scabbs. That was a man she could understand. He was a disgusting little rodent, which didn't differentiate him from most men, but he had simple needs: food, shelter, delousing. Yolanda shuddered and decided that after this bounty she needed to find new friends.

'COME ON GIRLS,' called Themis. 'We have a date with destiny.' She pulled the ripcord on her chainsword and turned toward Gonth and the Goliaths. 'Fate brought us to this dome. Vengeance will carry us home again.'

'Orders, ma'am?' asked Lysanne. She pulled at the bandages around her hand and jammed a plasma pistol in amongst the linen.

'If it growls,' said Themis, 'shoot it. Avoid grenades if possible. We can't afford to harm the guilders. If any 'Cats come through this, I don't want a bounty on our heads.'

'But don't be afraid to use the Guilder's men as shields,' added Lysanne with a smile.

'That's why you're my second,' said Themis. 'You're always thinking.' She turned to her gang. 'For the fallen,' she cried.

'For the fallen,' replied the Wildcats.

Themis revved her chainsword and strode into the dome. As she and the 'Cats worked their way around behind the battle, a guilder guard came running up to them.

'Ladies,' he called. 'Hey! Girls!'

Themis stopped and glared at the approaching guard. 'Did you say, "girls"?' she asked.

The guard smiled a broad, stupid, male smile. 'I heard you might need some help,' he said. 'Well, you girls stick with me and I'll make sure you don't get hurt.'

Themis licked her lips and smiled back. 'You'll make sure we don't get hurt,' she said.

The guard nodded.

'Well, who's going to keep you from getting hurt?'

Themis looked down at her rumbling chainsword. The guard glanced down as well, and his smile faded. With his attention on the sword, Themis snapped her leg up and out, kicking the guard a few centimetres below his belt. He fell to the ground, groaning.

'Come on, girls,' said Themis. 'And remember what Lysanne said about using the guards as shields.'

UP AHEAD, YOLANDA saw another three-way battle. Scabbs and his slave pals were caught between Redemptionists and a group of advancing Orlocks. There were a lot more slaves than she remembered – and many of them were better dressed than the average slave – but they were completely outgunned. And Scabbs seemed out of it. He sat by a couple of bodies lying upon some stones.

'Time to even the odds a little,' said Yolanda as she pulled out her laspistols. She let loose with a volley of blasts that hit the ground in front of the Orlocks. They stopped advancing and scattered, diving behind whatever cover they could find nearby.

She kicked over an ore cart and ducked behind it. 'Scabbs?' she called out. 'You armed?'

Three blasts hit the other side of the steel cart and bounced off after she spoke. A moment later, Scabbs called back. 'Yolanda? Is that you?'

'What kind of stupid question is that, you son of a ratskin?'

Scabbs didn't even reply. No sarcasm. Not even any pouting. Something must be really wrong with the little man. Two more shots clanged off her ersatz shield. Yolanda knew she had to return fire soon or the Orlocks would move to flank her. The last two shots had come from her left so she rolled left and fired right. As she suspected, the gangers on the left had taken cover again, but she caught one sticking his head up on the right and plugged him in the shoulder.

'If you have a weapon, Scabbs, I could use a little help here,' she said as she scrambled back behind the cart. 'It's called a cross fire. But it only works if you fire as well. Whatever's wrong, push it down for now. Focus on the problem at hand. That's how you stay alive.'

Another volley of shots ricocheted off the cart followed by a single shot that came nowhere near her.

'I got one,' yelled Scabbs. 'I got one.'

'Great,' said Yolanda. She thought he sounded a little too happy about it, but people dealt with pain in many ways. 'Gloat less. Shoot more.' She rolled to the right and saw one of the gangers repositioning to get cover from Scabbs. She fired twice, hitting him in the leg and foot. He dropped to the ground and screamed. The odds were definitely getting better.

As Yolanda rolled back to safety, she saw movement out of the corner of her eye right before running into a boot. She looked up into the barrel of a pistol. At the other end of the weapon stood the Orlock ganger who'd kidnapped Scabbs. He was smiling.

'Don't even try it,' he said. 'Drop the pistols and maybe you live long enough to know the pleasure of Ander.'

THEMIS AND LYSANNE had worked their way around the guilder line, leaving the rest of the Wildcats behind their walking shields to provide cover fire. Working in tandem, the duo had already taken down two Goliaths.

Lysanne would light them up with a ball of plasma in the chest. This did little more than stun the hulking behemoths, but it gave Themis time to close to melee with her chainsword. Even with blades rotating at thousands of revolutions per minute, the chainsword would have trouble cutting through tough Goliath muscle, and their underlying bones were like bars of steel.

Themis didn't bother going for the vital organs in the chest or stomach. She aimed a little lower. One quick slash through a Goliath's loin cloth dropped them to the ground in a whimpering heap. It was then an easy matter to kick their weapons out of reach and leave them curled up in a ball in the dirt.

They made their way toward the next Goliath in line. Luckily, the Guilders and the 'Cats provided enough distraction that their infiltration hadn't been detected yet. Themis nodded at Lysanne. 'Now,' she said.

Lysanne grabbed her bandaged wrist to steady the plasma pistol and fired, but as she moved in behind the ball of plasma, a huge explosion rocked the dome behind them, knocking both 'Cats to the ground. Lysanne looked back through the guilder line to see a fireball erupt into the air.

'What happened?' called Themis.

'Looks like someone in that other Goliath battle didn't get your message about not using grenades.' Lysanne rested on her good hand and pushed herself up to her knees.

The ground beneath them shook again. Dust rained down on them from the dome ceiling. Both women stayed on the ground.

'One more blast like that and this whole place will come down on our heads,' said Themis.

But Lysanne had other problems to worry about. As she struggled back to her knees, the Goliath she had shot reared above her. She raised her plasma pistol, but he slapped it away with a big, meaty hand. He kicked her in the chest, sending her flying back several metres. She landed on her back with a spine jarring crack.

The world around her went fuzzy. She shook her head to try to clear the gathering fog in her vision. The Goliath strode toward her, pulling out a shotgun and pumping a shell as he approached. Laser blasts and bullets slapped him in the chest and arms, but didn't slow him down.

Then, behind the Goliath, Lysanne saw something even worse. Gonth had appeared from out of the smoke and dust. With a single, massive hand, he grabbed Themis and lifted her off the ground by the throat. His other hand held her arm out to the side. With a quick flip, he snapped her wrist, and the chainsword fell from her grasp. It jumped and flipped on the ground.

Gonth looked over at Lysanne and the Goliath standing above her. 'Kill her,' said the Grak gang's new leader. 'Kill them all. This one I'll take home for a little fun.'

The Goliath lowered the barrel of the shotgun and pointed it at Lysanne's face.

'Do NOT PRESUME to meddle in my work, heretic,' yelled Crimson over his shoulder. 'After I cast down this witch, I will turn my attention on you. Leave now and your redemption might be commuted… for a while.'

Crimson's sleeves had fallen down around his shoulders, revealing his thin, bony arms. Kal had no idea where the Cardinal got the strength to hoist Francks over his head and hold him there. Certainly, he couldn't last long. Kal just needed to keep him talking.

'It won't end there, Crimson,' said Kal. 'Or should I call you Ignus?' Crimson flinched at the name but still didn't turn around. 'Francks was right,' he said out loud. 'Too many people already know the truth.'

'You don't even know what you know,' said Crimson. 'That's always been your downfall, heretic. Too little knowledge, too late.'

Kal slipped his laspistols from their holsters, drawing them out silently. He wondered why Francks wasn't struggling. The man had killed two assassins with his bare hands. If he couldn't take Crimson, something must be wrong.

Kal continued talking. 'Let me see if I can get close. You murdered that glowing guy down there a long time ago and Francks here is the only witness. That about sum it up?'

Francks raised his head and looked at Kal. There was an odd gleam in his eyes and he smiled broadly. Kal mouthed at him, 'Can you fight?'

Francks simply shook his head and closed his eyes.

'There's more in this universe than life and death,' said Crimson. 'But I wouldn't expect a heretic bounty hunter to grasp the intricacies of philosophy.'

'I figure the rest of the story is all Redemptionist crap anyway,' said Kal. 'Hardly worth my time. But that man is coming with me. You can walk away or not. It really doesn't matter either way to me.'

Kal saw the exposed muscles in Crimson's upper arms tense. He was getting ready to throw Francks over the edge. Kal had to go for broke. 'I can drop you where you stand, Crimson,' he called out. 'One thing I am good at is shooting people. I can make you fall any way I want. Francks will survive. You won't.'

Looking back, it might not have been the right tactic to try with a crazed fanatic like Crimson. Faced with death or losing, a fanatic will almost always choose death.

Crimson heaved Francks over the edge and dropped to his knees. Kal fired, but his blasts flew futilely over the Cardinal's head. Crimson rolled to the side as Kal continued to fire. The Cardinal dived behind a half-wall as Kal rushed to the edge to see if the fall had indeed killed Francks.

The prophet lay on his back in a crumpled heap at the base of the wall. His right leg bent nearly double at the knee while his left arm twisted back at the shoulder and lay under his body. Blood pooled around the body and Kal could see a jagged rock sticking up through his side. But there was movement, and even from this height, he could see the man's odd, swirling eyes.

Kal turned to advance on Crimson's position. He aimed his laspistols toward the half-wall. 'That was your third and final chance, Cardinal,' called Kal. 'You and your assassins have all failed. You're just not very good at killing.'

'You'd be surprised,' said Crimson. 'I'm just getting started.' He rose up behind the wall with a plasma gun in his hands. 'I left this here a long time ago for just such an occasion.' He jammed a power cell into the weapon and fired.

Kal dived to the side as a large stone beside him exploded from the released plasma energy. Shards rained around him as he hit the ground. He knew better than to get into a gunfight against a plasma gun. The energy shells were like grenades. You just had to get close. However, the next shot hit the top of the wall, blowing it apart around his hands, and dropping Kal over the edge.

10: OVER THE EDGE

CARDINAL CRIMSON RUSHED forward and pointed his plasma gun into the pit. He twisted his head back and forth, searching frantically for any sign of the heretic, Kal Jerico. The heretic must die! Both heretics. Jerico and that crazy false prophet, Francks. They would ruin everything. All he had built. All he had worked and fought and killed for over the years would come crashing down if those two heretics got their way.

He could feel it all slipping away from him. His heart beat so loud it pulsed and rang in his ears. His face felt flush and he laboured to get enough breath, wheezing through his lipless mouth. His tongue was like a wad of sandpaper in his mouth, and his hands shook so hard he almost dropped his gun into the worksite below.

Crimson's eyes went wide as he focused on the scene below. There were so many people down there. So many witnesses to his defeat: his guards, the slaves and those idiotic townspeople. Past that a completely different battle raged with even more people coming to uncover his secrets; to get between Cardinal Crimson and his mission on this world.

And then there was Francks. The false prophet lay below him, broken, but still squirming, still trembling, still alive. 'Why are you so hard to kill?'

Crimson pointed the plasma gun at Francks, but his trembling hand made it impossible to aim. He grabbed the butt of the gun with his free hand to steady it and tried to squint, forgetting that he had no usable eyelids.

'The Emperor damn him to the depths of The Sump,' cried Crimson.

'You just can't seem to finish the job, can you, Ignus?'

'Who's that?' screamed the Cardinal. He waved his gun around and scanned the wall and the pit below. He checked over his shoulder as well. The voice seemed to have come from below, but he couldn't be sure. It sounded like it was right next to him. 'Is that you, Bowdie?' he called. 'What do you want from me? Why can't you stay dead and buried like all the others?'

'You can never kill me,' said the voice. 'I am forever. I will haunt you to your dying day.'

That had definitely come from below. Perhaps it was Bowdie. Perhaps it was just in his head. It didn't matter. They all had to die now. Crimson fired his gun into the pit. The explosion nearly knocked him over the edge. 'Leave me alone!' he screamed. 'I'll kill you all. I will cleanse this place and raze it to the ground. Let's see you rise from that!'

He fired again and again, waving the weapon around randomly and squeezing the trigger to unleash powerful blasts of plasma in all directions. Shards of rocks, hunks of metal, and pieces of bodies flew into the air wherever the energy shells hit. Crimson laughed with gleeful abandon with every shot, dancing up and down the edge of the pit as he fired.

'I am the will,' he cried. 'I am the way. I am the holy rite of redemption. Feel my flame, feel my wrath and wither under my gaze. I am the will. I am the way…'

* * *

YOLANDA WRACKED HER brain for a sarcastic response to Ander's vulgar proposal, but the best she could come up with was, 'What, the pleasure of dragging your sorry butt in for the bounty?'

It was pitiful. With Jerico, she always had a zinger ready. It must be lack of sleep. She was off her game. That also explained how this idiot Orlock had got the jump on her in the first place.

'Last chance,' said Ander. 'Drop your weapon and call off your gang, or we'll wipe you out and dump the bodies in a hole. What'll it be?'

Ander had her in a bad spot. She was flat on her back and he stood behind her. His groin was too far away and she'd never get her feet around before he pulled the trigger. Yolanda hated to admit it, Ander had the advantage. But she'd rather die than give him the advantage he was truly looking for.

Yolanda loosened her grip, letting her pistols flop around her fingers. At the same time, she tensed her body for action. Perhaps a scissors move with her legs or a quick roll to the side to make him miss, followed by two quick gun blasts.

'That's better,' he said. His lips spread into a broad smile. 'Now, get up slow–'

The air above Yolanda sizzled. A bright light arced over her head, blinding her. She blinked away the tears that welled up and grasped her weapons. Now was her chance. If Ander had been blinded as well, she might get the drop on him.

As she aimed her weapons, Ander's pistol dropped from his hands and he fell to the ground next to her. His mouth lolled open slightly and his eyes had gone wide in surprise, probably from the large hole in his chest.

'Did I get him?' called Scabbs.

'Yeah,' said Yolanda, turning away from the glassy-eyed corpse. 'Nice shooting. Feel free to gloat about that one. Took you long enough, though.'

'Still a little busy here,' replied Scabbs. 'I've got Redemptionists breathing down my back, you know.'

'Okay,' called Yolanda. 'Gloat later. Shoot more now.' She grabbed Ander's gun and stuck it into her vest. 'Cover me,' she called. 'I'm coming over.'

Yolanda crouched behind the overturned cart. When she heard Scabbs's laser blasts, she jumped over and dived into a forward roll. She came up blasting and sprinted in a zigzag toward Scabbs.

As she leaped over the low wall surrounding the slave encampment, a large chunk of stone exploded beneath her. She hit the ground hard and lay there for a moment.

'What in the Spire was that?' asked Scabbs.

Debris rained down around them. The worshippers panicked and began screaming. Some jumped the wall and ran off, heedless of the battles raging around them. Others curled into a ball and whimpered. Energy blasts exploded all around the work site.

'Plasma gun,' said Yolanda. She crawled to an intact portion of wall. 'Can't tell where it's coming from. Damn!'

'What's wrong?' asked Scabbs. 'Are you okay?'

'I just thought of the perfect comeback for Ander.'

THEMIS HEARD THE snap of her wrist breaking over the whine of the chainsword. The pain shot up her arm like a laser blast. She tried to scream in pain but, with Gonth's hand around her neck, only a gurgle escaped her lips.

She pounded on his chest with her free hand, but he just laughed at her as he turned to leave. She could see the battle behind him. It appeared even more chaotic than before. The Guilder guards and her girls had broken ranks and were diving for cover. The Goliaths had regrouped and were starting to pursue.

Themis searched for Lysanne, hoping she had found some way to get out from under the barrel of Gonth's ganger. Then she saw her young lieutenant. She lay still on the ground, her wrap-around top covered in blood. The Goliath who'd been standing over her was no longer there. He must have gone off with the others.

She wanted to cry out. She wanted to weep for the loss of her girls, but the darkness invaded her mind. Lack of air was turning the world black around her. It looked like all was lost. Themis's eyelids drooped. She wanted to let go, let the darkness take her. But she knew what lay on the other side, and it wasn't death. At least not right away. She had to fight.

Grabbing hold of Gonth's hand around her throat, Themis pulled at his fingers and then his thumb. Just a little air would give her a few more moments. Maybe she could call for a retreat. Maybe she could find some way to get away from this brute. Anything was possible with just a little more air.

LYSANNE ROLLED OVER onto her stomach, lifted her chest off the ground, and puked. She wrung blood and vomit from her hair and looked over at the dead Goliath next to her. One minute he'd been standing there ready to pull the trigger, the next minute his chest simply exploded. The head had dropped and rolled between her legs while blood spewed from the lower half of his torso all over her face and chest.

She'd been so horrified Lysanne froze, completely forgetting about Themis and Gonth. It was the most repulsive thing she'd ever witnessed, and she'd seen her fair share of battles. Lysanne pushed the bloody vision out of her mind and concentrated on saving Themis.

She grabbed her weapon and ran through the chaos toward Gonth. Themis didn't look good. One arm hung limp at her side while the other pulled at the monstrous hand around her throat. She'd stopped kicking, as if she had no fight left within her.

Gonth slapped Themis across the face and blood sprayed from her mouth. At that moment, Themis seemed to get a small gasp of air and then looked right at her. Lysanne saw a little fire still burning behind those fierce eyes.

Themis opened her mouth and forced one croaking word out: 'Grenade!' she called and held out her hand behind the Goliath's head.

It was little more than a whisper, but Lysanne heard it clearly enough. She also knew better than to question an order from her leader, even one that seemed suicidal. She popped a frag grenade off her belt, pulled the pin, and tossed it.

It was a perfect throw. Themis snatched it out of the air, pulled her hand back, and slammed the bomb into Gonth's face. He immediately dropped her and began to claw at his head. Themis pushed herself up with her good hand and scrambled away as Gonth danced around frantically.

When he turned toward Lysanne, she finally understood what had happened. The grenade was lodged in his open mouth. He pulled and pulled at it, but couldn't get the bomb out past his teeth. Lysanne fell to the ground and covered her head with her hands. A moment later, the explosion rang out like thunder, and bits of bone and blood rained down around her again.

'Come on,' called Themis. 'We got what we came for. Get the 'Cats. This place is totally scavved.'

'WELL, THAT COULD have gone better,' said Kal under his breath. He clung to the wall just below Crimson, who continued to rant and fire his plasma gun. Luckily, Kal had been tucked under a bank of pipes and beams when the Cardinal peered over the edge. Now the man was so berserk, Kal doubted the Cardinal had any idea where or even who he was anymore.

He just wanted to scare him away, not send him into a psychotic episode.

Kal inched his way down the wall away from the lunatic, his fingers and toes clawing at thin, mortar-filled cracks. A few more metres to the side and he'd be hidden from view all the way down the wall. It was slow going and his shoulders were numb again. He'd spent too much time hanging from his hands today.

'I've got to learn when to shut my mouth,' he said. Kal glanced over his shoulder to see the chaos caused by Crimson's tantrum. The guard lines had broken and the few remaining Goliaths moved freely through the chaos, thumping and shooting anything that moved. The Wildcats were more disciplined than the guards, and they seemed to be edging toward the door. Smart girls.

Kal climbed down the wall as he kept an eye on the various battles. If the 'Cats were here, Yolanda must be nearby. He found her a moment later. It looked like she was arguing with Scabbs while shooting at the last of the Orlocks.

The slaves and townsfolk were either catatonic or running for the exit. Those lucky enough to escape the plasma blasts and the Goliaths might actually make it back to civilization in one piece. One slave girl's body lay draped across the miracle body. She must have died protecting it.

As Kal neared the bottom, he noticed that Crimson's guards had regrouped on the hill after the slaves fled from the plasma gun. They seemed uncertain what to do next. They looked back and forth between the miracle body in the middle of the sniper zone and their boss, the crazed sniper himself. Kal couldn't care less which way they went as long as they left him alone. He needed to get to Francks.

He dropped the last several metres and turned to run down the wall to his bounty. At that moment, a voice blared above the chaos.

'Stop this madness now!' screamed the amplified voice.

Kal twirled around to see who the hell was stupid enough to use a voice amp in the middle of this maelstrom. It was Tavis. What in the Spire was he doing here? The Guilder stood between the chaos at the door and the chaos surrounding the miracle body. Perhaps he thought he could bring some order with the force of his voice and his presence. To Kal, he looked like a lightning rod for more trouble.

'This is my dome,' he yelled through the amp. 'You are trespassers and I am well within my rights to have you all shot or sent to the slave mines.'

Kal didn't think it was the kind of rhetoric that would win him friends or influence people, but the rest of the dome fell almost completely silent. Everyone, it seemed, wanted to hear what the idiot with the amp had to say.

'Leave now or I put a bounty on all your heads,' he said. 'I can do that. I'm a Guilder and you... you are nothing. Nobody will even mourn your passing. Leave now. I want my dome back.'

Kal didn't have time for this. He turned and ran toward Francks.

'Leave,' continued Tavis. 'Do you hear me?'

'I hear you,' cried Crimson. 'This was my dome before and it will be mine again.'

Kal stopped and stared at the Cardinal. He fired the plasma gun. Kal turned back to Tavis. The Guilder's head, along with the amp and the hand that held it, exploded in a gory shower of blood, bone and plastic. The body stayed upright for a moment and then dropped over backward.

Kal was stunned. Crimson had just killed a Guilder, and on the Guilder's property. He wished he had a pict camera to record it. He ran to Francks's side. Along the way he noticed the Cardinal's men had made their decision. They ran up the hill toward their spiritual leader, probably to hustle him out before the Guilder's men took the law into their own hands.

'KAL JERICO,' SAID Jobe Francks. 'I knew you would come.'

The bounty hunter stood above Francks, a look of deep concern on his face. It seemed to Jobe that *he* should be the one concerned as he could no longer feel his legs and it seemed impossible to even sit up.

'How?' asked Kal. 'You don't even know who I am.'

'The tapestry is much influenced by your passage through this life,' said Francks. His breathing was laboured and it took him a few moments to refill his lungs so he could continue. 'You have touched a great many threads on your travels.'

'Do you always talk like this?' asked Kal. He smiled. 'Or is this a special occasion?'

The bounty hunter kneeled down next to Francks and gently poked and prodded him. Jobe could have told him not to bother. His wounds were all internal and well beyond Jerico's abilities to remedy, but he wanted the man to feel useful, so kept quiet.

'I mean meeting me must be quite a treat,' said Kal. He forced another smile, but Jobe could see the concern behind the bounty hunter's sparkling eyes. 'Especially for someone who's been in the Ash Wastes most of his life.'

Jobe wanted to continue playing this game of wits, but he could feel his essence draining away. 'There's not much time,' he said. 'I'm afraid I won't be able to come with you to see Mr Nemo.'

Kal raised his hands in mock defence. 'I don't know anything about...'

Jobe coughed and spit blood onto his new clothes. His lungs were filling, which made breathing difficult. He wouldn't be able to talk much longer. 'Please listen,' he said. 'This will all be for nothing if you don't let me finish.'

Kal nodded. 'I think I understand,' he said. 'Go ahead.'

He talked quickly, stopping every once in a while to cough up blood.

'Your friend,' said Francks. 'The scabby one. He has Bitten's journal. Every evil deed Ignus – Crimson – ever committed is there. I leave it in your care. I know you will do the right thing. Be careful, though. Ignus is well-protected. If you go to his lair again, you will die.'

Kal opened his mouth to protest or to ask a question, but then shut it again.

Francks continued. 'You will know what to do when the time comes. We all must play our parts. I thought mine was to find Bowdie. I now realise I was brought here to find you. I leave the fight in your hands. Bitten carried it as long and as far as he could. But now truth has its rightful champion.'

'I'm no champion,' said Kal. 'I couldn't even save myself this evening. I sent Crimson into a homicidal rage, and I practically forced him to throw you to your death. Believe me, you're better off picking another champion.'

Jobe smiled. His time was almost up, but he felt warm, contented, complete. 'I didn't choose you,' he said. 'The Universe did. And it has its reasons. This fight needs someone like you, Kal Jerico. And we both know there's no one else quite like you to choose.'

'I don't know what to say to that,' said Kal. 'I've never had much stomach for Cawdor or Redemptionists. Too preachy and holier than thou for my liking. I try to take people as they are, and not change them. But I can tell you're different from Crimson and his ilk. Honest and decent. I would have liked to have had the chance to get to know you. I'm… I'm sorry I couldn't save you.'

'Don't worry about me,' said Jobe. His left arm was numb and it felt like someone had placed a concrete block on his chest. 'My mission is complete. Syris and I are done here. We can move on. We can have peace.'

He gazed into Kal's eyes and his vision clouded over. 'But you,' he said. His voice sounded far away, as if echoing down a tunnel. 'You won't be at peace until you find Wotan. I understand. A man needs his faithful companion. I cannot go with you to Nemo, but I can give you two gifts that might help.'

Jobe pulled Bitten's envelope from his pocket and held it up for Kal. 'Take it,' he said. 'I have no need for it where I am going.'

Kal reached for the envelope. When he took it, Jobe grabbed him around the wrist. The clouds in his eyes swirled from white to grey to black like a sudden storm. 'Here is your second gift.'

After a moment, Kal pulled away and blinked. 'What the scav was that?' he asked.

'Information,' said Jobe. 'Memories. A vision of your cyber-mastiff, Wotan. Find him. Go to him. Finish your mission. Good luck.'

And then it was time to go. The blackness crept from his chest toward his head. The visions swirled and danced in his mind. His life. Bowdie's. Crimson's and Jerico's. The entire tapestry. A scene in a bar hovered at the edges of his consciousness. He pushed the others away. This he wanted to see. At the end, he laughed and laughed and laughed.

He could hear Kal speaking to him from down the tunnel. 'What's so funny?' he said. 'What are you laughing at?'

'Nothing,' replied Francks, although he wasn't sure if Kal could even hear him anymore. 'You'll find out soon enough.'

The tunnel brightened in front of Jobe Francks. He looked back at Kal once more and smiled. He then turned to his side and saw an infinite set of tunnels all running parallel to one another, but all headed for the same light at the end. He could see Syris walking down the next tunnel and knew they would meet at the end – at the hub. And it was good.

'KAL?'

'...'

'Wake up, Jerico.'

Kal's face was slapped. By the length of the fingers and the force behind the smack, he was certain Yolanda had done the slapping.

'What?' he asked. 'Why are you hitting me?' He sat beside Jobe Francks. Yolanda and Scabbs stood over him. Scabbs, at least, looked concerned.

'You've been sitting there for several minutes, Kal,' said Scabbs. 'We were worried.'

'The runt was worried,' said Yolanda. 'I just want to leave. Our friends the Goliaths are coming.'

Kal shook his head to clear away the fog. He looked down at Francks. Dead. How long? Had it all been a dream?

'*Now*, Jerico, or I leave you as a peace offering to the Goliaths.' Yolanda pulled Kal to his feet and pushed him toward the pile of rubble. 'Up there. Maybe we can circle around and get back to the portal.'

Kal let Yolanda lead for now. He tried to sort out what happened as they climbed the hill. 'My guns,' he said. 'I dropped them when I fell over the edge.'

'They're in your holsters, Kal.'

'Odd,' said Kal. 'And where did everyone else go?'

'The Wildcats retreated after Crimson went berserk,' said Yolanda. 'His craziness's guards hustled him away after he killed Tavis. The Guilder guards lasted a while, but now we're right back where we started, running from the scavving Goliaths.'

'And I've got my laspistols?'

Scabbs slapped him this time. 'Come on, Kal!' he whined. 'We need you out here with us. The Goliaths are at the bottom of the hill. We need a Kal Jerico plan to get out of this alive. There's no one quite like you at coming up with hair-brained schemes.'

Kal smiled. 'That's just what he meant, wasn't it,' he said. 'I'm Kal Jerico. I'm the hero.'

'Right,' said Yolanda sarcastically. 'I guess that makes us sidekicks, huh?'

Kal nodded, but he wasn't really listening. 'I've got an idea,' he said. 'You two keep running. Turn right at the top of the hill. Don't stop until you get to the wall of the dome. Bobo will know where to go from there.'

'Bobo?' said Scabbs. 'I didn't see Bobo come in with you.'

'He didn't,' said Kal. 'But he's up there. He came in through the secret back door.'

'Secret? What secret? How do you know all this, Jerico?' asked Yolanda.

'I don't know how,' said Kal. 'I just know. Now go.'

Kal stopped at the top of the hill. The Goliaths were about halfway up and coming fast. Their long, thick legs made climbing the hill seem like running on level ground.

He grabbed his leather coat with both hands and pushed it open past his holsters. They were forty metres away. Kal blew gently on his fingertips and lowered his hands toward his guns. Thirty metres.

'Kal,' called Scabbs from behind him. 'You can't kill Goliaths with your laspistols. Come on. Run!'

'Oh can't I?' said Kal.

Twenty metres. Bullets and laser blasts flew through the air, narrowly missing the stoic bounty hunter. Kal drew his guns and fired four shots in rapid succession. Not a single blast hit the Goliaths. He hadn't even been aiming at them. Satisfied that it was enough, Kal turned and ran.

Behind him, he heard a loud crack, followed by a low rumble, and then a ground-shaking blast. Kal took a moment to glance over his shoulder and admire his handiwork. Large chunks of masonry and metal beams fell through the air as the ceiling and side wall of the dome collapsed on top of the last remnants of the Grak gang.

Kal smiled. 'I do have a certain style,' he said. 'A certain unconventional way of doing things, don't I?'

A few minutes later, he caught up with Scabbs and Yolanda, who stood next to Bobo. 'The back door is right over here, isn't it Bobo?' he asked.

'YOU'RE CERTAIN ABOUT this, Jerico?' asked Yolanda, for about the tenth time.

Kal shushed her. 'Yes, I'm certain,' he whispered. 'I see it all in my head. And don't ask me to explain how or why. I just do. Okay? Francks said it was a gift to help me get Wotan back.'

'You're dog is in there,' said Yolanda. The sarcasm was so thick he would have had trouble cutting it with his sabre.

Kal just nodded. He was tired of this discussion. He stepped out from behind the stalagmite where they hid and crept toward the cave opening. They were in a huge cavern two hour's hike out from Down Town – the deepest, darkest settlement in the Underhive. Kal kept close to the wall of the cavern, though not for cover so much as to avoid falling into the pool of sludge that covered most of the floor.

Yolanda and Scabbs followed him after a moment. He heard a scuffle behind him and turned to see Yolanda push Scabbs into the wall to get around him. 'And why would Nemo bring your dog all the way down to Hive Bottom?'

'So the neighbours wouldn't complain about his barking?' suggested Scabbs.

'And speaking of neighbours,' said Yolanda. 'Do you have any idea what kinds of things live in these caves down here? Mutants. Monsters. Things that make Goliaths look like kittens.'

Kal pointed his torch at a small niche carved into the wall ahead. 'Screamer!' he said. 'Don't get too close or you'll set it off.' He waded out into the sludge to avoid the proximity alarm. Two splashes behind him told Kal that the others had followed suit.

'How did you know that was there?' asked Yolanda.

Kal pointed at his head and kept moving forward. They zigzagged their way to the cave entrance, avoiding all the screamers. Kal switched off his torch. 'Wait here for my signal.' He said. 'I don't want them to see us coming.'

'How will you see?' asked Yolanda.

Kal didn't answer. He moved into the cave with his eyes closed. If he concentrated, he could see every twist and turn in his mind. After a few minutes, he stopped and opened his eyes. Light spilled onto the floor from around the next turn. He waited, counting down from ten in his head.

When he reached zero, Kal slipped around the corner and came up behind the guard who had just turned to walk back into the lit chamber. Kal grabbed him from behind, wrapped his hand over the guard's mouth and stuck the barrel of his laspistol into the man's back.

'Don't make a sound and you'll live. Understand?'

The guard nodded his head. Kal pulled him back around the corner and smacked him in the back of the head with the pearl handle of his laspistol. He lowered the guard to the floor and began counting again.

A few minutes later, Kal crept back to the cave entrance, switched on his torch and motioned to Yolanda and Scabbs to follow. He led them back to the edge of the lit chamber and crouched by the bodies of two guards.

'Okay,' he said. 'Wotan is in there. There's only two more guards and they won't see us coming.'

'How do you know?' asked Yolanda.

'Just trust me this once,' said Kal.

He pulled out his pistols and stepped around the corner. When Yolanda came up beside him, he heard her stifle a laugh. Kal had to admit, it was pretty comical.

At the far end of the chamber sat Wotan chained to the floor. Beneath him lay one of the twin Delaque gangers employed by Nemo for grunt work. Wotan's front paws held the twin's leather coat to the floor on either side of his body. His haunches rested on the ganger's groin.

The twin – Kal thought it was the one who called himself Destroy as he had a blue neckerchief around his neck – was in obvious discomfort.

Seek, the other twin, was flat up against the wall in front of Wotan. His arms alternately flapped in front of his face and groin as Wotan snapped and growled at him.

'Get him off me. Get him off me,' said Destroy over and over again.

'If I move, he'll kill me,' said Seek. 'Get him off yourself and help me.'

'This is all your fault,' said Destroy.

'My fault?' whined Seek. 'You're the one who got too close. I was just trying to help.'

'Some help you are. Why didn't you go get the guards?'

'You could have yelled for them yourself. It's not my job to get the guards. Besides, they're gone.'

'Gone? Where are they? Why didn't you tell me they were gone? I'm gonna kill you when I get out of this.'

'Not if I kill you first.'

Kal stepped into the room. 'Need some help, boys?'

The twins looked at Kal. 'Now look what you did.' said Destroy from beneath Wotan. 'You let Kal Jerico waltz right in here.'

'I did that? I did that? Why did you have to get so close to the stupid mastiff?'

'That's it. I am so gonna kill you.'

Yolanda fired her laspistol into the wall behind them. 'Would you two shut up?' she yelled. 'Or I'll kill you both.'

'Here's what's going to happen,' said Kal as he moved into the middle of the room. 'We're going to tie you up. We'll even knock you out if you'd like. Then, we're going to take Wotan and leave you with the credits I owe Nemo.'

'Credits?' asked Yolanda. 'You didn't say anything about giving them credits. Where did you get credits?'

Kal ignored her. 'Now I know you two will give this money to Nemo,' he continued, 'because it's probably the only thing that will save your life once he finds out you lost Wotan.'

'Fine,' said Destroy. 'Just get this crazy mastiff off of me. I can't feel my legs anymore.'

'Get him out of my face first,' said Seek. 'I'm in danger of losing my future here.'

'Wotan!' commanded Kal. 'Down!'

Wotan stopped growling and snapping at Seek's crotch and laid down on Destroy.

After he and Yolanda tied them both up, Kal reached into his pocket and pulled out the thick envelope Francks had given him. He took out a massive wad handful of credits and started counting. Less than a third of the way through the stack he stopped and put the rest back in the envelope.

He dropped the credits in between the twins. Then he got another idea, which made him laugh so loud it echoed around the cave complex for a minute. He turned to Scabbs. 'Give me the journal,' he said.

Scabbs looked at him blankly. 'Bitten's journal,' said Kal.

Scabbs resisted. 'A lot of people paid a huge price for this journal, Kal,' he said. 'People died over it. We can't just give it to Nemo. It's not right.'

Kal draped an arm around Scabbs's shoulders. 'I know you went through a lot these last few days,' he said. 'I can't imagine what it was like for you. But we have to do this. It's the next best thing to giving Francks over to Nemo. Better, really. All Nemo wants is the information, so let's give it to him. Otherwise, even with the money, he'll still come after us. Trust me. I think this is exactly what Francks would have wanted.'

'I don't understand,' said Scabbs.

Kal pointed at his head again. 'Just trust me for now, okay?'

Scabbs shrugged and pulled out the journal. Kal took it and picked up the money. He placed the credits in a pouch which he laid on top of the journal and dropped the whole package between the bound gangers.

'We're through now,' he said. 'Do you understand? The next time I see you two, I let Wotan off the leash. Make sure your boss gets this or Wotan and I will hunt you down like the rats you are.'

With that, Kal turned and strode out of the chamber into the darkness. On his way through, he made sure to pass by all of the screamers outside, setting them all off. A horrendous screaming wail reverberated through the cavern. It wouldn't last very long, but it would certainly drive the twins into another screaming argument. Kal chuckled as he jogged into the darkness, his faithful cyber-mastiff at his side.

THE HIVE CITY docks were a study in chaos. Hundreds of people hustled around in odd, unpredictable patterns, hauling goods to or from the transports; onto and off the docks or into the adjacent warehouses.

Dock workers operated cranes, loaded crates onto skids, or just lounged on a convenient box while foremen ran around yelling and pointing and yelling some more. Large metal cartons were moved into and out of the warehouses, while men with clipboards wandered around, checking lists and getting signatures from other men walking around with their own clipboards.

Add to that the working girls and purveyors of other nefarious goods and services who made the docks their home and office, plus the guards who patrolled the area to safeguard the transportation system, and the average day at the docks began to resemble a beehive; a beehive the size of a small city.

At least that's what Guard Creed always thought. It was fitting, too, he figured. This was a hive and the people in Hive City were little more than drones, moving through their lives with no purpose other than working for the queen – or in this case, Helmawr and the Emperor. And like drones, they got little compensation and had no prospects for a future that didn't involve working until they died.

The drones would never even get a chance to enjoy or even see any of the wonderful goods shipped through these docks where they toiled. The goods either flew up to the Spire for the pleasure of the nobles, or into orbit to be loaded into interstellar transports that would take the hive's goods to fascinating worlds where people weren't forced to live in hives and work like drones.

Creed had time for such idle thoughts because he'd been posted at the far end of the docks between a broken down warehouse and a berth that was now only used for personal craft, and it was a rare event indeed when a personal craft landed in the docks. The last time had been some noble coming down from the

Spire with some famous bounty hunter. Creed hadn't been lucky enough to be on duty that day.

There had been that wild-haired, old man who had wandered through the docks a few days ago, but that had been on Juke's watch, and everyone knew Juke was a little crazy. This post would do that to you, if you let it.

So, Creed was understandably surprised when two old men wearing blue capes and orange body armour walked toward him, headed for the boarded-up warehouse across from his desk.

'Wait a minute, you old geezers,' said Creed. He put his hand on his pistol for emphasis. 'Where do you think you're going?'

'Home,' they said in unison. The men looked at each other and smiled.

'Well, you're not living in that old building. It's condemned,' said Creed. He stood up and moved to intercept the men, who were still walking. 'That's the rule. It's been a while since I read the notice on the wall over there, but I do remember it saying "No Entry".'

'He can read,' said one of the old men.

The other stared deep into Creed's eyes and smiled again. 'And he questions the order of the world.'

Creed was getting creeped out by the way the two men talked about him but not to him. And they hadn't stopped walking, which made him back up as he talked. He stopped and pulled out his laspistol, levelling it at the one with the cloudy eyes. The old man just smiled and stared at him – or, more to the point, through him.

'Turn around and head back to the City,' he said. 'Maybe you can flop at Madam Noritake's, if you got credits. If not, find some abandoned building in the Underhive. This is my post and I don't want any trouble.'

The cloudy eyes began to swirl and Creed became unsteady, dizzy. He felt like he was falling into them.

'Put away the weapon, Creed,' said the old man.

Creed holstered his weapon.

'Stand back and let us through. We won't be flopping in the warehouse today.'

The guard stepped back and returned to his desk. The world around him seemed fuzzy, as if he'd had one too many Snakes. Shapes moved through the swirls. He heard voices, but it seemed like they were a long way away.

'Tell him to read the books,' said one voice.

'He will,' said the other voice. 'It has to be his choice to read or not. But he will. I can tell. I can always tell.'

A few minutes later, Creed opened his eyes and looked at the abandoned warehouse. He was a little worried that he might have missed something when he fell asleep – that's what had got Juke fired – but as usual, there was nobody there and nothing happening. Just him and the loneliest berth on the docks.

'This job is so scavving boring,' he said. Then he noticed a couple books on his desk. He looked around to see who had dropped the books, but saw nobody around. He picked up the books and read the titles. One was called *The Universal Path*. The other was *Questioning the Truth*. Creed opened up *Questioning the Truth* and began to read.

EPILOGUE:
THE MESSENGER

'IT'S STRANGE KNOWING what's going to happen before it happens,' said Kal. He stuck his hand out as the barmaid walked by and caught the bottle of Wild Snake that fell off her tray. He thought about patting her rear as she left, but his cheek hurt just seeing her reaction in his mind. 'I don't know how Francks lived like this. It's a little disconcerting.'

'I thought his gift was only supposed to help you get Wotan back,' said Yolanda. 'How long is it going to last?'

'I don't know,' said Kal. He took a long swig of the Snake. 'But while I have it, I should go back to Nemo's gambling hole and clean up.'

Kal blocked Yolanda's hand without even looking and took another drink. 'Just kidding,' he said. 'With my luck, the gift would give out right as I made a big bet. No, I'm going to stay right here in the Sump Hole and drink with my friends – all of them.' He patted Wotan's head.

Kal pulled out the envelope Francks had given him. 'Tonight's on me,' he said. 'We've got money to spend and nothing will ruin this victory for me.'

'Hey, Jerico–' said Yolanda.

'Yes,' said Kal, pre-empting her demand. 'You two can have your cut now.' He counted out their shares of the Grak bounty and slapped two piles of credits on the table. 'That still leaves enough for me to blow on this cel-ebration.'

'What I don't understand,' said Yolanda as she grabbed her share, 'is where did Francks get this money and why did he give it to you?' She snatched up the creds and stuffed them down her cleavage.

Kal couldn't even imagine anyone dumb enough to try to steal her money from there. It'd be like sticking your hand in a bear trap. 'That's the best part about this party,' said Kal, pushing that image out of his head. 'It's paid for by our good friend Cardinal Crimson.'

The other two just stared at Kal. 'Near as I can figure, Crimson had paid Bitten to keep him quiet, and maybe for his part in setting up Francks for the assassin. Bitten had a change of heart and gave the money to Francks, but his past caught up with him in the end, anyway.'

'What I can't figure,' said Scabbs, breaking his silence finally, 'is why Francks trusted you with his deep, dark secrets about Crimson. You threw it all away, Kal. He gave me the journal and you just handed it over to Nemo. All those people died. Arliana died. And for what? So, the master spy could have dirt on Crimson?'

Kal let out a low whistle. 'You've been holding that in for a while, haven't you? I guess I owe you an explana-tion. Look, Francks told me I could only get Crimson from an angle, not head on. He even said I would die if I ever faced the Cardinal again.'

Kal ducked right before a bottle of Snake flew over his head and crashed into the wall behind him. He hardly missed a beat before continuing. 'I didn't think much of it at the time, but Francks could see things. I realised *that* down in the Hive Bottom. Plus he was eas-ier to talk to than any Cawdor I ever met before. He was okay, and I wasn't going to just ignore advice like that.'

'So you gave his secrets to Nemo?' said Scabbs again. 'To Nemo of all people? What kind of a plan was that?'

Kal smiled. 'A Kal Jerico plan,' he said. 'Nemo will use that information to slowly eat away at Crimson's power base. He's the only person in the Underhive powerful enough to hold that madman in check, and now he has the tools he needs to do it.'

'Okay,' said Scabbs. 'Maybe.'

'Plus, with the two of them feuding, neither one will have time to screw us over.' Kal stopped talking for a moment and stared at the wall. After a moment, he took a quick swig of his Snake and got up. 'I've got to leave soon. The debt collector for the Re-Engineers gang is on his way here again.'

'The debt collectors are already here,' said a gruff voice from across the room.

Kal looked up as two large, Van Saar ruffians pushed their way through the crowd to the table. They had no visible weapons but both of them looked like they could have given Gonth and Grak a run for their money in an arm wrestling contest.

'The Re-Engineers would like their money now,' said the one with the gruff voice. 'And don't tell us you ain't got it, cause we saw that stash in your pocket. You can give it to us now or we can take it after we break your arms and legs.'

Kal shrugged and pulled out the credits. As he began counting, he realised two things. First, he hadn't even got an image of them beating him to a pulp, let alone saw them coming before they spoke. Second, if these were the debt collectors the Van Saar gang had sent to collect for his guns, then he had no idea why that little guy had been hounding him.

After paying his debt, Kal dropped the empty envelope on the table and smiled.

'You're out of money, Kal,' said Scabbs. 'Why are you smiling? Did you get another vision?'

'No,' said Kal. 'Well sort of. I was just thinking about this little gem that I kept in reserve in case Nemo doesn't go after Crimson like I hoped.'

He pulled out a folded piece of paper and opened it up. It was the wanted poster he'd found in Bitten's hab. Tucked inside was a photo of Crimson shooting Guilder Tavis. 'Bobo shot this pict in the dome. It's from a vid of the entire battle. I wonder who might like to buy that vid and how much they would be willing to pay?'

All three of them laughed and Kal sat down again. He had not a care in the world beside getting drunk and celebrating his victory with his friends, his mastiff and perhaps a willing barmaid. Life was back to normal and he was perfectly content.

'Mr Jerico?'

Kal looked up. It was the squirrelly guy in the silk suit. He'd forgotten about that vision – his last, apparently. 'What?' asked Kal. 'What is it? Why have you been following me?'

'I have a piece of mail for you,' said the little man. He pushed his glasses up the bridge of his nose with a single finger and smiled as he handed Kal a white envelope.

Kal took the envelope and turned it over and over in his hand. On the back was his name printed in ornate lettering with glittering, gold, ink. The front was sealed with red wax embossed with a strange signet design.

He looked at the messenger and then back at the envelope. 'What is it?'

'It's an invitation to a wedding, Mr Jerico,' he replied.

'Really? But I don't know anybody who's getting married. Whose wedding is it?' Kal said.

'Yours, Mr Jerico,' the messenger replied, deadpan.

In the back of Kal's mind, he heard Jobe Francks laugh.